SATISFACTION
IN TIMES OF ANGER

JULIAN EDGE

Michael Terence
Publishing

First published in paperback by
Michael Terence Publishing in 2017

www.mtp.agency

Copyright © 2017 Julian Edge

www.julianedge.com

Julian Edge has asserted his right to be identified as the author of this work in accordance with the Copyright, Designs and Patents Act 1988

ISBN 978-1-549-57159-6

The characters in this book, their actions and statements, are all entirely fictional. They should not be associated with any real-life persons, living or dead, or seen as representing any actual groups, organisations or communities.

All rights reserved. No part of this publication may be reproduced, stored in a retrieval system, or transmitted, in any form or by any means, electronic, mechanical, photocopying, recording or otherwise, without the prior permission of the publishers

Cover image
Copyright © Sharon Yanai

*To all who refuse victimhood
and seize the chance to grow.*

SATISFACTION
IN TIMES OF ANGER

JULIAN EDGE

Chapter 1

Elli flicks her hair back over her left shoulder. It always goes better that side. She's done it a bit lighter this time. He likes that she's blonde. Not just that he likes blondes, he said. He likes that *she* is blonde. That's different. She hopes the foundation is covering the zits on her chin. It is so unfair. They always come on worse when she is going to see him.

Should she put on more lipstick? No, it's fine. Well, maybe a bit. It's an expensive one she bought with the money he'd given her. He likes pink, he said. She smiles to think of what he'd said next about what was pink and he also liked. He would like what he saw when she took her coat off. The new bra was not designed to keep secrets and she could just imagine how his friends would stare.

'Well, you can look, boys.' That's what her mum used to say. And then she'd laugh and throw her hair back. Just like that. Elli checks the time on her phone. He's late. She hates this hanging around on the street, but he says it saves him having to park and it wouldn't look right if he drove right up to the hostel. Well, he's not wrong there. Anyway, she knows he's busy. He wouldn't keep her waiting unless it was something important. And then he might be extra nice. One night, he didn't show up at all, but then he was so sorry and he gave her this really cool bracelet. Proper accessory kind of thing. If he doesn't come soon, maybe she'll text him.

'Hello, hello! What are you doing in that there doorway?'

They make her jump. Never saw them coming.

'Piss off!' she replies and looks away.

'That's not very nice, is it?' says the taller one. 'Is that nice?' he repeats to his friend.

'Oh, come on,' the other replies. 'We'll miss kick-off.'

'Aye, alright, I'm coming.' Walking backwards after his friend, he calls back to Elli,

'If you haven't had a customer by full-time, I'll give you a quick one on the way home.'

'Bloody hell, Bill,' his friend comments in a voice a lot louder than it needs to be. 'She only looks about ten.'

'But you'll have to wait for me, 'cause it might go to penalties, this one!'

'Piss off!' Elli shouts this time and reaches into her bag for her phone, wishing it was a weapon.

* * *

She has just finished texting him when she sees the white van coming. Her face falls. It's OK, but it's not like the Mercedes. She loves the Mercedes, the hard, smooth feel of it, the soft, leathery smell of it. He says he got it made-to-measure after he met her, so she could stretch out so nice on the back seat. Cheeky bugger. She'd rather be taller. Still, she probably hasn't finished growing yet. And those parts that count have already grown very nicely, haven't they?

She smiles. No point in looking miserable when he arrives, is there? Even if it isn't going to be that feathery blanket he spread out for her the first time. There'll be another time. She steps out of the doorway and waves. He pulls up and smiles that lovely smile of his, those beautiful white teeth in that handsome face.

'Hey, pretty one,' he says as she opens the door and gets in. 'I've got a surprise for you.'

'Oooh,' she says, putting her hand on his thigh and leaning over to kiss him lightly on the lips. 'I hope that doesn't mean you think I've got something for you.'

'Oh, but baby, I know you have,' he says in mock surprise. 'And I know just where you keep it.'

They both laugh as Amir does a u-turn and heads back in the direction he came from. He pulls a small joint from his shirt pocket.

'Why don't you light that for us?'

So she does, using the smart silver lighter that was one of his first presents to her. She takes three deep tokes and passes to him. Slowly exhaling, she kicks off her shoes and puts her feet up on the dashboard. She sees him glance across as her light skirt slides up her thighs.

'God, that feels good,' she says. 'Let's have some bloody fun.'

'Acha,' says Amir, passing the joint back, 'Let's do that.'

* * *

It isn't one of the great clubs. It opens too early and never really kicks off. But it's a Thursday night and it makes no sense to get back to the hostel too late. Just gives the old fella another chance to play crazyman. No point in that on a Thursday. And Amir has sort of promised to take her to the seaside at the weekend. In the Mercedes, he says. Probably.

They've had a few drinks and another joint on the way here and the music is better than usual. She's been dancing with Amir or one of his mates for a couple of hours now. He's good like that. If he wants a break, he doesn't mind if she dances with one of the others. Doesn't get all jealous-like.

Now they are at one of the few tables scattered around the walls. He pushes a slim black box over towards her.

'What's that?'

'Have a look.'

'Something for me?'

'Told you, didn't I?'

She pulls the lid off the box. Her eyes widen.

'Wow! It's beautiful! That is so cool.' She takes the watch out and tries it on.

'It's fantastic! Can we get the bracelet made smaller?'

'It's a Bulova,' says Amir, emphasizing the significance with raised eyebrows and a nod. 'Yeah, sure we can. Let me see. Hey, Mohsin!'

Amir looks how loose the watch is on her wrist, slips it off and holds it up in the air. Elli doesn't know whether to protest or not. She could easily go to Timpsons and get it done herself. Amir laughs at the expression on her face.

'No worries, little one. It's coming right back to you.'

Without turning to look at the fat youth behind him, Amir simply says, 'Take three links out of that.' Mohsin disappears.

'But I'm going to have to get off soon,' says Elli, still concerned.

'Won't take a minute,' says Amir, finishing his drink. 'Mohsin has the right tools. And yeah, anyway, it's time we were off. 'Specially if we're going to make a stop on the way.'

Elli tosses her hair back.

'Oh, I don't know about that. I think I might be a bit tired. And sweaty.'

'Well,' says Amir, 'at the weekend you can have a nice shower in a posh seaside hotel if you like.'

'Oh yeah? So, we'll wait till the weekend, shall we?'

'Nah, tonight you'll do sweaty.'

'Cheeky bugger! Anyway, I'm off for a pee before we go.'

Elli touches up her makeup and brushes out her hair. A girl has to make an effort. There is plenty of competition out there. She's seen them looking at Amir. And him looking back sometimes. But now he's given her a — what was it? — a Buvola. Not like a Rolex or a Tag, but it looks dead smart, with a black face and diamonds around it. Well, not real diamonds, obviously, but she'll look it up online and see how much they cost.

She dances across the floor towards him, swinging her hips and pulling her shoulders back, avoiding two attempts by others to dance with her as she passes. Back at the table, the watch is already lying in its open box. With a squeal of excitement, she picks it up and tries it on again.

'It's perfect. It's just perfect! Where's Mohsin? I have to thank him.'

'He's outside. I said we'd give him a lift.'

'Oh, I thought we were going to …'

'Don't you worry about that. You worry about showing that watch off too much. Somebody might want to nick it. Anyway, you don't want people talking. They'll want to know where you got it.'

'So what? It's from my boyfriend, innit?'

'Yeah, that's right.'

* * *

Out in the car park, there is no sign of Mohsin and Amir shows no interest in waiting for him, which is fine by Elli. He pulls out into the quiet streets and turns towards the old bus station.

'No, don't let's go down there,' she says. 'Let's go out where you parked under the trees. That was nicer.'

'Anything you say, Elli-girl. It'll make us a bit later.'

'Yeah, but it's nice out there.'

'Good by me' says Amir. He reaches back behind his seat. 'Look what I got.'

'Single Malt? What's single malt?'

'Try it. See what you think. But take it easy, it might be a bit strong for a lightweight like you if you drink it straight.'

'Oh, yeah? I'm a girl who likes something strong and straight. Thought you knew that.'

She watches the little smile play around the edges of his mouth. She knows he likes it when she's cheeky like that.

'Well, go ahead then. Help yourself while I drive.'

So she does.

* * *

Satisfaction in Times of Anger

Fifteen minutes later, he pulls up under the trees that Elli remembers. You couldn't call it 'in the country,' but the houses have grown less densely packed and they have turned down an only partly-made road that goes past some derelict storage units on the left, with a field bordered by a barbed-wire fence on the right.

'Whoooofff,' she hoots, and giggles. 'Want some?'

'Sure. Why not?' Amir takes a swig. 'Come on,' he says. 'I've got the mattress in the back.'

'Mmmm,' says Elli, woozily opening her door. 'Are there any stars?'

'Not in the back of the van,' Amir replies, taking her arm and steering her around the vehicle. As they pass, he bangs on the side of the van. And from inside, there is a bang in response.

'Bloody hell, what's that?' Elli jumps in shock and almost falls. Amir puts his arm around her to steady her.

'It's Mohsin. I told you, I promised him a lift. There's no room in the front for three.'

'Mohsin? What's he doing here?'

'Well, just right now, he's waiting for us to open the back door.'

'So he can get out?'

'So we can get in, you mean,.'

'I'm not getting there with him. He's a creepy little bastard, always hanging around, staring.'

'Don't worry, I'll be with you.' Holding her arm firmly with one hand, he opens the van door.

'Amir, what are you talking about?'

'A look,' says Amir. 'That's all. He just wants a look. He's never seen a girl's tits before.'

'Well, I'm not showing him mine!'

'Oh come on, Elli-girl! What's the harm? You said you want to thank him. For fixing your new watch. Come on, give the guy a treat.'

Spinning her around, Amir pulls Elli's coat off and throws it into the van.

She turns back to him. 'No, I don't want to.'

'Do it for me. I told him he could have a look. Don't make me out a liar.'

'Amir, please!'

'You want to make me look stupid? Like my girlfriend won't do what I ask her? Not one little thing? Hey?' There is a new harshness in his voice.

'Bloody hell, Amir,' tears begin to run down Elli's cheeks. 'It's cold. I'll catch my death.'

'Well, be quick, then.' He smiles, but the harshness is still there.

Quietly sobbing, Elli fumbles with the buttons of her blouse. When she has them undone, Amir pulls the blouse off and throws it after the coat. He turns her around to face the open door and pushes her up against the back of the van.

'Come on. Get on with it!' He stands close behind her.

'You do it if you're so fucking keen!'

'No, Elli-girl, you do it.' He grabs a handful of her hair and yanks her head back. Her whole body shaking now, Elli reaches around and undoes her bra, slips it down her arms and throws it in with her other things.

'There we are,' says Amir. 'You're such a good little bad girl, innit? Now, my brother, how do you like that? How do you like them? Look how they move.' Tightening his grip on Elli's hair, he pulls her head from left to right, right to left.

'Stop it, please,' Elli pleads. 'Stop it now.'

'OK,' says Amir, releasing her hair. He puts a hand on each shoulder and pushes the upper half of her body into the van.

'Oh, no! Oh, fucking hell! He's got his thing out!' Elli half-screams and tries to push back. Amir grabs her with both arms around her hips, lifts her off her feet and heaves her inside. One of her shoes falls off and lies on its side in the dirt at the edge of the road. As the cloud cover breaks up, the moon glows along the broken pattern of glass beads glued onto the shoe.

In desperation and growing bewilderment, Elli gets to her hands and knees on the thin mattress that covers the floor of the van.

'That's perfect,' says Amir, in a voice that Elli does not recognise, but seems to be absolutely his. How strange is that? Her head is spinning and she feels nauseous. He said, 'Perfect,' didn't he? She doesn't feel perfect, but she is losing touch with what is going on, so maybe ...

'Now you stay like that and you don't move till I say so. I told you I'd got a surprise for you, didn't I?'

Amir undoes his belt and gets into the van, letting the door half-close behind him. A treacherous blade of moonlight creeps in. If she opens her eyes, through the chaos of the dope and the wine and the scotch, Elli can see her new watch on her wrist. But mostly, she wants her eyes tight shut. Especially after Mohsin shuffles closer to her face.

* * *

They leave Elli in the back to get dressed as they drive home. After dropping off Mohsin and getting Elli around to the passenger seat, Amir pulls into an all-night petrol station where she can, 'make herself look a bit more presentable,' as he puts it.

Once inside the converted container, she throws up, uses the toilet, and throws up again. Semi-comatose and struggling to make sense of what is happening, she splashes water on her face and runs her fingers through her hair. Makeup seems out of the question. She stands for a while staring blankly into the mirror.

On the wall next to it is a notice that says,

THIS FACILITY IS CLEANED REGULARLY.
IF YOU HAVE ANY COMPLAINTS, PLEASE
REPORT THEM TO THE MANAGEMENT.

With a slight frown, she tries to engage with this. Looking around, she slowly resolves that she does not have any complaints. There is a smell of vomit, some of which is on the floor, but that is hers, and she can't really complain about that. The sink is a bit small, but it's probably only meant for washing hands. There are paper towels, and that's really good, because she's had to wash her face and she doesn't know otherwise how she could have dried it. She wishes she could brush her teeth, but you can't expect petrol stations to provide toothbrush and toothpaste, can you?

Trouble is that thinking about that makes the foul taste on her tongue seem even worse. She squeezes a tiny blob of liquid soap into her hand, adds a squirt of water and scoops it into her mouth. It tastes a bit weird, but not so bad. She whooshes it around. Then she tries gargling, but that's a mistake, because she swallows a bit and some of it goes up her nose and she chokes on the rest. Scummy water down her front. She wipes her mouth with another paper towel. The last one! That's lucky. Or is that something she should inform the management about? Not that she would want them to think it was a complaint ...

There is a knock at the door.

'Come on, Elli-girl. You just check your new watch and look how late it is. Time to get you home.'

'Yeah. Whatever.'

She drops the paper towel on the floor and opens the door. Amir reaches in, takes her by the arm and leads her across the tarmac. 'Don't worry, little lady, I'll make sure you get back safe. Won't be long till the weekend now, eh?' he smiles.

'Yeah,' says Elli again, steadying herself against the van. 'Whatever.'

Chapter 2

Call In and Learn About Islam - the banner says. Enough to make you throw up on the spot.

'I know as much as I need to know about you lot.'

Ryan Price looks around the busy shopping street and goes on muttering, audible only to himself, as if addressing the people passing by.

'Walking round in your pyjamas with your stupid, scraggy beards and your women all dressed up in bin-bags. And God knows how many of you packed into a two-bedroom terrace, and bringing over all your relatives, and half of them illegals who can't even speak English, and the stink of your cooking everywhere, and all the clever little bastards in school getting their GCSEs and taking all the college places and jobs.'

Ryan remembers a teacher telling them that Winton used to be a village before the city swallowed it up. On the other hand, Ryan's teachers said a lot of things and most of them were crap. A right bloody funny village it must've been, eh? Betting shops, charities, hairdressers, and fast-foods. And then all the Ahmeds and Mahmouds selling god-knows-what. And with some of them, not even the shop signs are in English. Oh, and the village church, of course. Except it isn't a church anymore, is it? It's a mosque now. Whoever heard of a village mosque? A call-in-and-learn-about-Islam-mosque. And what sort of plots do we think they're cooking up in there, eh? Won't be long before they take over the whole fucking country if somebody doesn't do something.

Well, perhaps somebody will. That's what the Great Whites are all about and getting in with them is the best thing that's ever happened to Ryan. Something to feel proud of. He beats his clenched fist against the shark emblem on his chest and shouts out their marching chant, just for the hell of it, just for how it makes him feel:

'ONOROL! ONOROL! ONOROL!'

He gets some funny looks from people passing by, but Ryan just stares them out. They'll learn soon enough. He lights up. Nice. Grabbed two cartons of the best from the shop they did the night before last. Wishes he'd taken more. They got so excited about the "cocktail" that they weren't thinking straight about what they could've nicked first. He looks at his lighter — a Zippo copy with a skull and crossbones on it — it wasn't his fault the bloody thing didn't go off. He'd done it just like they told him, but the flame went out.

Then Ryan has an idea that brings a wide grin to his face. What about a Zippo with a white shark on it? He's going to tell Kyle about that. Everybody's going to want one. They can get some made. Kyle'll know how.

Word is, Kyle is pissed off with him about the shop thing. Kyle wanted a proper big blaze to get in the papers, something to impress a visitor. Well, it wasn't his fault. Fucking typical. Everybody else talks and he goes out and does what needs doing and then everybody finds fault. Where were they when he was standing there with a bottle of petrol in one hand and his lighter in the other? Ryan flips the Zippo open and lights it. Snaps it to. Flips it open again. Lights it. Closes it. It feels good. Sound. Being in control.

Still, Kyle wants to see him, so he'd better get over there. Ryan puts the lighter back into the pocket of his hoody and zips it up. He pulls the hood up over his head, takes a long drag on his cigarette and lets it fall to the pavement. He steps into the path of a short, middle-aged woman carrying a shopping bag in each hand. Leaning forward, he shouts, 'ONOROL!' as loud as he can into her shocked face and makes as if to grab hold of her headscarf. She's partly blinded by the smoke and drops her bags trying to defend herself. Looks proper frightened. So she should be. Ryan runs giggling down the street, banging his fist now and again against the shark, and shouting, 'ONOROL! ONOROL! ONOROL!' in fine spirits, keen to see Kyle and other like-minded friends at The King's Head.

* * *

As far as Ryan is concerned, the pub, standing on the corner of Clarendon Street and Granville Street, is as much of a local shrine as it is a watering hole. Its front is covered in large, dark green tiles that still have some of their original gloss. The front door and windows are edged with brown, ribbed tiles, a few of which have been replaced with inferior copies or, in some cases, even blobs of cement, from back when the brewery let the place run down.

When you step off the street into the front porch, you see a faded, framed magazine article, telling you that The King's Head, "in its mixture of styles and influences, documents the architectural and social history of the English public house since the late nineteenth century." His old man made Ryan read that bit out to him god knows how many times. Then he'd say, 'Aye, that's right.'

And then in they'd go, straight on to the bar, feeling they were a part of something bigger than themselves, but also something that belonged to them.

The pub has had a loyal clientele, father and son, for generations. And Ryan can't get enough of the stories the old blokes love to tell. Like the Friday nights when two men would fight around the back, with what was left of their pay-packets as the prize. The crowd roaring them on would bet what was left of their own wages on the outcome. Those tales give Ryan — and everybody else he knows — a sense of their own history and birthright.

Another thing everybody agrees on is that the new owners have done a top job on the barroom, with the restored bar itself, brass foot rail, mirror and all, running most of the length of the long wall. It all just looks like a proper pub should: dark and shiny, but not posh. Some tables for them that want to sit and plenty of room for them as want to stand. Makes you feel at home, and makes you feel like *somebody* at the same time.

Bit like the landlord, Kyle thinks to himself as he gets closer. You wouldn't have thought how well Terry Smith fits in, with him being a southerner and that. But the new owners got it dead right with him, as well. You can have a laugh with Terry, and he isn't bothered if things get what he calls, 'boisterous,' but nobody messes him about. Early days, and Ryan was there with his dad, some Saturday night pushing-and-shoving kicked off. Smith comes out from behind the bar on the spot, swinging a baseball bat.

'You can take this out the back,' he bellows as he approaches the two men involved. 'As long as you keep away from the cars and don't scare the other customers. Or you can look around and see what absolute twats you are making of yourselves and sit back down. Or you can just leave. And three other things I'll tell you,' and by now his voice has dropped because everybody's gone dead quiet.

'One, nobody fights in my pub. Two, you do not want to know how much damage I can do with this thing. Three, if that looks like a tooth in the end of this bat, that's because that's what it is.'

'Come on Bill, sit thee down,' says one of the old-timers.

'Aye, come on, Dave, we don't want any trouble here,' says another.

'Can I have a look at that bat?' somebody shouts to Smith as the tension eases down.

'Sorry,' Terry replies with a smile as he strolls back behind the bar and slips the bat under it. 'Special occasions only.'

* * *

Ryan approaches the pub from the rear, cutting off Granville Street across the rough car park and past the toilet block to the back door. To get to the first floor, which is where Ryan is headed, he needs to go through the bar to the stairs at the front of the building. True, there is a rickety-looking, metal fire-escape that leads from the car park up to a large window on the first floor. He thinks about creeping up it and knocking on the window to give Kyle a surprise. But Kyle's sense of humour isn't something you can depend on. One time he can see a joke, and then another time, well, if Kyle doesn't see the joke, things can get right fucked-up. And anyway, that laddering might have met some building regulations at one time, but he wouldn't like to have to bet his life on it now.

Ryan nods to Terry on his way through the bar.

'Y'alright?'

'Yeah, you?'

'Yeah, not so bad. Kyle in?'

'Yeah. Him and Nick. I think I heard your name mentioned.'

'Oh yeah?'

'Yeah, something about a "useless tosser."'

Terry grins, which is not an altogether reassuring sight. Like all his bar-room staff, he is a big, muscular bloke with close-cropped hair. When he smiles, something happens to the tattoo on his left cheek. Ryan has long wanted to take a closer look, but the time has never seemed quite right.

Once through the bar, he turns left up the stairs to reach the first-floor landing. There are three rooms. To the right is an old box room that's had a toilet plumbed in at some point. Doesn't smell too great. To the far left is Terry Smith's office, which Ryan has never seen inside. The central room, the one the old fire-escape leads to, is the one Ryan hurries towards, excited to be here again and not at all worried by Terry's typical joke. The door is partly open, so he bursts in with a loud, 'ONOROL!' and a thump of his clenched right fist onto his proudly worn Great White Shark.

Nick spins around, arms outstretched, to block any path to Kyle. Despite this, Ryan sees Kyle duck lower in his seat as his right hand reaches out for the top drawer of the desk. The hand comes back as a fist armed in brass. Immediately, both men recognise Ryan and a cascade of obscene abuse comes across the room at him like projectile vomit. Just in time, Kyle calls Nick back from delivering the blow he is preparing. For a moment, all three stand in silence, Ryan pale and nervously grinning, Nick red-faced and furious, Kyle breathing slowly and deeply, deliberately recovering his composure.

'Sorry about the welcome, Ryan,' Kyle says, eventually. 'Take a seat. Help yourself.'

He points to the solid wooden chairs grouped around a coffee table and the cigarettes lying on it.

'That was a good lesson for us,' he continues.

'How do you mean, Kyle?' says Ryan.

'Well,' Kyle smiles. 'That was no way for us to greet a friend, was it?' He pauses. 'But on the other hand, we didn't know it was a friend coming in, did we? So, we have to get things a bit more sorted here, so we do know who's coming in, and we're ready to make them welcome. Or not. Wouldn't you say, Nick? That Ryan gave us something to think about we might get sorted?'

'Certainly did, Kyle. Certainly did.' Nick takes a seat and a cigarette from the packet on the table. Ryan pulls out his Zippo, gives Nick a light, and sits down himself.

'Bloody hell, Kyle,' he grins, 'you certainly scared the shit out of me! Who did you think I might have been?'

'That's a very fair question, young Ryan. Me and Nick have been in a few places together where somebody coming through a door like that might have been very, shall we say, 'unfriendly' towards us. I think we were just a bit caught up in our past, don't you, Nick?'

'Could be, Kyle.'

'Or preparing for our future, eh?'

'Some things do seem to keep coming round,

somehow.'

Kyle joins the other two at the coffee table and helps himself to a cigarette. Ryan lights it.

'Your lighter,' says Kyle.

'Yeah,' Ryan nods, enthusiastically. 'I've had an idea.'

'You fixed it, then,' Kyle continues.

'Fixed it?'

'Yeah, you dumb fuck,' Nick breaks in. 'So, when you spin the little wheel there, it sets fire to something. That's what was supposed to happen the night before last. Remember?'

'That wasn't my fault! Nor the lighter's!'

'So whose fault was it then, Comrade fucking Molotov's?' Nick shouts into his face.

'Eh? It went out! I lit the rag and I threw it and it went out. I wasn't going to go looking for a bottle of petrol in the dark with a lighter, was I?'

'So what did you do, Ryan?' Kyle takes over again.

'I pissed off, didn't I? What else was I supposed to do?'

'And which way did you piss off, you little pisser?' Nick bangs on the table. 'Let me tell you, you pissed off right through a set of cameras, didn't you?'

'I forgot about them. Anyway, how do you know? Oh, that sneaky little bastard, Bazza, told you, didn't he.'

'Doesn't matter how we know, Ryan,' says Kyle. 'Thing is that we do.'

There is a short silence while they smoke.

'Let me tell you, Ryan, about two different scenarios. Do you know what a scenario is, Ryan?' Kyle stubs out his cigarette in the half-full, heavy glass ashtray on the table.

'Yeah. Course I do. It's like a scene, yeah?'

'That'll do. Well, in one scene, we have a Paki shop going up in flames and perhaps somebody, some group, some organisation, maybe, claiming responsibility for it and showing what they can do when they want to. Get it?'

'Yeah, us, The Great Whites.' Ryan bangs his fist against his chest again and opens his mouth to shout. Thinks better of it.

'In another scene, Ryan, we have a Paki shopkeeper who has to do a bit of cleaning up, while the police have a video of some idiot in a Great Whites hoody who can't even manage to light a bottle of petrol or avoid running through a bank of CCTV cameras.'

'Yeah, well, like I said ...'

'Shut up, Ryan. You see, we are not messing about anymore. We are not just a bunch of angries off our heads at the weekend and giving some Pakis a kicking. That hoody you've got on, it didn't come from nothing.'

'I know that, Kyle ...'

'Shut the fuck up, Ryan!' Kyle scoops the ashtray off the table and into Ryan's chest. Ryan grunts at the shock of it, catches the ashtray in his lap and sits there holding it, upside down.

'You see this?' Kyle waves his arms around to take in the room. 'This isn't just an upstairs room at The King's Head anymore. This is an office. Do you know what that is over there?'

'Yeah, it's a filing cabinet, Kyle.'

'That's right. And this is not just an office, either.

Very soon it's going to be an HQ. Headquarters, Ryan. Because we're getting serious and we're getting organised and that is going to take some discipline and people doing what they are told. And that means finishing the jobs they get given. Are you with me, Ryan?'

'Yeah, yeah. I'm sorry Kyle.'

'I was saying to Kyle before you came,' Nick leans forward, 'Best way to make sure we get a bit of discipline in the ranks is to make an example of somebody. A bit of serious hurt.' Nick stands up.

'Come on, Nick. Bloody hell, Kyle. I just messed up that once.'

'Young Ryan,' says Kyle, 'that is the most sensible thing you've said so far. You know, I find it a lot easier to hear you say, "I messed up," than listen to you bitching on about, "It wasn't my fault." It makes me think you're prepared to take responsibility for what's on you. Is that right, Ryan?'

Kyle stands up and walks around the table. He squats down by Ryan's side and lifts the ashtray from his lap, leaving its contents behind. He puts the ashtray back on the table.

'Yeah, yeah, that's right, Kyle.'

'Yeah, good. I believe you. So, from now on, when you go out to do something as a Great White, you either come back with it done, or you don't fucking-well come back at all!'

Kyle's voice shifts from little more than a whisper to a scream and with his final words, he swings his brass-knuckled fist into Ryan's knee.

'Waaaahhh!!!' Ryan jumps to his feet and collapses to

the floor. Picking himself up, he limps towards the door.

'Fucking hell, Kyle. You didn't have to do that.'

'You might be right,' Kyle agrees. 'But just for a second there, I thought I did. Now there's something useful you can do. You ready?'

'What?'

'You ready?'

'Yeah, I'm ready. What?'

'Get the word out I want as many people here as we can raise tomorrow night. In the bar around nine.'

'OK.'

'And Ryan?'

'What?'

'Get yourself cleaned up. You look a right fucking mess. Not fit to wear the shark.'

Ryan hobbles down the stairs rubbing his knee. It hurts like hell. Instead of any more banter with Terry, he leaves through the front door and sets off for a café where he reckons he'll find some of the old gang.

Chapter 3

Two of them. He rings the bell. She looks down at the crumpled tarmac pavement. They wait together separately as another November evening drizzles in. At the rattle of the safety chain, they exchange glances and become a team.

The door opens. A man in his mid-sixties: balding, grey ponytail, baggy jeans and a Led Zeppelin sweatshirt that was probably once blue.

She speaks first.

'Good evening. Mr Thompson?'

'Yes.'

'I'm Detective Inspector Mason. This is my colleague, Detective Sergeant Bent.'

'Good name for a policeman. ... Sorry.'

'I think Sergeant Bent has probably heard that one before.'

'I bet he has.'

'Mr Thompson, I wonder if we could have a few minutes of your time?'

'Your lot have already had a fair bit of my time.'

'Yes, I realise that. You were recently the victim of an act of vandalism.'

'Aye.'

'The shed on your allotment was trashed.'

'You could say that. He busted the door off its hinges, broke the windows, smashed up the plants I'd potted, pissed over the mess he'd made and stole my tools. But you know all that, don't you?'

'The culprit, Billy Tanner, was arrested and convicted and given a community service sentence.'

'Are you trying to wind me up?'

'No, Mr Thompson, I'm really not.'

'A "community service sentence."'

'Yes, as you know, it's part of our Restorative Justice policy ...'

'Oh, aye, I know all about that: "It helps the poor criminal realise the effect of his crimes on his victims, and everybody lives happily ever after."'

'We have had some very positive results ...'

'Positive who for?'

'Well, in some cases it really has helped the criminal realise that he was actually harming and hurting a real person, someone like his own parents, maybe. And some do want to put things right. Our figures show this approach is helping cut re-offending and keeping people out of prison, where things would probably only just get worse. So, ...'

'Do you have to learn all this shi... ...stuff?'

'Well, Mr Thompson, it's what I see going on in front of my eyes.'

'Well, what *I* see going on in front of *my* eyes is this poxy little shit turns up at the allotment one day with his social worker and with this sneer on his rat-face, while he says these things he's been told to say. He hangs around till she's gone, pretending to do something half-way useful, and then he says, "Fuck this, I'm off."'

'Yes, we saw your report and it is being followed up.'

"Fuck this, I'm off," he says. I don't like to use that sort of language, but that's what he said, and with my wife there.'

'Yes, it's not on.'

'And just for goodbyes, he spits on the veg as he's walking off.'

'Yes.'

'And, "it is being followed up," is it? Am I going to get another apology? A bit more "Restorative Justice"?'

'I don't think another apology would give you much satisfaction, would it, Mr Thompson?'

'No, it bloody well wouldn't. I'd like to break the little bastard's thieving fingers, that's what ...'

DS Bent, who has so far been silent, leans forward. He does not really move as such; he just leans a little. Standing at six feet three inches and weighing fifteen stone, or two hundred and ten pounds as they like to say at the gym, a small movement can have a very definite effect. Mason and Bent both know that.

'Yes, Mr Thompson,' he says quietly, his slight accent adding a sense of Michael Caine pressure to his delivery. 'That's just the sort of thing we'd like to talk to you about. Do you think we might come in for a few minutes?'

Thompson seems almost to flinch. He steps back, holding the door open and calling to his wife.

* * *

The living room is small, but still, the traditional three-piece suite has been squeezed in, oriented towards the television. There is a slight whiff of an absent family dog.

Mason takes the lead again.

'Yes, this issue of satisfaction is what we have come to talk to you about.'

'Well, ...'

'Although I'm sure you wouldn't really want to break the young man's fingers, would you? I mean, physically bend his fingers back until the bones break . . . '

'Of course, he wouldn't! It's just a way of talking.'

'Yes, of course, Mrs Thompson, just a way of talking. But I have to check, you see, because one thing can lead to another.'

'Oh, well, I don't know about that, I'm sure. We, er ... The kettle's just boiled. Would you like a cup of tea?'

'Mmmm. Yes, please, that would be grand. Milk, no sugar, please.'

'Right you are.'

She turns questioningly to Bent.

'Same, please.'

'Would you rather have coffee?'

'No, tea's fine, thanks.'

'It's no bother, we've got both.'

'No, really, I'd like tea.'

'All right, then. Do you take sugar?'

'No, thanks, just like DI Mason would be perfect.'

'Do your own decorating?' Mason speaks into the silence while Mrs Thompson is out of the room.

'Yeah. Why d'you ask?'

'Nice job on the wallpaper. They're hard, those big patterns.'

'And you waste a lot,' Thompson nods, looking grudgingly pleased.

'Here you are,' says Mrs Thompson, returning with two mugs of tea. 'Ours are on the side.'

Her husband steps into the kitchen and returns with two more mugs.

'City fan, then?' Mason nods at one of the mugs.

'Man and boy. Long before we had all the Arab money. Not that we mind it,' addressed to Bent. 'You're not from around here.'

'No,' Bent replies. 'Millwall was my local team.'

'Woah! That can't've been easy!'

Bent lets it go,

'Can't be harder than following the Trotters,' Mason throws in. Then she picks up where she left off.

'Anyway, you see, we have had some real successes with our Restorative Justice approach but, equally, there has been some dissatisfaction. Well, nothing's perfect, is it?'

'No, I suppose not.'

'So we are following up cases where the victims don't feel they've been fairly treated. Like you, Mr and Mrs Thompson.'

'And what does "following up" do for us?'

'Well, two things, Mr Thompson. First, we want you to know that this is not over. We are not forgetting about it. Unduly lenient sentencing can be challenged.'

'And second,' Bent leans forward. Once again, the effect on Thompson seems almost physical. 'We want to warn you.'

'Warn us?'

'Yes, you might be approached by some dangerous people.'

'How do you mean?'

'Well, there was this one youth thought it was funny to get drunk and kick in people's garden fences on his way home. His mates thought it was a bit of a laugh, as well, so they lied to cover up for him.'

'Give him an alibi, like?'

'Exactly. He was given an official warning, but that just seemed to encourage him.'

'Too bloody right.'

'So, one night, his back door got kicked in, with a message — that things could get worse and next time it wouldn't be just his door.'

Thompson grins. 'And who got to kick the door in?'

'It seems likely one or two victims of other crimes were involved. People like to help out.'

"Course they do. Decent people would. So, are you saying that I could get somebody to, say, chuck a brick through that little bastard Tanner's window ...'

'John!'

'Sorry, love.'

Mason and Bent exchange glances.

'No, Mr Thompson,' says Mason, leaning forward. 'What we are actually saying is that if you were to get involved in anything like that, you would be just as much of a criminal as Tanner himself.'

'That's the real point of the story,' Bent goes on. 'You might think that something like that would make you feel better, but it wouldn't. It would just get you into trouble.'

'So why the hell are you coming round here telling me about all this?'

'Because we are starting to see a pattern,' says Mason. 'As though there is some kind of a misguided vigilante group behind some of these actions. There is organisation. There is planning.'

'Somebody might make you an offer,' says Bent.

'Make us an offer?' says Mrs Thompson. 'Whatever do you mean?'

'Well, just like Mr Thompson said. Somebody might suggest they could put a brick through Billy Tanner's window for you. One night when you have a good alibi.'

'Why would they do that?'

'Because some sweet day, Mrs Thompson, they would come back and tell you what kind of a favour you can do for somebody else, to give them some so-called satisfaction.'

'Well, we wouldn't want to get mixed up with anything like that, would we John?'

Thompson looks at the floor and shakes his head.

'Nah, not for us.'

'You haven't heard of a scheme like this, then, Mr Thompson?' Mason asks.

'No.'

'Not been approached by anyone?'

'No! I told you.'

'Must be a mistake, then,' says Bent.

'What's a mistake?'

'Your name being mentioned.'

'Mentioned by who?'

'What we're saying,' Mason takes over again, 'is that any kind of vigilante work, even if it's well intentioned, is a slippery slope and will have very serious consequences. You're good people, Mr and Mrs Thompson. There will be a follow-up to the Tanner case and you will be asked to make a statement of how all this has affected you, so please give that some thought.'

'And if anyone should contact you about the possibility of arranging some "satisfaction" for you,' Bent continues, 'please tell them you want nothing to do with it, they are putting themselves and others in danger, and they are wasting police time we would rather spend on nicking criminals.'

'Always remembering,' Mason comes back, 'they are turning themselves into criminals and we will enforce the law.'

'So, you've really come round here to threaten us. Is that it?'

'John, there's no need to talk like that!'

Mason and Bent stand up.

'No, there really isn't, Mr Thompson,' says Mason. 'We are on the same side and we want to make sure that we stay that way.' She lays a card on the table. 'In case you hear anything.'

'Aye, well,' says Thompson, heading for the door. 'We'd best not keep you any longer, so as you can get back to your nicking criminals. Good luck with that.'

* * *

Mason and Bent walk back to the nearby housing development where they have parked their car.

'Involved?' Bent asks.

'Or if not, he fancies the idea.'

'Her?'

'No. But if he does get into it, she'll stick with him.'

'I hope that's not what they call gender stereotyping, DI Mason.'

'That's what they call *nous*, DS Bent, and being able to read character. You may get there in time.'

'Oh, I think I got their number all right.'

They get into the car.

'Don't tell me you've got them pegged as racists, too.'

'Oh, you think not?'

Mason unwraps a piece of nicotine-gum and starts chewing.

'What did they do?' she asks. 'Teach me.'

Bent squeezes out a very thin smile as he drives them out of the estate and away through the narrow streets surrounding it, past the massed ranks of wheelie-bins.

'Always game to try, boss. Always game to try. That whole business with the coffee? What do you think that was all about?'

'She meant it wouldn't be any bother to make you a coffee if you wanted one.'

'It meant that, and it also meant that she saw me as *different*, more than she would have if it had been a white bloke sitting there. I'd already said what I wanted.'

'Bollocks.'

'For sure.'

'Even if that was true, it would just mean she *wasn't*

racist, she was just being open and flexible.'

'Uh-huh.'

'I'm thinking you are not exactly agreeing with me.'

Bent sighs. Shakes his head.

'The whole of bloody society is racist the way you tell it,' Mason adds.

'That's a good place to start. Take it as the norm and you won't go far wrong.'

'And you're always angry about it.'

'I don't do anger, boss. It is what it is. I work with things the way they are.'

'Sure.'

'But just answer me this,' Bent goes on. 'If one of his mates asked him now to describe us, what do you think he would say?'

'What do I think he would say?'

'Yeah, if somebody said, "What did they look like, them two?"'

'Thin woman and a big black bloke.'

'Yeah, so do I.'

'So, what's your problem with that?'

'He wouldn't say, "A big bloke and a thin white woman, would he?"'

'Well, he probably would if he was black, and if he was talking to somebody black.'

'So, we agree.'

'You do lose it on this sometimes, you know.'

'Yes, boss. But I'll tell you one thing — I'm black and I wouldn't describe us like that whoever I was talking to.'

'So, how would you describe us, then?'

'Skinny middle-aged woman with this really good-looking young fella.'

'Oh, shut up!'

'Yes, boss. Sorry, boss.'

They are both grinning as they drive through the glass and steel monuments to corporate higher education that mark the southern approach to the city centre. Then, as they crawl into the traffic chaos of the endless road works and tramline extensions, the mood changes. Bent looks across at Mason. He knows how easily, when they are together with nothing immediate to do, he drifts away from workaday concerns and banter, getting lost in his own issues.

Like him, he feels, there is a place she goes to in those silences. Interesting that they both seem comfortable in each other's company without having to talk all the time. There is something like a sense of kinship. Funny word. But the feeling is different from professional and definitely not sexual. Almost as though they have different pieces of a picture they haven't yet seen, but he would like to. He can't explain it even to himself. He gets so far in thinking it through, and then ... well ... well ... Why not try? Why not now? He makes a decision.

'About the name,' he finds himself saying. 'Bent.'

'You must enjoy it. You ask everyone to use it, rather than your given name.'

'It's not that I enjoy it, like a joke. It's like a scab. I use it as a reminder. You scratch it off and it stops itching. It's sore.'

'What??' Mason stares at him.

'*Bent* isn't a joke about my honesty. It's my slave name. Comes from the eighteenth-century British planter who owned my family.'

'What? You know this?'

'Oh yes. Stories from my grandma about stories from her grandma and so on. It's not so long ago. And I've read up on it a bit ...'

'Bloody hell ...,' he hears the pause before she says his name, '... Bent. Do you ever think of changing it?'

He looks across at her. 'Of course. In each generation, I guess. Until we learn that changing the name doesn't change the history, it just hides it. So we keep the name and we honour our history.'

There is a different kind of silence before Mason says, 'I've just been thinking. That history, two hundred-odd years, all those wrongs that can't be put right. It must make "Restorative Justice" feel a bit puny.'

'Well, you have to do your best to make things right in the here and now, don't you? Even this grubby allotment shed business. I have my sympathy for John Thompson's anger, but revenge is no place to look for satisfaction, not if satisfaction has anything to do with peace of mind. That's something else grandmothers teach you.'

'Bent, how do those very civilised and sensible thoughts fit in with scratching off a scab to remind yourself it hurts?'

They are out of the city centre again and nearly back to base. The rain comes on with the darkness. Bent clicks the wipers to fast.

'Can't see how forgetting or denying it would help.'

'I don't really know what to say. Except, "Thank you." For telling me. I appreciate it.'

'Hmmm,' Bent nods and raises his eyebrows in acknowledgement.

He turns into the police station compound and pulls up to the entrance.

'I'll drop you off here, boss. Good to go?'

'Oh yes, thank you,' she replies. 'Never better. Let's go solve some crime!'

She swings out of the car and heads for the door.

'Certainly beats getting heavy with victims and protecting criminals,' he murmurs wryly to her retreating back. Then he drives on to park.

Chapter 4

Mason takes the stairs to the second floor. As she enters the large, open-plan workspace, she hears her name.

'Wendy?'

'Sir?'

'Just a quick word. My office, please.'

Mason follows Superintendent William Barrett between the desks to his glass-fronted office.

'Close the door. Take a seat. Just a couple of things .'

'Sir?'

'Incident, couple of nights ago. Corner shop. Seemed straightforward. Might not be. I want you to have a careful look at it. With your "communities" hat on.'

'Anything in particular, sir?'

'Bob Poole will bring you up to speed. He's been looking at some CCTV. The point is, I want this taken seriously. We don't want any come-back about the police not protecting ethnic minorities.'

'No, sir.'

'And at the same time, we don't want to go making mountains out of molehills. The thing about "communities" is that you're just as likely to stir up strife by making a fuss about nothing.'

Mason looks questioningly.

'While obviously,' Barrett continues, 'we need to come down hard on anything that is actually prejudicial to good community relations.'

'Yes, sir,' Mason feels obliged to say.

'Good. I'll trust your judgement on that. Keep me

informed.'

'You said, "a couple of things," sir?'

'Yes, yes. About these follow-up calls you're making — Restorative Justice, rumours of vigilante action, how's that coming along?'

'Well, sir, something's going on for sure. These aren't just random incidents. There hasn't been any violence yet, but there will be. If we are going to get on top of this, we'll need more resources.'

'Mmmm,' Barrett, pulls a sour face. 'Something we haven't got a lot of. Especially when you factor in gender and ethnic considerations. We might have to do a bit of a re-think. Shift that to the back-burner. Assistant Chief Constable's pet project, of course. And you work well with James Bent, by all accounts.'

'Yes, sir. Bent's a good police officer.'

'Oh yes, and that's another thing. Why does everyone call him, "Bent" all the time? Why not James, or Jim, Jimmy, Jimbo — whatever. OK, perhaps not "*Jimbo*" for obvious reasons ...' Barrett rolls his eyes in mock horror. Drawing no response from Mason, he continues, 'It stands out.'

'Yes, sir. Not an issue, really. I address DS Bent as '*Bent*' simply because he prefers it. I suppose I've got used to it. It sat a bit oddly with me at first, too. Sounded a bit public school — "all chaps together."'

Barrett's stiffens in his seat.

'Sorry, sir, I have absolutely no experience of public schools, so I wouldn't know. As you say, it is not usual, but neither does it signify anything other than respecting a fellow officer's wishes.'

'Not a question of your antipathy to public schools,

then?'

'I confess to ignorance, sir. I hope I am not prejudiced against anyone because of a background they can't possibly have chosen. And,' she continues, despite Barrett's obvious intention to respond, 'if I may, sir, I would like to thank you for your sensitivity in noticing such a fine point so soon after your arrival and for bringing it to my attention. It's very helpful and I sincerely appreciate your leadership and care.'

'Mmmm.'

'Are we good, sir? I think DS Poole is waiting on me.'

'Yes. Yes, I suppose *"we are good."* Thank you, Wendy.'

'Sir.'

* * *

Mason's smile as she leaves Barrett's office is not visible on her face, nor, she hopes, detectable in her walk. It feels pleasantly warm inside. What to do? One can go only so far in trying to manage one's superiors, even a wanker like Barrett. Bloody Bent and his name thing. And as for *"Jimbo"* ... she doesn't even know if she is going to tell him about that one ...

'Bob!' she calls. 'What's up?'

'Oh, have I got news for you, boss!'

She perches on his desk and leans towards the computer screen. Poole points to one of two hooded figures that can be made out in the corner of the digital image.

'Watch this little twat here.'

'Not much of a picture, Bob.'

'No, but at least the thing was working.'

The two men stand together, fumbling with something. Then there is a flash of light.

'Is that them trying to light the bottle?'

'Yep.'

'What kind of idiot tries to firebomb a building that close to a filling station?'

'This kind of idiot,' says Poole, pointing again.

One figure throws the lighted bottle in through the broken shop window and then the two of them run away in different directions, disappearing from the picture.

'Mmmm,' says Mason. 'So bloody lucky that thing didn't go off.'

'What about that!' Poole chuckles. 'Lands on a pile of mashed up ice-creams they've tipped out of the freezer and trampled on, bottle doesn't break and the rag just fizzles out. Not enough petrol on it. Probably worried about burning their fingers. You have to laugh.'

'Doesn't tell us anything we didn't already know, though, Bob, does it?'

'A-ha!' Poole replies. 'And now for my next trick …'

He clicks on a different recording.

'One of the little beggars ran off up Charles Street, but the other one …'

'Runs straight across the forecourt and into another camera!' Mason finishes his sentence and pulls up a chair. 'So, what've you got for us?'

'No face, I'm afraid, you can see him pulling his hood down as he runs. It's male, anyway, medium height, light build. But look at this.'

He pauses the recording.

'This is pretty primitive equipment. I can't zoom in or clean it up. But I think we know what that is.'

He points to a white patch on the chest of the hoody that the youth is wearing.

'A shark,' Mason sighs.

'A Great White, by any other name.'

'And that's the name these idiots choose to call themselves, The Great Whites: "One Nation, One Race, One Language." That's their schtick, isn't it? I didn't think that we'd got them up here in any serious way.'

'Depends what you call serious, boss. We've always had our hooligans, always had our racists and always had our racist hooligans. Now and again somebody gives it all a more political focus, British National Party, English Defence League, something like that. They have a surge and then it blows over — or blows up, more like, because they haven't got the wit to organise anything that'll hold together.'

'And you think this lot's different?'

'Probably not. Not in the long run.'

'But in the long run, we're all dead?'

'Mmmm,' Poole nods and lets the recording run on until the youth has disappeared from the screen.

'Yes. And since I spotted this, I've run a few checks and they've started turning up in reports across the north, so it would figure that we'd get them on our screen — literally! — at some point. Thing is, it's been a while since we had any serious racial violence. Now, that could mean things are getting better, or it could mean we're due for another round.'

'And we're not overwhelmed with evidence of things

getting better. That what you mean?'

Poole shrugs and pulls a face. 'Youth unemployment, benefit cuts, immigration, housing, Brexit, Islamist propaganda, snuff videos, terrorist plots, hate crime, pressure on Muslims to condemn this and inform on that ...'

'OK, Bob, you've made your point.' Mason stands up. 'Get us some more, would you, on this lot? What do we know about Great Whites here in our neck of the woods? Names? Addresses? And what is the word nationally? And check back with the shop owner again ...'

'Mr Khawaja.'

'Yes, ask about any threats, any hassle — beyond the usual — and if he's noticed anybody with this shark design on their jackets.'

'OK, boss. Will do. I'll get onto it tomorrow. Bit late now. Taking my girl to gymnastics tonight.'

Mason checks her watch.

'Yeah, you're right. Time flies when you're fighting crime, eh? How was the match last night, anyway?'

'Rubbish. Went to penalties. But it was a good result, so the lads enjoyed it.'

* * *

Bent has waited in the parked car, wondering if the rain is going to ease off. He turns on the radio just in time to catch the end of what sounds like a grim report about young girls in care.

'Sometimes not a lot of care in care,' he murmurs to himself. 'And if there's nobody outside who cares very much about what's happening to you, it's got to be a bit of a one-sided battle.' His thoughts run on along those lines as the radio presenters banter their way towards the next item, which turns out to be about dog-grooming salons. He decides to make a run for it.

'Ah, James, a word,' Barrett's voice greets him as he enters the Operations Room.

'Sir,' Bent replies and sets off for the Superintendent's office.

'No need to close the door. Did you hear the news this evening?'

'Anything in particular, sir?'

'Yes, this local, care-home, under-age sex thing, or whatever it turns out to be.'

'Ah, I only caught the tail-end of that, I'm afraid, sir. Don't really have much of a picture.'

'No, none of us does as of right now, but I'm afraid we'll all be seeing a fair old bit of it soon enough and, as pictures go, it's not going to be a pretty one. Possibly a very varied demographic. Social services up to their necks in it. Local politicos sniffing for an advantage. Press sharpening their sense of outrage and preparing to mix their metaphors. And there will be a racial element to it. Not your ethnic group, nor mine either, and that's where we are going to have to be very careful indeed.'

'Yes, sir. I can imagine.'

'So, I want you to get up to speed on this. Not quite sure yet what your role will be, but a person only has to look around this place to see that ethnic diversity is not our longest suit.'

'No, sir.'

'Well, in my book, the old "colour-blindness" is no way

to look ahead. Mind you, we don't want to get caught in any "political correctness" nonsense, either. We simply need all the different perspectives we can get.'

'Yes, sir. I see that.'

'Good. I've had a word with DCI Shriver, so you report to her. If you see any particular problems ahead, either with your own involvement or that of any other officers, I want you to let me know asap. Be ultra-sensitive and run up flags at the first sign.'

'Yes, sir. I'll keep that in mind.'

'And this will mean shelving your follow-up work to the Restorative Justice Project. Pity.'

'Yes, sir. There are things going on out there that we need to keep an eye on.'

'Yes, so I understand. We certainly don't want any kind of vigilante nonsense taking hold. On the other hand, we have to cut our cloth these days, you know. We are obliged to prioritise and, well, DI Mason and yourself, quite obviously, you do have characteristics that we have to deploy with care.'

'Characteristics, sir?'

'Yes, yes. So, tidy up any loose ends with DI Mason and put a knot in them. For now, anyway.'

'Yes, sir.'

'Good. Right you are. Thank you, James.'

'Thank you, sir.'

Bent counts on his imitation of impassivity to see him out of the room. He trusts that he will not feel obliged to push Barrett with regard to the details of his "characteristics," or tempted to put a knot in anything else.

Chapter 5

The pools of water that form around every blocked drain extend well out into the road. Bent weaves their way through the heavily parked streets on which two-way traffic is only an occasional possibility. He takes care not to send waves of muddy water in the direction of the unfortunate pedestrians picking their way through the sodden mush of uncollected leaves on the pavements. Some motorists respond too enthusiastically to a chance to accelerate, and there is a shout and a shaken fist.

'Another angry victim,' Mason comments.

'There's a lot of it about,' Bent responds. 'And you can just hear the motorist saying, "But it was an accident. I didn't mean to."'

A few minutes later, he parks outside one of their "loose ends." Nice neighbourhood. Nothing fancy, but neat semis. Well-tended lawns and flower beds for the most part, except for where the kerb has been lowered and the garden replaced with a forecourt for parking. The occasional loft extension. Some mock-Georgian windows.

'Yeah. Yeah,' says Mason, continuing from where they left off. 'So, are we all to be held responsible for the unintended consequences of our actions?'

'Oh, that's a lot of philosophy for this time of day, boss.'

'Well ...'

'But the general answer is: Probably, yes. And the specific answer is: Definitely, if you accelerate through a puddle close to the pavement.'

'Yes,' Mason smiles, 'I didn't think it would be too

much philosophy for you to have an answer. And so to the Langleys. Remind me.'

Bent raises his eyebrows. Getting no response, he takes out his notebook, flips it open and reads:

'Laura. 19. Raped. Guilty verdict. Judge Sebastian Rawnsley decides not to follow sentencing guidelines. Hands down a minimal community order, with two years' supervision and compulsory enrolment in an alcohol treatment programme.'

'Why?'

'Both parties were drunk. Judge believes the defendant might have misunderstood the situation, *and* he showed remorse.'

'Plus,' Mason comes in, 'he calls in a gang of his mates to testify that Laura was a regular easy shag. Laura disputes their evidence, but breaks down under extremely hostile cross-examination. Friends are photographed celebrating with convicted rapist outside the court.'

'Yes, boss, I didn't think you would need very much reminding about this one.'

'Just getting into the mood.'

'And the reason we are here is that the victim's father and brother issued direct threats against said rapist and have gone so far as to confront him.'

Bent closes his notebook and waits. He senses that there is more and he knows enough about listening to know that this is not the time to ask questions. Or say anything at all. He watches the rain and waits for Mason to put into words whatever it is she is working on.

Mason shifts in her seat, tips the backrest a little and leans into it, staring up at the car roof.

'You've been assigned to this child-sex-abuse case.'

'Yes, Barrett has this idea I will bring something to it. I'm not sure if he really means what he says about getting a different ethnic perspective, or he just wants to have a black face around to give some sort of cover.'

'Black-face validity?'

'Very funny. I'm not sure about him.'

'You mean he's not the first person you would choose to mind your back?'

'That's right. I get the feeling he's more interested in getting people in front of him in case the shit starts to fly.'

'And you think it will?'

'Yes. Under the usual conditions of confidentiality …'

'Uh-oh.'

'The story so far is very much the tip of a large and ugly iceberg. That was the gist of the briefing we got.'

Mason is silent. Bent looks across at her. It is as if she has closed down. Brow creased, eyes almost closed, lips reduced to only the faintest of lines across her face. Her chin is pulled down onto her chest and her arms are folded tight across her body.

'Hmm?' The noise she made seems like a question, so Bent goes on.

'All we see for sure right now is some kids on the street. That's the best-case scenario.'

'And? Otherwise?'

'Maybe different groups of men involved and girls farmed out on demand.'

'Farmed out?' Mason spits the words through her teeth.

'It seems like a suitable expression for what might be set up like a livestock operation.' Bent's tone is now emotionless.

Mason takes a deep breath. And another. Finally, she re-sets her seat and sits forward.

'Wheels within wheels, Bent.'

'Meaning?'

'Later. Let's go and deal with the Langleys' aspect first.' She reaches for the door handle.

'Woah. Just a minute,' says Bent, making no move to leave the car. 'What do you mean, "aspect"? There is no connection between the Langleys and the abuse investigation. Not as far as I know, anyway.'

Mason looks back to him as she swings her feet out of the car. Her face is stony.

'You are right absolutely right. Take particular note of the "as far as *you* know."'

Bent notes the emphasis, but hears it not so much as an accusation, more as an expression of the pain that seems to flicker across her eyes.

'Maybe some things are connected even before they happen,' Mason adds.

'And you will explain this to me later, ma'am? Not much later, I hope.'

Mason takes another deep breath and blows it out noisily.

'No, not much later. But first, the Langleys — steady as she goes.'

'Aye-aye, cap'n,' says Bent.

By the time he has caught up with Mason at the door, he has compartmentalised the exchange and filed it under, 'To Be Continued.' It is a talent that he is aware of having and a skill that he has consciously developed. Some people, he knows, regard him as cold in this regard. He sees the ability as a strength in an environment where every learned advantage might be crucial. Crucial, too, in getting yourself into a position where you really can let your passions rip when that is what you want to do. Wasted heat can just leave everything lukewarm, and then entropy will get you for sure.

* * *

Half an hour later, they are back on the street. In the living room, they have left two men: the older one sitting on the sofa, quietly weeping and the younger standing in front of the painting over the fireplace, not seeing it, apparently not breathing at all.

The crisis point of the meeting comes when the younger man says,

'I'll tell you what. I'd like his body to be found with a broken bottle stuffed up his arse, that's what.'

It is at this point that his father begins to cry.

'Really?' says Bent. 'Is that what you want?'

The father shakes his head.

'Let it go, Pat. Let it go.'

And as his son moves to speak again, he goes on, through the tears.

'Let it *go*. There is no satisfaction to be had. The only way out of this is to accept that.'

'That doesn't sound like you. That sounds like my mother, lighting candles and talking about forgive and forget. Not even she believes it.'

'That's not what I'm saying, Pat. And your mother's right in her way, for herself. I see it now.'

'And what about your daughter?' asks Mason.

'She doesn't want anything to do with it. She's going away for a while. We have relatives in Canada.'

After a short pause, Mason and Bent look at each other and stand up.

'Let's leave it there, then, shall we?' Mason says. 'I think you're on a good road, Mr Langley.'

Bent shakes hands with the son.

'Stay close to your father, Mr Langley,' he says. 'He needs your support. And, if you'll excuse me saying so, so does your mother. "Forgive and forget" is no easy path. And it is very helpful to a lot of people.' He holds eye contact with the young man for several seconds before turning to his father.

'Mr Langley, what you said about "satisfaction" is exactly right. I hope you will both remember that if anyone contacts you and talks about it. What they are talking about is revenge.'

'Which is not only illegal,' Mason adds. 'It would also increase your pain. And you would be caught. And the consequences would be severe.'

'We have your number. If anybody contacts us, we'll get in touch,' the older man replies.

'Mr Langley?' says Bent, turning to back to the son.

He nods and looks away. Mason and Bent let themselves out.

* * *

Satisfaction in Times of Anger

The rain has stopped and the clouds are breaking up. Evening has closed in and the temperature is dropping. Once inside the car, Bent starts the engine and turns up the heater.

'"No satisfaction to be had,"' Mason quotes.

'It's a hard pill to swallow,' Bent responds. 'We keep saying it. We believe it. Did it feel different this time?' He waits, opening up space for Mason to take the conversation back to where they had left it.

There is a long pause. And then it turns into a silence. When Mason speaks again, there is no obvious connection to what has gone before.

'Ever heard of a bunch of idiots call themselves *The Great Whites*?'

'Mmmm.' Bent nods slowly. Then shouts, 'On a roll!'

'What? Jesus, you made me jump! What is, 'On a roll'? Some kind of burger ad?'

'Damn, DI Mason, you are quick!' Bent shakes his head in admiration. 'But no, unfortunately not. They have a slogan they chant, punching the air and all that sort of thing. It sounds like, 'On a roll,' which is how they want to present themselves, you know, getting stronger, but actually it's ONOROL, oh-en-oh-ar-oh-el,' he spells it out.

'Which stands for?'

'One Nation, One Race, One Language.'

Mason groans. She folds herself together into a ball, tight against the seat belt, head down, arms across her body, knees pulled up.

'Oh, no! In fact, I am very slow. Sometimes. I knew the slogan, but I didn't get the chant. Oh, bloody hell.

Now, where have I heard that sort of thing before?'

'Take your pick,' Bent responds. 'I think it was those nice, slave-owning Greeks, who we thank for our democratic culture, who also gave us the word, *xenophobia*, but there's absolutely no reason to think they started it.'

Mason unwinds herself.

'OK, let's skip the history lesson. I'm almost sorry I asked. What about these Great Whites?'

'New. Newish, anyway. Roots in London and the south-east, though it seems to be catching on 'Up North'— Bradford, Barnsley, Wakefield for starters. The odd fringe demo, a few posters and leaflets. Natty line in black hoodies with a Great White Shark on them, hence their clever name. Don't know that they have much real organisation. And I haven't heard of them around here, either.'

'Well, you have now. I wish I'd asked you before. I should have known that you'd be up to speed. Well,' she adds in mock disparagement, 'More than most.'

'They're here?'

'Mmmm. Bungled fire-bombing of a corner shop next to a filling station. Could have been very nasty indeed.'

'"Bungled" would fit. Still, fire-bombs are a league up from trashing somebody's shed and pissing on their potted plants.'

'Oh, yes. So is farming out young girls as some sort of livestock operation.'

'So, given the cuts, I suppose we have to say Barrett is right about priorities, at least.'

Mason's only reply is to unwrap another piece of gum.

'I have this feeling I am not quite keeping up,' Bent presses.

'In my own time, DS Bent. In my own time.'

'Seems to be getting colder, ma'am,' says Bent, and turns the heater up a notch.

Mason sighs. Stares out of her side window. After a while, she speaks again, the sharpness gone from her voice.

'What you told me about your name. About the history of it. About the scab.'

'Mmmm.'

'I appreciate it. And there is a connection. But I'm not sure what it is. It might have something to do with, "Forgive and Forget."'

'When you say it, I can almost hear the quote marks.'

'I struggle with forgiving.' She turns to look at him. 'And I have no idea at all what people mean by forgetting. I understand being able to move on. I can do that.'

'But?'

'*And* that comes a lot easier once you've got even.'

Bent nods as he adds,

'But it's not that simple, because some things you can't get even for.'

Mason speaks now as if to some mid-point out in the rain ahead of them.

'Against some people, if that's the issue, you can get some kind of payback. You can also try to make a difference here and there, but you can't ever get *even*.'

Bent lowers his window a little, takes a deep breath, closes it.

'And anyway, it's you,' Mason murmurs.

'You don't mean, me?'

'No, I mean, it's you, yourself. It's you that's wrong.'

'I'm not with you anymore.'

'You can't make it right. You can't go back and make it right. You just have to keep on, holding together what you can, but you know you're not right. It's like you use as much of yourself as isn't fucked-up to steer, and then you try to take out as many of them as you can before you crash.'

Mason is still staring ahead through the windscreen. Bent looks repeatedly across to her.

'But even then,' she goes on, 'you can't be sure about who it is that is doing the steering, because she is fucked up as well, just like the rest of you. You have to hope the hands on the wheel and the brain behind the eyes are true ...'

'True?'

'Yes, true. True to something. True to something that has survived.'

There is a long pause.

'Do you want to tell me about "survived," DI Mason?'

'Maybe I do, DS Bent. Maybe I do. But that doesn't make it a good idea.'

More silence.

'Yes, OK, I get that,' he takes it up. 'I mean, I get up every day and put my black face out there to be patronised, and I put my sweet black arse on the line for people who see me as a useful statistic on their ethnic recruitment and promotion checklists, and for others who want what they want when they want it and then wish I just wasn't there. So where do you fit into this madness, DI Mason? Where yo goin' fine yo satisfacshun?'

'You are terrible at that accent.'

They both smile.

'That's the whole point, though, isn't it?' he says, suddenly bitterly serious again. 'There *is* no satisfaction, but we keep pushing for it. Yes, I want to know what drives you. But only if and when you want to say.'

She looks at her watch.

'You free tomorrow night?'

'I certainly could be.'

'So careful, DS Bent! So guarded!' She pushes on before he can speak.

'No, sorry, you have every right. Forget I said that.'

'Done.'

'Right! Well, according to what I see on tv, I think we are meant to creep off to a dingy bar somewhere and get fighting drunk, or fuck, or sink into an alcoholic stupor, and I don't intend to do any of those things. But I could fancy something tasty to eat and a half-way decent bottle of wine.'

'There's a newish place down by the station,' says Bent. 'Called *Straits* — it's a mix of Chinese, Malay and Indian.'

'Ah,' says Mason, 'As in Singapore Straits. Hmmm. I'm afraid they aren't going to be doing much custom with our LGBT community.'

'Funny! And I do wonder if they thought that through.'

'Unless it's a double bluff and they hope everybody

gets the joke.'

'Half past eight good?'

'Yes, fine. And perhaps by then, we'll know more about what's happening with these girls that you're looking at.'

'And your little white dogfish.'

Chapter 6

Ryan is buzzing as he looks around the barroom. This is not the normal crowd at The King's Head. Not just the normal crowd, anyway. Kyle is going to be pretty pleased with him this time. He has put himself about, reached out, and got the place absolutely hammered. Some of the regulars are moaning, but then, when don't they? Those that like to sit down can't get a seat, much less what they like to think of as 'their' seat. And those that like to stand at the bar find themselves getting jostled now and again, which has already led to a bit of light aggro.

'Hey, Nick,' he calls out.

'What?'

'Good crowd, eh?'

'You think?'

'Where's Kyle?'

'Upstairs having a "private meeting" with his "Very Important Guest."'

Hearing Nick's tone, Ryan tries to change the subject.

'Who are all this lot?' He nods towards a group of men strung along the bar: all close-cropped, jeans, black leather jackets over black T-shirts.

'Turned up at the same time. Seem to know Terry. Sound like him, as well.'

'Londoners?'

'Something like that. Arrogant bastards. They come on like they know what's up, while we just hang around waiting for something to happen.'

At ten o'clock, Terry produces an old handbell and rings it. In the moment's silence that follows, Ryan feels all the tension in the room gather in his chest. He hasn't heard a bell like that since the fights his dad used to take him to. He feels his fists clench.

Then Terry shouts, just once,

'Free beer!'

Terry and his barmen start pulling pints of bitter, pouring pints of lager, and lining them up on the bar. A roar goes up. The strangers at the front start passing the pint pots and glasses back into the room to anyone who wants to take them. More and more willing hands are found. Ask no questions. People are getting their phones out and calling their mates. The beer keeps coming as fast as the crowd can drink it. Pretty soon, it's like a four-nil over Bayern bloody Munich, the raucous room sweet and sour with beer and sweat. Ryan relaxes into it. That feeling of belonging.

At half-past ten, Terry rings the bell again, longer this time.

'Hey, you!' he shouts, to one of the strangers now in the middle of the room; tall bloke, big waistline, with the shoulders to carry it off.

'What do you say to somebody who gives you free beer?'

'What do you say to somebody what gives you free beer?' the man bellows back. 'I don't know, Terry. What *do* you say to somebody what gives you free beer?'

'You ignorant bastard,' Terry hollers. 'You say, "Thank you very much, you're a White Man!"'

'Right,' comes the reply. 'Thank you very much, you're a White Man! Everybody, now! Thank you very much, you're a White Man!'

He punches the air with his fist as he leads the room

in the chant:

'THANK you very MUCH, you're a WHITE MAN! THANK you very MUCH, you're a WHITE MAN! THANK you very MUCH, you're a WHITE MAN!'

Ryan joins in, feeling at one with his people. And Nick seems to have cheered up, thank god. A few people leave, one mixed-race bloke Ryan sort of knows and two of his friends. Curious, Ryan follows them towards the door.

'Can't take a joke, eh? Got no sense of humour?' one of the strangers by the door shouts. 'Don't hurry back. We like a bit of a laugh around here. Where are you from, anyway?'

'I'm from around here. Where the fuck are you from?'

'Oh, why don't you tell me your address? A few of us could call round later. You could tell us where you got that nice tan.'

'Come on, Wes, this isn't worth it.' One of his companions puts his hand on the man's arm. 'It really isn't.'

After a tense moment, they turn and leave.

Back in the bar, the chanting is dying down when Terry rings his bell again.

'Right! Now then. As you're all feeling so grateful, and as you've all learned to be so polite, I think it's time to say another thank-you to the particular white men who just stood you all those drinks. So, make a bit of space and put your hands together for somebody you all know: our friend, Kyle Redwood, and a special friend of his who's got a few words to say to you.'

The man at the entrance seems to have become a kind of security guard. He holds the door open as Kyle and his companion come down the stairs and, when Ryan tries to step forward and high-five Kyle, this bloke grabs his arm and pulls him back.

Also wearing jeans and a black jacket over a black T-shirt, Kyle is looking excited, high almost. It's the jacket, with a Great White embossed on the left chest, that catches Ryan's attention. As pumped as Kyle himself looks to be wearing it, Ryan guesses that he hasn't seen one before, either.

The man with him looks in his fifties. Not as tall as Kyle. Slim. Greying. Looks fit. He's wearing a dark blue suit and tie. Ryan has seen the tie close-up. Very cool. The repeating white pattern that looks abstract from a distance is a shark's head, showing its teeth.

Terry passes a beer crate over the bar and Kyle steps up onto it.

'Thanks for coming tonight. Don't worry, I don't have a lot to say. And there will be time for another round of free beer!'

Cheers ring out, along with a couple of voices returning to:

'THANK you very MUCH, you're a WHITE MAN!'

Kyle grins and waves his hands, palms down, for silence.

'You are not wrong! And I'm proud of it!'

Cheers.

'And that's what tonight is all about and why we have a visitor to talk to us. We all know what's been going on now for a long time. Help the immigrants. Give 'em benefits. Give 'em housing. Give 'em schooling. Give 'em pensions. Give 'em jobs. Give 'em cars. Anything else you'd like? Eh? Eh?'

The crowd, silent at first and now prompted, starts to respond with shouts of agreement and anger.

'Whites can form a queue over there!' Kyle shouts. 'Queuing for what? Queuing for what? Eh? Fuck knows! 'Cause there isn't any houses, and there isn't any jobs and they've cut your benefits and the schools are full of pickaninnies that don't speak English!'

'Too fucking right!' comes back.

Kyle waves his hands for silence again. Now the silence is expectant, eager.

'Yes, Whites can form a queue over there. And that's where you can stay. With a bit of luck, somebody'll come along in a bit and give you some forms to fill in so's you can qualify for jam tomorrow. And what do we know about tomorrow, eh?'

'Never comes!' voices shout back.

'That's right! Tomorrow never comes. So, if we are going to do something, when are we going to do it? When, eh?'

'Now! Now!' voices call back.

'Yes, now!!' Kyle looks ready to take it up again at full pitch. But just at this point, his companion raises a finger and his eyebrows.

'Yes!' Kyle takes a deep breath. 'Right now is when we are going to do something. And what we are going to do right now, is, er... to listen to our guest from London. Give him a big hand. Step up here Mr C!'

Kyle claps enthusiastically as he gets down from the beer crate. Ryan joins in the applause and moves to stand next to Kyle. The other man steps up.

'Thank you, Kyle. Thanks, everyone, for coming along

tonight. I won't keep you long. And then we can all enjoy that promised round before we go home and get ready for work tomorrow.'

'You're a white man!' someone calls out and the speaker smiles.

'As Kyle was saying, a working man deserves a job, a house, and hope for a better future in the country he feels at home in — his country. And even if we might not have a job, there's always work to do. Different kinds of work.'

Ryan looks around. The atmosphere is changing. You can see it in the faces, just like you can feel it in your guts. It's partly to do with the man's voice. It isn't a London voice, nor a local voice. It's a voice that doesn't tell you where it comes from, but you don't mind. It's a confident voice that makes *you* feel confident just listening to it. It seems to get inside you and then take you with it.

Ryan feels unfamiliar, complicated emotions rippling through him. This is a voice that expresses your own hurt and loss and bewilderment and lets you know it's OK to feel the way you do. More than that, it's *right* to feel that way. It explains to you, as though you are listening to yourself, that we are not at fault so much as we have been misled. What our parents and grandparents struggled for, fought for, suffered for, has been taken away and given to others. Our generosity has been abused. We are being victimised through no fault of our own.

But it is not too late. It is never too late for people of goodwill to put things right. And we are good people. We are *real* people, *the* real people of this nation. We don't feel bitterness, but our disappointment needs to be

Satisfaction in Times of Anger

addressed. We are not violent, but our strength needs to be respected. We are a proud nation, open to the world, and also a particular race with a famous history and a bright future. Every other nation in the world wants to learn our language and it is our language, the English language, that rules the world. Other people, other nations, might come and go, like all the different fish that swim around in all the oceans on the planet, and so they should. But among all those flapping fins, the Great White Shark knows what it is. It doesn't have to make a fuss about it. It goes its own way, knowing its rights.

For the first time in his life, Ryan feels not just spoken *to*, instead of being shouted at or ignored, he feels spoken *for*. He feels the togetherness of the crowd around him. Like you do at a match, but now a part of something even bigger. As the speaker goes on, still calm, still in control, you can feel the wave coming at you. No, coming *for* you. It feels like an invitation to get up on it and ride. He listens intently as the voice takes on even more authority:

'That is how we need to be in this country. We who are this country: One Nation, One Race, One Language. We are not violent, but we demand to be respected. We know who we are and we know our rights. One Nation, One Race, One Language. We are generous to others, but we also know that charity begins at home. One Nation, One Race, One Language. We believe in democracy. We invented modern democracy.'

The crowd murmurs its approval.

'We are not a political party. Not yet. But we are becoming a movement. One Nation, One Race, One Language. Look around you.'

Several of the men in black leather jackets take them

off and turn to show the Great White motif across the back of their shirts.

'You can pick up a shirt as you leave. Keep your eyes open and look out for the shirt. Keep your eyes and your ears open anyway and notice what is going on around you. You know what is going on and you don't like it. You can learn to like it, or learn to do something about it. You can't vote for us yet, but you might find ways to lend a hand until you can vote for us — and vote for yourselves. One Nation, One Race, One Language. No, we are not yet a political party, but yes, we are a movement and there will be opportunities for you to put your shoulders to the wheel. You can make this your movement. You are in at the beginning. You can take control. And we are on a roll, we are ONOROL, Oh-En-Oh-Ar-Oh-El, One Nation, One Race, One Language: ONOROL!'

Voices take it up, punctuated by the triple-clap of the football crowd:

Clap-Clap-Clap — ONOROL! — Clap-Clap-Clap — ONOROL! —

Clap-Clap-Clap — ONOROL! — Clap-Clap-Clap — ONOROL! — Clap-Clap-Clap — ONOROL!

The speaker smiles, waves and steps down.

'You stay here,' he shouts into Kyle's ear. 'Call me later at my hotel.'

Ryan watches as burly figures ease the man's way through the back-slapping crowd to the door. The security guard leaves with him.

'Last round!' Terry bellows, ringing his bell, as they line the pints up along the bar.

'What do you say?' he shouts.

'Thank you very much, you're a white man!' the crowd choruses back gleefully. Occasionally, another round of ONOROL! breaks out.

By 12.30, finally, they have gone.

'Leave it, lads,' Terry says to his barmen. 'Just leave it. Big night. Good job. I've got some women coming in in the morning. They can do it. And there'll be a bonus for you.'

'Thanks, boss.'

'Cheers, Terry.'

Ryan tags along as Kyle and Nick go back upstairs to the office. He watches from the doorway as they sit at the low table and stare at each other.

'Come in and shut the door,' Kyle tells him. Make yourself useful. There's a bottle in that cupboard.'

Ryan joins them gratefully.

'Fucking hell,' says Nick.

'What a night,' says Kyle.

'Fucking hell,' says Nick.

'Seen what I got?' Kyle asks.

'What? The jacket? Yeah. Smart.'

'Nah, not the jacket.' Kyle reaches around behind his back, leans forward and lays something solid on the table. 'In case you're wondering,' he says, 'it's a not-quite-new, untraceable, semi-automatic Glock 17.'

'Fucking hell!' says Nick.

'Yeah,' says Kyle. He leans back and a broad grin spreads across his flushed face.

Chapter 7

Amir has had a skunk of a day. Putting plans for Blackpool in place has kept him running around, phoning, texting like he was everybody's servant instead of the man in charge. Some people will only talk face-to-face; some people want to keep you at a distance like you've got Aids. Some people want to see pictures; on their phone, or not on their phone. Some people want 'a surprise.' But that doesn't mean they won't complain about what they get on the end of their dicks.

If he could have a bit more control over the whole operation, he could make such a better fist of it than the half-wits in charge now. But no, he is supposed to be rustling the cattle, getting the cows to market, serving up the meat, keeping the customers happy and cleaning up afterwards, all without getting a sniff of the gravy.

He has just finished making a special delivery. Dog-tired, he pulls onto the forecourt of the rambling old Victorian house he shares with his parents, grandmother and sometimes an extended family member passing through. He stiffens as he sees the silver Prius hybrid parked there.

'Not now,' he mutters. 'Please, Lord, not Saint Tawfiq now.'

He really does not need a conversation with his brother. The star pupil. The graduate. The lawyer. The integrated-into-British-society and also true-to-his-roots paragon of a pain in the arse.

He gets out of the van. Tawfiq gets out of the Prius.

'As-salaamu alaikum,' Amir greets.

'Alaikum as-salaam. Where have you been?'

'Yeah, it's good to see you, too.'

'It's past one o'clock in the morning.'

'And you're sitting in your car outside my house like you haven't got a home to go to.'

'I do have a home to go to, but I also have my mother in my old home telling me how worried she is about you and how I have to do something.'

'So, do something. Tell her not to worry and everything is fine.'

'Is it?'

'Isn't it?'

'Where've you been?'

'Is there an echo around here?'

'Mum says she doesn't see you for days on end.'

'She exaggerates. Come on! Don't you remember what she was like when you were at home?'

'At least you could make sure to eat with them sometimes.'

'I do eat with them — a lot.'

'When was the last time?'

'The night before last.'

'No, you didn't.'

'What?'

'What did you eat?'

'I don't remember!'

'You weren't here at all the evening before last. That was why mum phoned me yesterday. Are you working?'

'Of course I'm working.'

'Still at Farid's?'

'Yes.'

'No, you're not. He hasn't seen you all week.'

'What is the matter with you? Started working for the police?'

'Why do you ask? Are you worried about the police?'

'Why should I be worried about the police?'

'Because one, you're a liar,' Tawfiq calmly ticks the points off. 'Two, you tell stupid lies that don't check out. Three, you've got money without working for it. Four, because I can smell the dope on you from here. And five, because you think you're clever when you're not.'

Amir flares.

'Oh, in that case,' he spits out. 'Guilty as charged, your honour. I am the moron in the family, you see. I plead extending circumstances, m'lord. My brother got all the brains and everyone was so pleased with him and so busy praising him that nobody noticed how stupid I was till it was too late.'

'People tell me you're down Robson Street with white girls. Under-age white girls.'

'Oh, people do, do they? Well, you can tell people I'm just waiting for my parents to fix me up with a nice wife from a nice family with loads of nice money so I can go round feeling superior to everybody in my nice fucking car.'

'I'll talk to you another time. When you're not ripped on whatever it is you're on right now.'

Tawfiq turns towards his car. Stops. Looks back.

'Listen, little brother. Those girls. They are also somebody's daughter, somebody's sister.'

Before Amir can respond, he goes on,

'And whatever you think about that, listen to this: There may soon be arrests. I know two girls have made complaints and the police are looking into it.'

'Complaints?' Amir lifts his chin. 'Believe me, I'm not getting any complaints.'

Tawfiq sighs, shakes his head.

'Go and see Farid tomorrow. He says you're welcome to go back. He says you're good at what you do. He just needs to be able to rely on you.'

Amir lights a cigarette as he watches the Prius slide silently away.

'Perfect car for my brother,' he thinks. 'Classy, but not showy; makes a thoughtful statement, but quietly. Damn! Why didn't I light up before? Is that still a hangover from the "respect for your older brother" shit?'

He looks over to the parked van. Yes, he had better take it back before Farid tells his brother about that, too. And hope the old man doesn't find out about him "borrowing" the Mercedes. But first, he needs to get the mattress out of the back of the van and dump it somewhere. It's starting to smell. Unsurprisingly. One of those silly bitches pissed on it at some point.

He thinks about his brother's warning. Tawfiq underestimates him, as usual. There aren't going to be any complaints from his girls. They are getting what they want. They get drunk, they get stoned, they get presents and they get fucked. And they aren't anybody's daughters or sisters, either. They are just greedy little cunts.

Amir finishes the cigarette. Steps on it. Spits. Goes into the house.

Chapter 8

Bent has phoned ahead to reserve, asking for a corner table. He also arrives early to make sure they get one. He is greeted by a middle-aged Indian woman who calls a young European waitress to seat him. When she asks (Bosnian? Bent wonders), he orders a beer.

Along the canalside, the restaurant has a lot of glass frontage, where most people prefer to sit. Opposite is an open-plan kitchen where dishes steam, flame and sizzle. Waiters shout orders in and a large, bald Chinese man is in charge of dispersing information and food in relevant directions. A young woman with a computer (Malay? — going by the dress) is also clearly involved, but Bent cannot quite figure out how. Just so long as the bill tallies.

'Happily multiculturally Eurasian here, then,' Bent smiles ironically to himself.

He has changed out of his working-day suit and tie and decided for informal rather than casual: open collar shirt and a short, dark-blue sports jacket. He wonders if Mason has also been thinking about how to dress, how much of an effort to make, and in what direction. Is this only an extension of their working relationship into a different time of day? Or is it a shift in that relationship?

She arrives punctually.

'You stood up,' she remarks as she reaches the table. She takes off her coat and drops it over the back of her chair.

'It wouldn't have crossed my mind not to. You're wearing a dress.'

They stand looking at each other for a moment.

Laugh. Sit down.

'Isn't standing up a bit old-fashioned?' she asks.

'I'll have to think about it. I suppose it's true I wouldn't have stood up for Bob. Or would I? No, I guess I wouldn't,' he smiles.

'Must be something about the way Mrs Bent brought her boys up, then.'

'Yes, must be.'

'Along with a tendency to be surprised by dresses.' She pours herself a glass of water from the carafe on the table.

'Oh, excuse me! It's, er ...'

'Mmmm?' She raises her eyebrows quizzically, sips the water.

'OK,' he says, raising his hands as if in surrender, 'You got me. I like dresses.'

'Must be difficult to get your size.'

He chuckles. Shakes his head. Takes a swallow of beer.

'Look around,' he says, without looking around.

'Women in pants, women in jeans, women in skirts, women in leggings, women in jeggings, women in trouser suits. How many women in dresses? I don't mean fancy, off-the-shoulder creations for big occasions, but just an everyday dress ...'

'You think this is just an everyday dress?'

'Ayeeeee! I did not mean it like that. In fact, I did not mean to comment on your dress at all, just that it was a dress. Is a dress. And I like dresses. I like to see dresses. I like to see women wearing dresses. No, just a minute,' he raises a hand again, this time in protest as she starts to speak.

'*And*, I wish in no way to take up a position on what women ought to wear or not wear, *and* I do like the actual dress you are wearing. *And* I hope you will either overlook or forgive the fact that I have not only formed an opinion of your clothing, but also expressed it.'

'Mmm. Are you sticking with beer or shall we have a bottle of wine?'

They move on to the menu.

'OK to share?'

'Surely.'

They order a number of dishes of the spicy Singaporean fusion food that the restaurant specialises in. And a bottle of Shiraz. They talk about the food, about the restaurant, the clientele, the staff. And from that, they move on, inevitably, to shop.

'I wonder if they're noticing it?' Bent asks. 'Abuse of minorities, anybody who looks like an immigrant.'

'Must be,' Mason responds. 'And it might be more than that. That's why this Great White business is starting to look more serious.'

'How so?'

'Nothing for sure, but signs. I mean, once, a gang of youths might have done a corner shop, and the owner might have been an ethnic, but the point would have been what they could nick, no matter how trivial. Now, it's more like the whole point is the trashing of the shop, and the owner definitely non-white minority.'

'You make it sound like ethnic cleansing.'

'That's going too far. And it might be that these Great Whites are just a bunch of thugs with a clever symbol.'

'Or?'

Mason sips her wine.

'Or, a generation of cannon-fodder is being prepared. Out of "the precariat" — dead-end youths who get their first feeling of ever belonging to anything. Creating the kind of mayhem that leads to demands for a crackdown on "the immigrant problem."'

'At which point,' Bent takes up the theme, 'some political group "spontaneously" steps forward to act in response to "genuine public demand."'

'I've never been a conspiracy theorist,' says Mason. 'But what you suggest could fit very unpleasantly with what's happening on the ground. Just rumours for now.'

Bent listens and takes it in. He feels the coldness inside him. A sense of data being logged. Analysis and calculation will follow. Action too, perhaps. If real action ever becomes possible against such a long-lived, insidious enemy.

'Thank you,' he says. 'Not my case, but you are right, I do want to know what's going on there.'

'And the girls?'

'It's not good.'

'It was never going to be.'

'Truth is, we're still not sure what we've got there, either. At one level, there's a lot of juvenile excitement based around a few iffy clubs. Places like *Paradise Garden* and *Lotus*. You know them?'

Mason shakes her head.

'The girls just clam up about themselves, but they've all got stories to tell about their friends, unnamed.'

'Makes them easier to ignore.'

'Don't give up on me just yet. Most of the girls are, or have been, in care. They are groomed with the usual: attention, presents, drink, drugs and they end up getting passed around.'

'Age?'

'Young. Some as young as thirteen, maybe younger.'

'If they're old enough to bleed.'

'What?'

'One of my favourite lines on the subject.'

It seems to Bent that the skin is being pulled tighter over the bones of Mason's skull as she continues:

'"If they're old enough to bleed, they're old enough to cut." Read it somewhere. Videos?'

'Not that we know of.'

'Yet.'

'No, but there is mention of "special events" that take place. Sounds more than just the local lads with a bit of extra cash to flash.'

'And?'

'Task force being set up – us, social workers, healthcare, psychologists, counsellors, local politicians and,' Bent pauses at this point, '"community leaders". This is what everybody's getting excited about. There's no way around the fact that the groomers are British Asians, "Pakistanis" as far as the girls are concerned, which might also mean Indian or Bangla Deshi, Somali, Arab or Afghani. They refer to each other as "The Brothers," according to one of the girls. Those set above us regard this as "sensitive," as the saying goes.'

'Yes, that would be "sensitive," wouldn't it?' Mason's face has closed into a mask. 'Unlike the girls.'

In the silence that follows, Bent is reminded of that unique moment before the fight starts, when you send your presence out to explore your opponent's vulnerabilities and you sense him reaching out across the ring for you. But this is different. He feels himself being assessed, but not for his weakness or capacity for violence. Nor is she an opponent. What is coming?

They both shift as if to speak. Mason is first.

'I've just realised something very, very important ...'

'Wha...'

'No, listen. Jesus, there are so many layers to this ...'

Bent leans forward, saying nothing, listening. Mason laughs,

'Yeah. Like I said. Lots of layers.'

'You could start at the surface and dig,' he suggests. 'Or start at the bottom and burrow on up.'

'I need a cigarette.'

'No, you don't.'

Her eyes flash.

'I meant that in a good way.'

'Yeah.'

'And I happen to know that you always carry a packet of cigarettes with you so you can keep on choosing not to have one every time you think you "need" one.'

'My father started to fuck me from when I was twelve.'

Bent holds her gaze. His eyes narrow as the wave of pain that washes across the table crashes over his body. The salt stings his face.

'I decided on the second approach.' Mason smiles a thin smile and unwraps a piece of nicotine gum. 'Start at the bottom.'

'Yes, you did.'

'Now you're going to wait for me to start burrowing on up, are you?'

'Yes, I am.'

'I'm not sure if I have a lot of burrowing strength left in me. But I'll tell you this: there is something, a something, some things in you like there are in me and I believe we want to know what that is all about.'

'You doing show-and-tell?'

'Yes, you smart-arse, I'm doing show-and-tell.'

'I didn't mean that in a trivial way.'

'I know you didn't. That's another layer.'

'Is it OK if I listen for a while longer?'

Mason sits back in her chair. Bent does the same.

'Yes,' she says. 'I chose the time to talk, so I'll talk.'

The waiter approaches. They wave him away. Bent pours more wine, emptying the bottle.

'Leave it at that?' he asks. She nods. Takes out her gum. Has a drink of water. A sip of wine.

'You know much about parents abusing their kids?'

'I know about kids getting knocked about. That's why some of us were down the gym, learning to look after ourselves. But not what you're talking about.'

'No. Did it help?'

'Learning to fight?'

'Yes.'

'Not according to what the others told me. It's not the

same, they said. When it's your dad coming at you, you can't just punch him out like you would some other bloke. You defend yourself and get out of the way.'

'It wasn't your problem, then?'

'My dad? No. Never was.'

'They were right, your friends. It's not the same when it's your dad coming at you.' She stares into her wine.

'I don't know what to say.'

'Just ask me something. Help me get going.' She looks up at him. It feels half like an instruction, half like a plea.

'Age twelve?'

'Yes. I remember him saying, 'So, you're going to big school now. You don't have to be Daddy's little girl anymore. Now you can be Daddy's big girl.'

'Jesus.'

'I swear to you, up to that minute, I had no idea. And after that, I didn't know what to do.'

'How long did it go on for?'

'Till I was fifteen, on and off.'

'And then it stopped?'

She takes another sip of wine.

'My brother found out. Sort of. Came home one day when he was supposed to be playing football. Not that he caught us at it, but we were both in a bit of a state and he got confused and upset. Didn't want to think about it, I suppose.'

'I suppose not.'

'Then a couple of weeks later, we were all sitting watching telly, the four of us, and this Crimewatch-sort-of program came on. We used to watch it now and again. But this time it was about child sexual abuse. I wanted to turn it off, but didn't dare. I think probably everyone in the room felt the same way. Every one of us probably thought it was addressed to us personally. And there were these girls on, talking about their fathers and mothers and brothers and sisters. They kept mentioning this helpline number and I couldn't stop myself memorising it.

'Then I started to cry. I thought someone would ask me why I was crying, or tell me not to get so upset, but nobody said anything. Then my mother started crying. Then my brother got up. He was eighteen then and a big lad, already bigger than my father. I will never forget that scene.'

She pauses, takes another drink. Bent does the same, remaining quiet, his face creased in pain.

'He reaches into his pocket and pulls out this black thing. I didn't know what it was at first. Then he flicks the blade open and throws the knife into my father's lap. "Keep this with you," he says. "You might need it." Then he left.'

'Left?'

'Well, left the room, left the house. But in a sense, he left for good. He joined the army soon after. We never really talked about what happened that evening, or what it was all about. The last thing he said to me was, "If you need me again, I'll always come. And next time, I'll bring a gun."

'But you didn't need him. Not for that, anyway.'

'No. It was finished with my father. He never said anything or came near me like that again. And my brother was dead within the year.'

'In action?'

'No, a stupid accident with a truck in training. But he's just as dead.'

'I'm very sorry to hear that.'

'Yeah, thanks.'

'And your parents?'

'I stayed at home till I went to university. Never went back much after that. Got jobs or stayed with friends in the vacations. A few years back, my mother told me he was getting dementia, couldn't remember anything or anybody. "Good move," I told her and left them to it.'

'They're dead?'

'He is. He had to go into hospital for some tests. He must have got up in the night, disoriented, and fell down some steps. Broke his hip. Then one of those super-bugs finished him off. She's in a home. I pay for it.'

'I hear you and I feel you, but I don't know what to call it.'

'Call what?'

'That feeling. That emotion. The one that isn't there. That space, that gap, where you might think a feeling would be.'

'Bloody hell, Bent. You do tell it like you see it, don't you?'

'Sorry. I didn't mean to sound harsh. But yes, that's also how Mrs Bent brought her boys up. No disrespect intended.'

'No need to apologise. You nailed it. It's a sign you were listening. Really listening. I tell you the story and you bring your pain to it. But you are so smart you also notice that it's your pain you are feeling. The pain should be coming through in the telling, but it's not there, because ...'

'Because,' Bent joins in. 'Let me risk this one. You have got the hurt buried so deep that the story doesn't touch it. It's down in a vault somewhere and that story does not contain the combination to unlock the door.'

'Then let me risk this one,' says Mason, her voice almost a whisper now, 'You're talking about yourself.'

'Living in Bluebeard's castle,' Bent seems to acknowledge, although in a mock-dramatic voice that shifts the mood.

'With the keys to all the rooms,' she follows the lead.

'But one room you really must not open.'

'Because that way lies madness.'

'Or something equally unpleasant.'

They both sit back in their chairs, only then noticing the extent to which they have been leaning forward, bodies tense, over the table.

'I think that's enough of that for tonight,' says Mason. She takes cigarettes from her bag, opens the packet, holds it to her nose and takes a deep breath.

'Disgusting!' she comments and puts them back into her bag.

Bent waves to a waitress and mimes signing.

'Do young people mime punching a PIN number, or just waving a contactless card?' Mason wonders out loud.

'Well, you're a detective, DI Mason.'

'Mmmm. Yes, let us observe and gather some evidence on that one before discussing it further.'

'Tomorrow?'

'No, sorry. Can't. Day after?'

'Mm-hmm.'

'Good.'

They add a tip and split the bill across two cards.

As they get up, Mason starts as though a shock has run through her. She reaches out a hand to Bent's arm.

'Jesus!'

'What's the matter? Are you OK?'

'Yes. No. I just felt something. Can you have an idea here?' She presses her other hand against her stomach.

'Do you want to go for a drink somewhere?'

'No, no, let's call it a night. Let me think.'

'So, give me a clue.'

'No. No. Not yet, not quite. But when I had that ... whatever it was, I also had this sensation of something so ... right. In a bad way. Leave it with me. Maybe, "Ah have a dream."'

She winks at Bent, her face now bright with animation. They wish each other goodnight and go their separate ways. After a dozen paces, he stops, concerned, and turns, but she is already out of sight.

Chapter 9

Elli is far from happy. There she is looking forward to the trip and, yeah, the new trainers are mega-cool, but when she tells Amir she doesn't trust him anymore, she's expecting at least an apology and a promise it won't happen again. Instead, he says she should bring a friend if that'll make her feel better. She doesn't want to bring a friend. She just wants to make sure that her boyfriend doesn't bring along one of his friends again and expect her to do stuff for him.

But she can't tell him that, can she? She'd look stupid. So she says, yeah, she'll bring a friend. So then, who to ask? Most of her mates are at the hostel. Karen can be a good laugh, but she's a right slapper and might have her eyes on Amir. Might have her hands on him, more likely, if Elli doesn't watch out. There wouldn't be any trouble like that with Bev, 'cause Bev's as ugly as sin and Amir wouldn't fancy her, but she can also be a miserable little bitch when she wants to. And weird.

So then Amir asks her if she's invited anybody. When she says no, he says, what about her with the long hair you were talking to at the club last week? Sarah? I don't think so. Why is he so interested in Sarah? Stuck-up cow. Thinks she's better than us. Struck lucky with the foster-parents. Nice work if you can get it. Dresses a bit different now.

So, fuck it, Elli asks Karen. Oh yeah, Karen's keen. Then what? Turns out Amir has asked Sarah if she'd like to 'go along with her friends.' Says he thought that's what Elli wanted — take some friends along, the more the merrier. So Elli tells Bev and, oh yes, Bev's keen. No problem, says Amir. I know a place we can all stay. If anybody wants to know, tell 'em you're staying at Mrs Atkins' guesthouse. Here's the number, ask for Mrs Atkins.

Next thing is, Sarah announces her foster-mother has phoned up and spoken to Mrs Atkins and she seems very nice and used to work at a hostel and likes to do her bit now and again to give 'disadvantaged' girls a treat and they'll all be looked after, no worries. Her mum ('mum' if you like!) is well put out with the 'disadvantaged' bit, but sucks it up so as not to make a fuss. But you just ask Sarah what her 'mum' thinks about Amir and she goes very quiet. Elli reckons that Sarah has spun a bit of a yarn about how they're getting there and back. That's not so bad. It means she's not quite so little-Miss-better-than-us after all.

So, here they are, in the Merc, with Elli in the front and three in the back. Amir asks if the others want to take turns in the front. And before Elli can say, 'No fucking way,' those three cackling and chatting in the back shout up, 'No fucking way!' And that leaves Elli a bit pissed off as well. She can only make out half of what they are on about. Bev is telling some story she's got from Carmen. Thing with Carmen is that she is fourteen, but looks about six, so she can't get into the clubs and doesn't have a lot of friends. She's mixed-race, too, so most of the guys aren't interested anyway. Upshot of that is Carmen's always making stuff up so she can come on big. And, to be fair, she is up for anything.

So, according to Bev, Carmen gets taken to this posh hotel and up the back stairs to this room and there's this old bloke sitting in an armchair in the dark, stark naked. And there's something about this pair of silk pyjamas she has to put on — pure white silk and covered with 'golliwogs,' whatever they are. So she gives this old bloke a blow-job and there's fifty quid. Fifty quid! Is this likely? But the other two just go Ooooh and Aaaah as if they believe it all. And Bev tries to big herself up as if she knows what's going on. Says she's seen the pyjamas. Lying cow. And bloody Amir keeps turning the music up and she has to keep turning it down. Oh yeah, great time we're having.

And then when they stop for a coffee, all of a sudden it's,

'Oh, OK, I'll take my turn up front,'

and bloody Sarah slides her round little arse in her tight fancy jeans into the front seat and plonks her neat new trainers on the dashboard.

Not much Amir can do at that point, really, but he tries to make Elli feel special again by passing back the makings and asking her to roll up a smoke. That shows them all that really she's the one with him.

It's uber-strong stuff. Amir passes.

'Not while I'm driving you lovely ladies,' he says.

By the time the second one's gone around, Bev is out of it. Sarah is singing quietly to herself and Karen is helping Elli hassle Amir about needing to pull over somewhere and buy some chocolate, or cake, or both.

'Double chocolate chip muffins!' says Elli.

'And some cider,' Karen adds.

So they do that and then they're into Blackpool. Bev wants to go straight to the funfair. Karen wants fish and chips. Elli wants to go to the front and get dive-bombed by the seagulls. Amir says they have to go to Mrs Atkins' place first and say hello and drop their stuff off. Then it's seaside, fish and chips in paper and on to the rides.

Sarah says that sounds good to her. Then she asks Elli to pass her the gear and she rolls up another one. This time Amir takes a toke and says, 'Nice.' Which pisses Elli off again.

'Not very near the sea, is it?' she says, as they drive through narrow streets of old terraced houses, broken up occasionally with clear spaces that look as though somebody might have wanted to do something there at some time, but gave up. The street they pull up in has bigger, three-storey houses, some with dormer windows built out at the attic level. Mrs Atkins' is on a corner and larger than the others. There are three steps up to a solid green front door that hasn't been decorated for a while. There is no sign to say it's a bed-and-breakfast place, but Amir bounds up the steps and bangs away with a big metal knocker that looks like a woman's hand holding a ball. He waves at the girls to get out and join him. They do, each carrying a little rucksack of overnight things and something to change into for the evening.

Mrs Atkins is a large woman in stretch jeans and a fleece top. Her hair is grey for the most part, long and unsuccessfully pinned up. She is neither friendly nor unfriendly. She looks at the girls but speaks only to Amir.

'Second floor at the back.'

'Come on, then,' says Amir. 'I'll show you your rooms.'

They troop up two flights of stairs and follow Amir across a landing. The place starts to look even bigger than it appeared from outside.

'You know your way around, then?' says Elli.

'Oh yeah,' Amir replies. 'We used to come here when I was a kid. Here we go, 32, 33, 34, 35, pick whichever one you like, but don't fight about it. They're all the same, anyway.'

Elli gives him what she calls her 'death stare.' She points to him and to herself a few times and raises her hands, palms up, in question.

'Yeah, don't worry about it,' says Amir with a wink. 'Just pick a room.'

The others have already opened the doors and looked at the rooms. They really are all the same. The walls are magnolia and the woodwork a yellowed white. Each room has a double bed, with a bedside unit and a table lamp. Also, a wardrobe, a small table and straight-backed chair, a mirror on the wall over the table and a central ceiling light. There is a window that looks out over the alley behind the house and the backyards of the houses beyond. The only distinguishing feature is the curtains. They are all in a check pattern, but 32 is blue, 33 red, 34 yellow and 35 green. Sarah, Karen and Bev have already taken the first three, leaving Elli with green, her least favourite colour.

'The bathroom's down the end,' says Amir. 'There's towels and extra blankets in the rooms. Settle yourselves in and come on down to the dining room.'

'Do we get keys?'

'You don't need to worry about keys. This place is as safe as houses,' says Amir. 'You've seen Mrs Atkins. Nobody messes with her or her guests.'

The girls drop off their rucksacks, go to the loo and regroup on the landing.

'Bit of a dump.' says Bev.

'Sod it,' says Karen. 'We'll have some "fun-o-the-fair" this afternoon, come back here and get our kit on, get off round some clubs tonight and we won't be much bothered about this place.'

'I hope I've got enough money with me,' says Sarah.

'I don't expect to be paying for anything, myself,' Karen shoots back.

'Yeah,' says Bev. 'Karen's just as keen on getting her kit off as getting it on, aren't you, Ka?'

'You're crude, you,' Karen replies. 'Boys just like buying me things, that's all.'

'Come on, you lot! Fish and chips!' Amir shouts up the stairs, and down they go.

They were expecting to eat walking along the sea front, but Mrs Atkins has got loads in from the local chipper and there are no plates, so it is still sort-of 'out of the paper.' Plus which, Amir has produced a couple of bottles of white wine to go with it, so there is nothing to complain about. They eat and drink and get a bit noisy. There is a knocking at the door and more guests arrive, but Mrs Atkins takes care of that and Amir pours more wine.

'Pleasure Beach!' shouts Bev, banging her glass back down on the table. 'I want a ride!'

'Off to The Big Dipper!' Karen agrees, emptying her glass.

'I want to go on the Wild Mouse!' says Sarah.

'The what?'

'The Wild Mouse. I've read about it. It's one of the old wooden ones — there aren't many left.'

'Bloody Hell, Sarah,' says Elli. 'This isn't a fucking museum trip, you know. I want to get back on The Big One! It's like five hundred feet up in the sky and you just drop out of it, straight down for about a mile. We went on it before, didn't we, Amir?'

'Certainly did, Elli,' says Amir. 'Let's just finish this bottle and we're off. Don't want to have to throw it away.'

'Nah, I've had enough,' says Bev. 'For now, anyway.'

She stands up and immediately sits down again.

'Woah! Wooh. Phoo. I might have had a bit too much!'

'Take it easy,' says Amir, 'We've got plenty of time. How are the rest of you doing?'

The girls look around the table.

'Pretty good.'

'Not great,'

'Bit tired.'

'Probably shouldn't have mixed the dope and the wine so early in the day,' says Amir.

'No worries!' says Elli. 'You keep it coming. I'm just getting my second wind.'

'I thought I could smell something,' says Karen and Bev gets into this really annoying cackling noise, like somebody's throttling a cat.

'Yeah,' says Amir. 'Well, like I said, we've got plenty of time. Why don't you all take a quick nap and then we'll get off?'

'A nap?' Elli snaps at him. 'We're not children!'

'I feel sick,' says Sarah. She stands up and leans heavily against the table.

The others get up, likewise, unsteadily.

'Hey,' says Elli, 'It's like the room's going round.'

'Come on,' says Amir. 'Let's call it a lie-down.' He puts an arm around her waist and leads her towards the door.

'Just hold on, girls,' he calls over his shoulder. 'I'll be right back.'

'Jesus,' says Bev. 'I can't see straight.'

'Close your eyes,' Karen suggests.

'That's even worse,' says Bev. 'Who are you?'

Elli looks back to see who she is talking to. But then it seems like there are three Amirs in the room. And the doorway comes closer. Then it moves sideways, but then there are other hands helping her line up with it again. Which is nice. But the stairs seem impossible. Elli tries putting one foot in front of the other, but that only works about half-way. Then it 's more like she's being pulled up the stairs, which isn't so nice. She can feel a seam splitting under her arm. She wants to stop, but the arms around her are too strong. It's a relief to get to the top. She steadies herself against her helper and takes a couple of steps, but then her knees go and the arms around her tighten again.

Then someone else is there. Mrs Atkins, perhaps? She's opening the bedroom door. Seems to be opening all the bedroom doors.

'Sorry, Mrs Atkins,' Elli mumbles.

Then she's sitting on the bed. She hears the door close again. Somebody is undressing. She can smell sweat. Somebody is undressing her. Quickly. Roughly.

'No,' she says. 'No, no. Amir?'

But everything is very vague and her hands don't do what she wants them to. She remembers them talking about getting their kit off at some point. Not like this. But it is all off, so that's that. She hears what sounds like a grunt. She lies back on the bed and passes out.

Chapter 10

Mason is going off duty when she hears the commotion. The distress in the woman's voice draws her over.

'Can I help?' she asks.

'I was explaining that we can't actually register a missing person after a few hours,' the duty sergeant says.

'Especially if it's a teenage girl fostered from The Greenfields,' the woman adds, bitterly.

'No, madam, that's not what I said.'

'It's what it sounded like to me.'

'Perhaps you could just come and sit down and tell me about it,' Mason suggests. 'Thank you, sergeant.'

'Thank *you*, ma'am.'

The story pours out of Mrs Lowe:

'Sarah arranged to go away to Blackpool with a group of old friends from Greenfields. The home is providing transport. They wanted to stay overnight. I wasn't keen on that, but you don't want to be overprotective, do you? I phoned the Guest House and the woman sounded nice. She said she used to work in a hostel herself and would keep an eye on the girls.

'They all went off this morning. Then around six, I thought I'd check that everything was alright. But I heard Sarah's phone ringing upstairs. It was in her room. That is so unusual. She never goes anywhere without her phone.'

Before Mason can speak, Mrs Lowe goes on:

'No, I am not stupid, or naïve, and yes, somebody might leave a phone behind if they didn't want to be contacted for a while. I get that. So I phoned the B&B again, but now there's no answer.'

'A landline?'

'No, a mobile, and I left a message. Three messages, in fact. And then I phoned Greenfields. The person I spoke to said she didn't know anything about a trip. It sounded a bit unusual, she said, but yes, they do have a mini-bus. No, the person who would know for sure wasn't available. She didn't know where the log for the mini-bus was, that wasn't her responsibility.'

'Do you know who else was going on this trip?'

'Sarah told me some names, but I don't know any of them. I met the foster parents of one of them, Elli, once, but we didn't get on very well and, anyway, I don't think that worked out. Look, Sarah is fifteen. She's doing well at school. She doesn't have a boyfriend. She likes dancing. She's very normal. I don't know what else to say.'

'Where does she go dancing?'

'Oh, a few places: *Bundles* is one. *Macro-Micro*. *The Lotus*.'

'*The Lotus*?'

'Yes, that's become her favourite recently. I know she's under age, but I drop her off and pick her up. You can't keep them under lock and key 24/7, can you?'

'No, no, you can't,' says Mason, now making connections that she does not want to be making. 'What sort of a crowd do they get there?'

'Mixed, she says,' Mrs Lowe replies, a little warily.

'Mixed?'

'Well, I mean, all sorts, you know.'

'Racially mixed, you mean?'

'Not necessarily, but I hope so, don't you? How else are we all supposed to get on? They say there's a lot of racial prejudice in the police, don't they?'

'I have heard that, Mrs Lowe, but I hope you didn't hear any of that in my question. I'm just trying to get a picture.'

'Mmmm.'

'As the sergeant was saying, your daughter has not been away for very long and there doesn't seem to be a definite reason for alarm. But,' she continues in the face of Mrs Lowe's protest, 'what about this girl, Elli? Do you have any contact information at all for her?'

'No! And the woman at Greenfields wouldn't give me her phone number.'

'Well,' says Mason, taking out her phone, 'Let's see if we can do something about that. Have you got their number?'

Mrs Lowe reaches into her bag and takes out her phone. Mason notices her hand shaking and she feels a strong wave of compassion for this woman, doing everything she can to do right.

Before Mrs Lowe can check the number, however, the phone in her hand starts to ring. She clearly does not recognise the number.

'Hello?'

'Mum, mum, help me!'

'Sarah!' Mrs Lowe jumps to her feet. 'Where are you, luvvie?'

'I don't know!'

'Are you all right?'

The phone sobs.

'Please!' says Mason and takes it.

'Sarah, my name is Mason, I am a police officer. I am with your mum. We are coming to pick you up. Where are you?'

'I don't know.'

'Are you in a house?'

'No, I'm in a phone box. I haven't got any more money.'

'Sarah, look at where you hang the phone up. There's an address there. What does it say?'

'Oakmount Road. Blackpool. FY2 6RX.'

'Good girl. Stay there.'

'No, they'll see me!'

The pips signalling the end of the call started to sound.

'Sarah,' says Mason, fighting back questions, 'Find somewhere to hide where you can see the phone box. A police car will be there in a few minutes. Do you understand?'

But the line goes dead before she reaches the end of the sentence.

Mason gives swift instructions to the duty sergeant.

'Tell them all bells and whistles and let me know where they take her. I'm on the way.'

'Mrs Lowe,' she turns to the woman who has followed her, handing back her phone. 'Go home. That's the best place for you to be and I will bring Sarah to you.'

'No chance. She'll want to see me. I'll come with you.'

'No, that's not possible,' says Mason, heading for the car park.

'Then I'll see you there! I've got a GPS. I can find FY2 6RX and the nearest police station!'

'She won't be there by the time you get there.'

'Somebody's after her, aren't they?'

Mason stops and turns to face her.

'Yes. So that gives us three possibilities: the police have picked her up; whoever was chasing her has found her; she is on the run. If it's the last of those, where will she try to go? She will go home,' Mason answers her own question. 'I need you there to cover that possibility. Right now you are wasting time. Give me your number and go home. Call me if anything happens.' Mason hands Mrs Lowe her business card and pulls out her phone to take the number.

'A young girl with no money can't possibly get home from Blackpool before we can get there. If she does, she'll find my husband there. If she has a chance to get in touch again, she will phone this number and you want to know what she says,' Mrs Lowe blazes back at her. 'I am coming with you and it's you who's wasting time.'

'Yes,' says Mason and leads the way to her car.

Ten minutes later, as they leave the city streets and join the evening traffic heading west, Mason's phone rings, activating the in-car system.

'Yes?'

'Local lads say no sign of her.'

'Keep looking. Real fear of abduction. More detailed description coming up.'

Without further comment, Mason indicates to Mrs

Lowe that she should take over, which she does, in a voice fraying under tension.

'Five foot six, slim, fifteen years old, long hair, light brown, fair complexion, lovely smile, nice teeth, blue jeans, black leather ankle-boots, yellow, well, gold blouse, blue, crew-neck sweater, short, black, belted raincoat, cream-coloured little rucksack, with ponies on it …' at which point she breaks down.

'Got that, sergeant?' Mason asks.

'Yes, ma'am.'

'Keep in touch,' she closes the exchange.

'Well done,' to Mrs Lowe. 'There are tissues in the glove compartment.'

A filling station appears on the left and Mason pulls in, parking away from the pumps.

'What's the matter?' asks Mrs Lowe.

'Just a minute. Just a minute. Let me think.'

'Can't you think and drive?'

'Yes, but I don't want to be thinking and driving in the wrong direction and I can't think and talk to you at the same time.'

'Yes, you can. Talk your thoughts to me. Put them into words. All of them. Make me understand. It will help you understand what you're thinking.'

Mason gives her a long look and begins.

'Girl hangs out at the Lotus. People she's likely to have met there. Men she's likely to have met there. And girls. Girls she used to know. Lies to her mother and goes away for the weekend. Something goes wrong. She is not getting what she expected or what she wants. She tries to get away but that is stopped. She is back with the people she tried to get away from. So, the question is no longer what will she do, but what will they do.'

'She might have just run away again.'

'In which case the Blackpool police will take care of it and we can't be that much help. Be quiet and listen.' Mason pauses for a moment. Takes a deep breath.

'They will be damn near as scared as she is. Just of different things. Consequences. As far as we know, we are dealing with some young, self-regarding lowlifes who think they are on a free ride. What they want now is for her to disappear and shut up. Pretend nothing happened. They don't want to hurt her. They want to get rid of her. — In a good way,' she adds, as she sees Lowe wince. 'If you ask me, they are on this road, driving in the opposite direction, trying to get her home as fast as they can.'

The two of them sit and look at the passing traffic.

'You can't be sure.'

'All I am sure about is we are doing no good sitting here. I have finished with my thinking and my talking and I thank you for your listening. Now I have to do something. And the only thing it makes any sense to do is what just came out of my talking and thinking. Not so, counsellor?'

Mrs Lowe gives a wan smile.

'That's the theory.'

'Then let's put it into practice. We have some time. We'll pick up your car from the station and you can show me the best way home.'

As they drive, Mrs Lowe talks. Yes, she is a counsellor. She works for a charity called *Pathways* that offers counselling, coaching and career advice to young people. She and her husband met too late in life to have children. They decided to foster some years ago and it has, for the most part, worked out very well. Some heartache, some disappointments, but some great times, too.

'Sounds like most families, then,' Mason comments. Lowe smiles and nods.

Sarah has been with them for nearly six months now. They feel very close to her. They have even been talking about adopting, but they do not know if she would like that.

'Your husband is at home?' Mason asks.

'Yes. You're wondering why he isn't out here.'

'No. Well, maybe. But if I was, it was a stupid thing to think.'

'My husband's a wheelchair user. We play to our strengths.'

Mason looks across at her.

'If he has strengths like yours, you must be a pretty formidable team.'

'United, never defeated,' says Lowe. 'That's my car there. Thanks for the ride.'

Mason watches her cross to her car and then follows her home. On the way, she checks in for more information, but there is none.

They both pull up outside the Lowe's bungalow. Mason gets out and walks to the other car. Mrs Lowe opens the window.

'Leave your car as usual,' Mason tells her.

'That'd be on the drive.'

'Fine. Look. I'm not going to tell you to go to bed and

sleep.'

'Really!?'

'No, but think about how your house usually looks at this time of a Saturday night, and as the night goes on. Where would there be lights on? Where not? Would it be different as you're not supposed to be expecting Sarah home tonight? Make it look as usual as you can. I don't want to put anybody off.'

'What about you?'

'You have your job here and I have mine. Let's play to our strengths. Your husband must be worried.'

'Yes,' she acknowledges. 'But our basic understanding is that no news is good news. He knows if there was anything he needed to know, I would have told him.'

'I suspect he also knows that if you knew where Sarah was, you would have told him that, too.'

'Yes,' says Mrs Lowe. 'You'll call if you hear anything. At any time.'

'Yes. And likewise,' says Mason. She puts Lowe's landline and mobile numbers into her phone and returns to her car. Once Mrs Lowe is in the house, Mason pulls down the street a little and turns into a side-street. She makes a u-turn and pulls back up the side-street to park close to the corner, from where she can see the Lowe's house.

She hopes that what she has so confidently predicted to Mrs Lowe is correct. There is no guarantee, but there is a logic to it. It makes sense and it creates one version of the world in which she, Mason, is in a position to do something.

'Hmph! Possible worlds,' she says to herself. 'And wanting to do something.' What she says next is,

'Fucking men!' She feels her anger at the endless, narcissistic male drive to exploitation and abuse. And herself in a position to do something.

She takes her constant packet of cigarettes from her bag and opens it. She extracts a cigarette like the poisonous foreign body she knows it to be and looks at it. She breaks off a centimetre, puts it in her mouth and starts to chew. Immediately, with a spasm of disgust and anger, she spits the foul mess out into a tissue that she screws up and puts back into her bag with the packet of cigarettes. She takes out another tissue and wipes her eyes.

She sits with the taste for a while. The sourness of it.

'Fucking men!' And herself in a position to do something.

'It's the good old neo-cortex that makes us human,' she says, 'But some decisions are still made in the gut.' Then she unwraps a piece of nicotine gum and settles down to wait. And think.

Chapter 11

Amir is driving fast, hoping not to be too fast and attract attention. But he has to be fast. He has to get this one out of the picture and himself back to Blackpool in time to keep some sort of control over what is going on. He does not really have much faith in Mohsin, or Ali, especially if they start on the white stuff.

Yes, OK, this one is his mistake. He's tried to take things too quickly. Maybe she isn't quite like the others. How the fuck is he supposed to tell the difference? They all like the flattery, they like the cars, they like the booze, they like the dope, they like the presents, they like to get their tits out and, sooner or later, they like to get their pants off. And yeah, this one is a bit different. That was the point, wasn't it? He had known exactly who would fancy this one and appreciate him, Amir, for bringing her along. He should have fucked her himself first. That would have got her into line. But the big fella likes 'em fresh, doesn't he? Talk about can't do right for doing wrong — it's like you never get the appreciation you deserve.

Well, at least she's quiet now. He looks in the rear-view mirror. On the back seat, she seems to be asleep. The doors are child-locked, so she can't make another run for it. They have a deal. He'll get her home and she'll keep quiet. Tell her parents they had a great time, but she didn't feel well, then she fainted and banged her face, so the driver offered to bring her home. Not to make a fuss about it, or he might get into trouble about the extra mileage on the mini-bus.

He pulls over. She sits up immediately. Perhaps she wasn't asleep after all.

'Must be around here somewhere.'

She looks out.

'Yeah. Take the next left and it's about half way along on the right.'

He follows her instructions, driving slowly.

'That's it!' she says.

Amir slows right down, looks at the house.

'Yeah, well I don't want to stop right outside, do I?'

He turns into the next side-street, makes a u-turn and pulls up behind a car parked just short of the corner. He gets out and opens the rear passenger door.

'If you talk to anybody about what's happened tonight, you will be very, very sorry. AND I know where you live,' says Amir, in as threatening a voice as he can manage, while thinking, 'I shouldn't be here. Stick to the girls from the hostels, God knows there's enough of 'em.'

'Are you listening?'

'Yes. OK. I've got it. It's not something I exactly want to talk about.'

'Shut up, then. Come on.'

He takes her arm and pulls her out of the car, pushing the door to behind her.

'I'll take you to the corner.'

'No need.'

'I want to see you go into the house, innit? Make sure I've got the right one.'

As they turn, Amir still holding Sarah's arm, the driver's door of the car parked in front of them opens and a woman gets out. She walks around the front of her car, steps on to the pavement and stands directly in their way.

'Hello, Sarah. Who's your friend?' the woman says, conversationally.

Sarah flinches and pulls away from Amir. He grabs her arm again and she squeals. Amir turns to the woman.

'None of your business.'

'Might be.'

'Get out of the way.'

'No.'

Without letting go of Sarah with this right hand, Amir takes a stride forward in order to sweep this stupid little woman out of the way with his left. Except she takes half a step back and pushes his arm out wide of her on its swing. Then she steps forward and brings her left knee up hard between his legs. Amir gasps, lets go of Sarah and doubles up in pain, holding his crotch. As his head arcs down towards the ground, the woman rolls back onto her left foot and launches her right knee up into his face. He sees it coming just before his nose explodes and everything turns red. He spins away from her, gurgling for air. He feels a kick in the back of the knee and falls, banging his head against the pavement. As it bounces back up, it meets something hard coming down. Amir does not move again.

Mason stoops and turns his head to one side, contributing another layer of skin to the flagstones. She checks that breath is still bubbling through what looks like a pan of chopped tomatoes.

'Are you OK, Sarah?' says Mason.

'Who are you?'

'Take it easy,' says Mason, pulling out her ID. 'My name's Mason, Detective Inspector Mason. We spoke briefly on the phone. I was with your mum. She's waiting for you at home.'

The girl relaxes visibly. She looks down at Amir.

'Can anybody learn to do that?'

'It takes a while, but I could recommend some courses.'

'It's not exactly Tai Chi, is it?

'Er, no. There is probably a fundamental principle in common: Avoid violence if at all possible.'

'And then?'

'Principle number two: If you are going to be violent, act so as to bring your violence to an end in the shortest possible time. Principle number three: What goes down does not get up. That's about it. Philosophically speaking.'

Sarah smiles weakly. She leans back against the garden wall behind her.

'I'd like to go home now.'

'Yes, we'll do that. But first, I need to know something, so excuse me for being direct. Have you been sexually assaulted?'

'No.' Sarah looks down.

'Sarah. Look at me.'

They lock eyes.

'Has anyone had sex with you against your will, or with your agreement? Or pressured you into doing things you didn't want to?'

'No.'

'Are you sure?'

'I think I'd know, don't you?' Sarah snaps. 'Sorry. I mean, I guess that's what they wanted, but it never came to that.'

'How many of you were there?'

'Four. Me and Elli and Karen and Bev.'

'Family names?'

Sarah gives them.

'All from Greenfields?'

'Yes.'

'Do you know what's happened to them?'

'No.'

'Do you know where you were exactly?'

'No.'

'Could you find the place again? If we go back to the phone box, could ...'

Sarah bursts into tears and, at that moment, Mrs Lowe comes running around the corner and she and her daughter fall into each other's arms.

'I saw the car,' she says to Mason after a short while. 'I saw the car slow down outside our house and then turn up here. I thought it must be them. I couldn't wait any longer,' she sobs.

Mason watches the two of them while she firms up on her earlier decision to steer this one down an unmade path of her own choosing. Even as she does so, she suppresses thoughts of what might have happened, or be happening, to the other three girls. Having nothing to pray to, she can only calculate and hope.

'Mrs Lowe, Sarah,' she says quietly, 'Please go home

now. Sarah, I want you to tell your mum and dad, and it is important that it's both of them, together, exactly what's happened. That means how it came about, including all the things that you don't want them to know, as well as what has happened today. Do you understand?'

Sarah nods.

'This is your big chance, Sarah,' Mason continues. 'Your big chance to evacuate all the stuff you have to get rid of, including the messes that you have made yourself, and to have a real, fresh start with people who love you. Don't miss it. Do not mess this up. You will regret it for the rest of your life if you blow this chance. Do you hear me?'

'Yes,' says Sarah, 'I hear you.'

At that point, Mr Lowe comes around the corner.

'Thank God!' he says. 'You're all right. Are you all right?'

Sarah embraces him.

'I'm so sorry.'

'That's OK, girl. Nothing we three can't handle.'

'I believe that,' says Mason. 'But there is more.'

'More? What do you mean?'

'What has happened here is part of a bigger picture, with a number, perhaps a large number, of other girls involved.'

'And men,' Mr Lowe adds.

'Yes, and men.'

'Men like him?' Mrs Lowe gestures towards Amir.

'Let's just say 'men' for the time being,' Mason replies. 'What I want you to do is to take Sarah home and keep her at home tomorrow. Look after her and listen to her. She has told me that she has not been sexually abused, so there is no absolute need to take any physical evidence right now.

'There's no need for you to contact the police, either. I'll take care of that side of things and I'll check with Greenfields about the others. I'll call round to see you tomorrow evening, probably with a colleague who is involved with the larger case I mentioned. We'll take a statement then. In the meantime, Sarah, you will have told your parents as much as you know about what is going on. When we meet again, I want you,' she nods to Mr and Mrs Lowe, to tell my colleague and myself everything that Sarah has told you. Sarah, you can listen and make sure that there isn't anything you want to change or add. Then we will tell you what we know and how we want to proceed.'

'Yes,' says Mrs Lowe. 'Sarah tells us, we tell you, Sarah checks. Sounds like a good procedure.'

'Around 6 or 7 in the evening be OK?'

'Is something going on?' asks Mr Lowe.

'Yes,' says Mason. 'Trust me till tomorrow?'

'Yes,' say Sarah and Mrs Lowe in unison. He shrugs.

'What about him?' he asks.

'Please just go home,' says Mason. 'I'll look after him.'

'We're not actually so worried about him right now,' says Mrs Lowe. 'See you tomorrow.'

The three of them leave, with Sarah half leaning on her foster father's wheelchair and with her other arm around her foster mother.

Mason waits for them to turn the corner before

pulling on a pair of throw-away, latex gloves. She turns Amir over onto his back. He groans. She checks his pockets and finds his wallet. She takes his driving licence and puts the wallet back. She finds his phone and, on it, dozens of pictures of young girls that raise again the sick anger that curdles her stomach. She tastes the bile at the back of her throat.

Also in terms of physical sensation, she feels the increasing force of her earlier decision made only partly logically and mostly in the gut. It gives her such a strong connection to that moment in the restaurant with Bent. Now she is sure.

She continues her search of Amir's pockets. There is a small Moleskine notebook with pages of names, addresses and numbers.

'Too good to be true,' she mutters to herself.

She rips the pages out and slips licence, phone and pages into an evidence bag. She takes a pen from Amir's inside pocket and writes into his notebook, using a simple form of block capitals that she has taught herself to produce with her left hand: STAY AWAY FROM HERE. I HAVE YOUR PHONE AND CONTACTS. YOU ARE MINE. WHEN I CALL, YOU JUMP. Then, with a humourless smile, she signs it: *GW*.

She puts the notebook back into Amir's pocket and rolls him into a safe position that should stop him choking on his own blood or vomit. He groans again, louder, and starts to crawl along the pavement. Reassessing the situation on the basis of his semi-consciousness, she part-drags him towards his car. The door is still unlocked, keys in the ignition.

'Good,' she says to herself. 'Less of a public spectacle.'

She opens a rear door, prods and pulls him to his feet and pushes him inside. With a struggle, she tucks his feet in and looks down on him. She rubs her knee and relives the moment.

'You have no idea how much,' she says and bangs the door.

She returns to her car and drives away, wondering if there is still time to sleep and when Bent will be awake.

Chapter 12

Driving home, Mason asks the duty sergeant to contact Blackpool: emergency over, girl found, report later, thanks for support.

Once home, to her surprise, she sleeps immediately. But not for long.

... her childhood bedroom door opens soundless as a snake; light seeps in from the landing; the silhouette enters; the room darkens again; the whispered, 'Shshshsh;' her hands tighten into fists; pressure on the mattress; she sinks into the swamp ...

She wakes with a silent scream filling her head.

'Nah!' she shouts, loud now. Sitting, she shakes her head. Unclenching her fingers, she switches on the bedside lamp and reaches for the glass of water.

So, it's back. After all this time ...

It took long years to learn how to slam that mental gate shut and keep the repressed anguish roiling behind it.

She gets up, makes tea, wanders slowly around the renovated factory worker's cottage she bought three years ago. She touches things, feels herself back into this safe space. The developers had done the kind of job that appealed to people like her. She laughs.

'People like me! Who's that?'

Someone who lives alone? She supposes so. There have been men. She lived with one somewhere else for a while. Another one lived here for a brief period. Did not turn out well.

Yes, someone who lives alone and prefers a good-sized

bathroom to a second bedroom, connecting arch knocked through the dividing wall downstairs to give more feeling of space. The old 'back-kitchen' extended and re-fitted with modern appliances. That eats into the size of the back yard, of course, but that has been repaved and walled with sympathetic stone and brick, leaving border spaces she has planted with bamboo. It's a good and private place to sit out when the weather allows. Tonight, she watches the bamboo dance wet and wild in the wind.

She makes another mug of tea while reflecting on the previous night's events and how they fall into a pattern already forming. She realises that, while planning what she might achieve, she is also evaluating all that she has to lose. Not a little. But how sad it would be if it all added up to only a little!

She looks at her watch. Texts Bent. Suggests meeting as soon as convenient that afternoon. Heads in to work.

On the way, she pulls into her local petrol station and fills up.

'As-salaamu alaikum, Bashir,' she greets the young man behind the counter.

'Wa alaikum as-salaam, ya Wendy,' he replies. 'How are you?'

'Fine, thanks. You?'

'Very well, thank you. Al hamdu lillah.'

I wonder if you can help me ...'

'In sha Allah. What is it?'

Mason takes a small piece of paper from her pocket. It is the page that separated out the section of names, addresses and numbers in Amir's notebook. It has one word written on it in Arabic script.

'What does this say?' she asks, showing him the page.

'He glances briefly at the paper. It says, "Al-Ikhwan." It means "The Brothers" in Arabic. The writing isn't very good. Not very educated man.'

'Thanks, Bashir,' she says and pays for the petrol.

'Where did you get it?'

'Found it. Does it mean anything else, apart from "brothers"?

'No. And maybe not really "brothers," either. You know, we use the word "brother" a lot — a friend, someone I know, maybe just another Somali or another Muslim.'

'Yeah,' Mason smiles. 'I have my "sisters," too. Have you heard of a group called "The Brothers" — Al-Ikhwan?'

'Round here, you mean?'

She nods.

'No, never.'

'OK, shukran, Bashir.'

'Afwan, my pleasure, Wendy. Ma'a as-salaama.'

'Take care. Bye!'

* * *

Bob Poole looks up as she enters.

'Hi, boss. More stuff in on the Weeny Whites — national and local.'

'Local?'

'Mmm, word is they're forming up into something more, well, "official," if you like. Got a place to meet, an office, even.'

'Address?'

'Yep.' Bob waves an email print-out at her.

She pauses for a moment.

'Let's go see. Get a sense of this thing. Perhaps we can nip it in the bud before anything silly happens. Or if it looks serious, let's know about it.'

She and Poole drive across town to The King's Head. It's not an area that Mason knows well.

'Used to be solid working-class, lots of Irish,' says Bob. 'Including some of my family a couple of generations back. Then the old houses were cleared and council estates built. Functional, but not bad, a hell of a lot better than the slums that were here before. Then the Thatcher years, the unemployment ...'

'I know the story, Bob: to those that have shall be given.'

'War is peace, love is hate and we are all free.'

'Greed is good.'

'The market will provide. All we need is more competition.'

'And here we are,' she says. 'The King's Head. This must have been a fine old place in its day. Love the tiles. So, let's see what the human cost adds up to these days.'

The barman's ready smile fades as he asks politely to see some ID and acknowledges that there is an office upstairs with a shark painted on the door. He asks Mason and Poole to wait while he phones ahead to announce them.

'That's really not necessary,' Mason suggests.

'Oh, but it is,' says Terry with a smile. 'It's a part of the service that we provide here at The King's Head.

Yes, hello, sir. There's a Detective Inspector Mason and a Detective Sergeant ... ?'

'Poole.'

'Poole, on their way up to see you, if that's convenient? Right, I'll tell them.'

Terry puts his phone away and looks back to Mason.

'Yes, you're lucky. He says he can just fit you in. Back into the hall, up the stairs to your left and it's the middle office. You can't miss it.'

'Anymore than I can make out what you're up to,' Mason thinks to herself. She and Poole follow his instructions. They knock on the door and a voice tells them to go in.

The room is very clearly only in the process of becoming an office. A filing cabinet with its packing corners still on stands against the right-hand wall, along with a large metal cupboard. Its doors are open and piles of what look like leaflets have been roughly, perhaps quickly, stacked on its shelves. To the immediate left of the door, a small laptop-plus-printer workstation has been set up. Straight ahead is a large desk with a landline on it, as well as In/Out trays, both empty.

The two men in the room introduce themselves as Kyle Redwood and Nick Muldoon. They are clearly excited about something, but it might just be a visit from the police. Kyle leaves his place behind the desk and all four sit around the coffee table.

'This is really just a courtesy call,' says Mason.

'That's very nice,' says Kyle.

'And a bit of a warning.'

'Oh?'

'Yes. We have CCTV evidence of a member of your group involved in a cack-handed attempt to burn down a shop. Luckily for him, he's also a bit of an idiot, or he might have hurt himself. But when we arrest him, he will be charged with attempted arson, among other things.'

'No, no, no,' Kyle replies. 'You misunderstand. We are basically a cultural institution. A meeting place for discussion and the exercise of our right to freedom of speech.'

'We didn't come here to listen to you repeat your lines, you daft little monkey,' says Poole. You are getting fair warning that any criminality will get stamped on.'

'You can't hold us responsible for who buys our hoodies,' says Nick.

Kyle breathes in sharply. Mason and Poole exchange looks.

'You are even more stupid than you look,' says Poole.

'Hoodies, T-shirts, jackets,' says Nick, blushing furiously, 'We sell all sorts of stuff like that. Raises money for a good cause.'

'As my colleague was saying,' Mason continues. 'Any criminality will be dealt with, as will any attempt to stir up racial, ethnic, or inter-communal problems.'

'Quite right,' says Kyle. 'We certainly don't want any racial, ethnic or inter-communal problems. We'd like to get rid of them altogether. Once and for all.'

'That'll do for now,' says Mason. 'You have been warned. We know where you live. You can tell him that we'll be around for him when it suits us.'

She drops onto the table a still photo of Ryan running across the garage forecourt.

'We'll let ourselves out.'

Downstairs, Poole excuses himself to visit the gents. Mason steps back into the bar. Terry is polishing glasses.

'You the landlord?'

'Yeah. Terry Smith.' He offers a hand and Mason shakes it.

'What are you doing with those punks upstairs?'

'Oh, they're not so bad. Bit young, but they're learning.

'What exactly?'

'Responsibility, organisation, discipline — that kind of thing.'

'So, are you involved with this Great Whites business?'

'Me? Involved? No, I just rent the room out. Could be the Rotary Club as far as I'm concerned.'

'But you're in sympathy with them? White supremacy?'

'Nah, that would be racist, wouldn't it? I don't think they're racist. They just want their own people to take a pride in who they are, same as others do. Black Power, Gay Pride, Women's Lib — seems like they're all OK, but if it's White Men, that's racist, yeah?'

'Well, look, Mr Smith ...'

'Terry, please,'

'OK, look, Terry, you seem a more sensible bloke than those two upstairs. Just let me tell you what I'm worried about.'

'What's that?'

'Well, do you know a place called the *Lotus*, for

example?'

'Yeah, a club, music, dancing. Tend to get quite a few of our brown cousins round there. Drugs. *Paradise Garden*'s another one.'

'Well, maybe it's nothing, but there is some chatter about some of those people you're talking about, calling themselves, 'The Brothers,' getting off with young girls, I mean, *young* girls.'

'White kids, 'cause they can't get any of their own, and real women have got more sense,' says Terry, putting a glass down on the bar with maybe more of a bang than he intended, Mason thinks.

'Thing is,' says Mason, 'If there is anything like that going on, just when a group like this,' she raises her eyes to the ceiling, 'is setting up, it could lead to trouble.'

'You mean they might see it as something they ought to do something about? Yeah, well, they just might — if the police aren't, somebody needs to, don't they?'

'That's just my point, Terry. If the Great Whites want to be taken seriously, they need to leave things like this to the police. There's no future in taking the law into your own hands, even when you think there might be. Even if you think it might be popular with some people. I'm sort of hoping that you might pass that message on.'

'Interesting' says Terry. 'I'll definitely do that. You can count on it.'

Poole returns and he and Mason walk out to their car.

'What can we count on, boss?'

'I told him to pass on a message that if that bunch of dildos up there start any trouble, we'll come down on them with a lot more than warnings.'

'You think he's involved with them?'

'Oh yes. I'm not saying he's the organ grinder, but I think he might know some of the people who pay the piper.'

* * *

When Mason and Bent meet, she brings him up to date about Sarah Lowe and Amir.

He looks at the phone, the pages from the notepad and Amir's driving licence. She enjoys his amazement.

'Have you checked any of this out?' he asks.

'Not a lot,' she replies, but three of the landlines stand out: two because he phones them a lot, and another because he phoned it a few times on Friday.'

She lets him wait.

'One is the central booking number for a taxi firm, one is the *Lotus*, and the third,' she pauses again, 'is the Council.'

'The City Council?'

'The very same.'

'Boy howdy!'

'You have some very strange expressions, you know.'

Bent updates her on the official investigation.

'Poor security and record-keeping mean it's really difficult to keep track of who can be accounted for at any one time. Overall picture of young white girls, singly or in pairs, sometimes groups, in the company of older Asian males. The girls usually the worse for wear, coming and going in taxis at all times of the day and night. All so common that it's no longer really noticed. Still not clear if there's enough actual evidence to proceed with a prosecution.'

'That,' says Mason in a cold, flat voice, 'will be because the victims are stupid little sluts who get what they asked for and no decent citizen would believe what they say or give a toss about what happens to them.'

'Not only,' Bent sighs, 'but there is some of that in it.'

'And now there is Sarah Lowe,' says Mason, 'And this.' She points to Amir's belongings.

'You haven't reported any of this, have you?'

'Not entirely, no. But I have checked that the other three girls are back at the hostel.'

Another silence.

'What's going on, boss?'

'I'm not sure.'

'So, there is something.'

'Mmmm. I had a flashback last night.'

'A flashback? Oh, Jesus, to what you were telling me about? That must have been awful. Does it happen a lot?'

'Used to. Not for years now.'

'You need to get off this case, boss. In fact, you're not even on it. So what if I take these?' he gestures to the phone, pages and licence. 'I'll contact him and tell him that he's toasted cheese unless he cooperates. I'll get him to tie all these numbers to names and cough the whole story. For that, he can have this lot back and I'll try to leave him out of what happens next. I'll just say an informant has come forward. That'll please Barrett no end regarding his deep racial sensitivity in putting me on to this case.'

'Sounds good. But you don't offer any kind of immunity. If this scumbag gets caught up, he gets caught up. It's enough for him that all his "Brothers" don't get to know he's the one pissing on them.'

Bent nods his agreement.

'The only problem,' he says, 'is this makes me the star when it's you who's done the work.'

'Not a problem. Satisfaction comes in many and varied ways. And,' she adds forcefully, 'I am always on this case. I was on this case before it was a case. I have been waiting for it and it has been waiting for me.'

Bent looks at her through half-closed eyes. 'So that's how we move ahead, yes? I take this stuff and we go for all the convictions we can get. That's what we do, yes?'

'Mmmm.'

'OK. So, we have to talk to the Lowes. If we can square those ends away, we're back on track.'

'Yeah.'

'End of detour.'

'Has to be, doesn't it? For me and for every stupid little slut who gets what's coming to her and doesn't know any better and nobody gives a toss about. Yes, I want to see convictions.' She takes a deep breath. 'And I want to see some pain out there.'

'Like what? Like more bodies on the pavement?'

There is no answer.

'I'm getting a bit worried here, boss.'

Still no answer.

'Would this Amir recognise you again?'

'Possibly, but I doubt it. The nearest streetlight was behind me and I kept my chin down. Once he got close, he didn't see a lot more.'

'Lowes and girls, then?'

'Yes. Then I'll answer your question.'

'Which one?'

'The one about the pavement.'

Chapter 13

At the Lowes' house, the atmosphere is both tense and subdued. Mason and Bent listen while Mr and Mrs Lowe re-tell Sarah's story. They appear shocked, defensive and protective.

'I hated having to go through this,' Mr Lowe says. 'The lies, the drugs, the ... behaviour. Apart from anything else, it made me feel like we failed and I don't know what we could have done differently.'

'It's not that we're naïve, or stupid,' Mrs Lowe adds. We know all this sort of thing goes on, it's just new for us to be a part of it. And,' she pushes on as she sees Sarah close to tears, 'we do get it — what you said to Sarah, DI Mason. I mean, you can only start from where you are. And from where we were last night, she's been honest and brave and we are proud of her.'

'Yes, we are,' says Mr Lowe. You have to back yourself to know sincerity when you see it and hear it, or what's the point? We're ready to move on, the three of us. Stronger than ever.'

An almost voiceless, 'Thank you,' from Sarah.

'Sounds good. Sounds very good,' says Mason. 'OK. Now, if you're feeling up to it, I would like to talk about moving on.' She looks around the room. 'There are some details we have to tidy up and we need to talk to you by yourselves, Mr and Mrs Lowe.

'Does that seem right?' asks Mr Lowe. 'Isn't Sarah a part of all of this now?'

'She is, Mr Lowe, she is,' Mason replies. 'She has her part to play, just like the rest of us. But we adults have another responsibility. We have to step back from the parts we're playing and get a view of the bigger picture. What is it that we're playing a part in? We have things we want to take responsibility for and we do not want Sarah to have to take responsibility for.'

'You're a philosopher, DI Mason.'

'I'm a police officer, Mr Lowe.'

'Sarah,' says Mr Lowe, 'How about if you and I go and take a look at that art project? Just pull some background stuff together?'

'Yeah. Yeah, That'd be great. Or maybe a bit later? Maybe I'll just go and read a bit till you're finished here.'

'You sure? You OK?'

'Yeah, sure. I'm good. See you in a bit,' to her parents. 'Thank you again,' — this to Mason, who nods an acknowledgement.

Then the four of them talk.

'We all know we're out of order,' says Mrs Lowe. 'with no social worker here. And you talked about a bigger case, and that means Sarah could be called to give evidence in court.'

Mason lets her talk.

'I'm not sure,' says Mrs Lowe. 'I get the point. These people have to be stopped. That's the general good. But we have to think about the potential harm to Sarah. She would have to go through all that story in public, and then be cross-examined by an aggressive barrister who'll want to suggest she's brought it all on herself. I don't know if we'll want to press charges.'

'It's not really down to you pressing charges,' Bent

comments. 'This will be a criminal prosecution.'

'Still,' says Mason. 'It might be possible to keep Sarah out of the case.'

Bent turns to her.

'But just leaving that aside for a moment,' Mason goes on, 'What kind of punishment do you think would be appropriate for these people. What would give you the feeling that justice is being done?'

'Well,' says Mr Lowe. 'I have to admit I didn't mind seeing that man on the ground last night. It's not something that you could argue for. But when it's not a question of arguing, when it's a question of somebody coming for your child …' Two tears roll down his cheeks. 'In most ways, I have got used to this chair. I don't think any more of what I can do and what I can't do. I just think of what I do and what I don't do. But last night, after all those hours of waiting, I so much wanted to get up and quite literally kick his head in.'

'That's why we have the police and courts and justice, Donald,' says Mrs Lowe quietly, 'so we don't get involved in revenge and violence. We depend on the police to protect us from ourselves.'

'I think I hear you both,' says Mason. 'We depend on the law to deliver justice in the kind of society we want to live in. And still, sometimes, there is a kind of punishment that the law can't deliver, and we miss that when we see our own in danger, or in pain. And especially when we see wrongdoers get away unpunished.'

'We certainly wouldn't want to see that,' says Mr Lowe.

'It seems as though you're giving us a choice here,'

says Mrs Lowe. 'as though we can keep this "off the books" ...'

'But perhaps we should leave that for this evening?' Bent interrupts.

'DS Bent?' says Mason.

'Excuse me, ma'am. It just crossed my mind that Mr and Mrs Lowe have been through a lot very recently and perhaps the complications of the situation might be a lot to take in right now.'

There is a silence.

'What exactly do you mean by, "complications"?' asks Mr Lowe.

'Mmmm,' says Mason. 'As DS Bent has suggested, it is not altogether straightforward. I think we all agree that we want to protect Sarah and we want to see appropriate punishment meted out, however that relates to the judicial system.'

'"*Relates to* the judicial system"?' Mr Lowe picks up. How does that work — ethically?'

'You're a philosopher, Mr Lowe?' says Bent.

'I'm a foster-father in a wheelchair, Detective Sergeant Bent.'

'Yes,' says Mason. 'We will leave that with you for now, on the strict understanding that you will not discuss it with anyone, including Sarah. And you will ask her not to talk about what's happened. Is that agreed?'

They nod.

'Good. Try to get some more sleep. I will be back in touch tomorrow.'

Mason and Bent stand up. The Lowes thank them

again and see them out. They march stiffly to the car. Get in. Bent drives away.

* * *

'What the fuck?!?' Mason shouts.

'You tell me, ma'am!' Bent replies, coldy.

'Don't ever do that to me again!' Mason storms, searching for her nicotine gum.

'Ma'am,' Bent responds, 'With all due respect, you can't pull rank on me when you are so far off-piste I can hear the snow cracking up the mountain. This is a big investigation, with all kinds of people crawling all over it. And you were playing those two. This is about what you want. You're looking to involve those people in whatever your agenda is, and it's not their kind of thing.'

'Pull over, will you? Just fucking pull over!'

Bent stops the car. Mason gets out and walks a little way away to where an old tree comes poking its way through its tiny allotted space in the pavement. She takes out her cigarettes, lights one and inhales deeply. When she finally breathes out, there is little smoke to be seen. She draws on it again and looks up at the sky. After the third drag, she pinches the end off the cigarette and puts it back into the packet. She returns to the car.

'How was that?' Bent asks.

'Glorious,' she replies. 'Disgusting.'

She hands him the packet.

'Would you throw that away for me, please?'

'Surely. Or do you want me to keep them?'

'No need. I've quit.'

They sit for a while and then Mason starts to talk,

getting louder and faster as she goes on.

'Three things. You said three things. One, it's a big investigation with a lot of interest. And it is going to get bigger. I am ready for that. I thought maybe you were, too. I thought that's what we were talking about the other night. Big stuff. Two, this is what I want. Yes, it is. I also thought that was what we were talking about — making a difference where it counts and being honest about why it counts. Three, you said these people aren't up for it. I don't know. I think you're wrong. And I don't think I was pushing them. I think you bottled it.'

'You think I bottled it.'

'Yes, I'm afraid I do. It's a big case, that scares you. You don't want to dig that deep into your own stuff, that scares you. And there is something about the Lowes that spooks you, too.'

'Have you finished, ma'am?'

'I'm afraid so.'

'One, I stopped doing things because somebody dared me to when I was about ten and I don't intend to start again now. Two, I very deeply appreciated what you told me over dinner. There are things I want to tell you, too. And then we can talk about what they mean, and what counts. Three, you saw how they were. Whatever kind of frustration they feel, their instincts are to uphold the law and protect the girl.'

His voice is low and calm. He knows, and supposes that by now she guesses, that is what happens when he gets angry. He has a cold anger that freezes out other feelings. Under some circumstances, it isolates him from the people he is with. Sometimes, that allows him to think with clinical calculation. Sometimes it allows him to respond with serious violence. At his best, he says, and when the situation demands it, he does not have to choose between the two.

'Protecting the girl is what I am counting on,' says Mason. 'But before we go any further with that, I'd like to ask you something and tell you something.'

'So ask.'

Whatever happens, can we please have that conversation that you just mentioned?'

'Yes.'

'OK, there's more to tell you. I am working a different case, remember.'

'The Great Whites?'

'Yes.'

Mason tells him about the visit she has made with Poole, about the strange nature of the set-up at The King's Head, and about Terry the barman.

'You told him about The Brothers. Why would you do that?'

Mason does not answer. After thirty seconds, Bent does.

'You're goading them. You want to kick off some kind of race riot. Have you completely lost it?'

'No. Not a race-riot. With the information we've got, and with Amir, we can bring about some kind of a meeting involving as many of the Ikhwan as possible. They're going to be feeling some heat by now, anyway. We can make them see the need to come together to get their stories straight. Once that is set up, we can leak the information to the Great Whites and give them a chance to get revenge on these bastards who've been raping these girls. We allow them a bit of a head start, and then we go in mob-handed and round up the Great Whites for racially-aggravated violence. We may even need to defend ourselves with some force. It still needs more detail, but that's the outline.'

'So, you are thinking, you get some satisfaction from having the rapists beaten to a pulp, and I get some satisfaction from seeing the racists worked over.'

'Very crudely, yes, something like that, though I do think there's more to it. And, anyway, what the Ikhwan are doing is also a kind of racism, isn't it? I guess you want to see that punished, too?'

'And how d'you think it'll play?'

'Play?'

'If what we think has been happening is happening, anyone beating the shit out of these Brothers is going to be a hero to most of the local population. Not to say national population.'

'Not when people get a view of what they're really about.'

'And who's got that view of what they're really about?'

'There are far-right connections, fascist even, maybe. There is evidence around, we can pull it together.'

'No matter how much people disapprove of racists in principle, they'll still say "Well done!" for beating up the "Pakis." And every person of colour will try to walk a little quieter and not go out at night.'

'Then that's where we have to make it clear that these Great Whites are just as much a threat to our society as this Ikhwan brotherhood is. Nobody likes a Nazi. Show people the kind of groups that these Great Whites are tied in with and it will be up to all sides to come out and condemn what is rotten in their own communities — to own and to disown.'

'Good luck with that.'

There is a silence.

'And what have the Lowes got to do with this?' Bent asks.

'Perhaps not more than keep their heads down and not talk about what happened last night. That breaks the loop. Gives us a free hand to play Amir. And from their point of view, stops social workers getting nosey about their fostering arrangements and parenting habits.'

'She works with young people, you know, it's not just about Sarah for her.'

'No, that's right. Nor for me.'

Another silence.

Mason puffs out her cheeks and blows.

'OK, now I've said it. I've said it and I've heard what it sounds like. And just right now, I'm not sorry.'

'Thank you,' says Bent. 'For the telling. You know, you might just be having a bad time. You've built a whole career on the other side of this argument. And we've all had our training course warnings about "noble cause corruption." That's what you're talking about. Thinking you can justify illegal means to reach some greater goal that you've decided on.'

'I know that, Bent. You're the one who said there might be a bigger picture and we might have different pieces of it. Yes, I have spent a career climbing this mountain and what that's done is get me to a place where I have a view. I believe I see where I need to go.

And I will risk the avalanche. Anyway, we have work to do. The kind we get paid for.'

'For sure. Can we talk more? Big picture?'

'Tomorrow?'

'I'm tied up tomorrow night. Night after?'

Good. And till then, we keep this tight.'

'Yes.'

Chapter 14

DCI Margaret Shriver is business-like but complimentary. She is not particularly happy about having Bent foisted onto her, or quite sure of how best to employ him, but she believes in credit where it's due.

'Thanks to DS Bent's informant — nice work, Bent — it looks as though we are going to cast a wider net than we thought. Those inquiries are in hand. It's going to mean holding off on any early arrests so as not to alert any of the bigger beasts up the food chain. In the meantime, we are going to focus on liaison with social services, seeing how much more evidence we can gather from the street, from the girls concerned, and see if any more of them are prepared to come forward with information.'

She goes on to detail duties that include Bent going to Greenfields hostel to liaise with a social worker and interview a girl who seems prepared to talk. When he sees the name Elli Washington, Bent can't help but think of a 'Thought for the Day' he heard recently on the morning radio: "Fate is the cards you get dealt. Destiny is how you play them." Corny, but this is how the cards are falling.

* * *

Bent meets up at Greenfields with Kathleen McMahon, the social worker assigned to the case,

'Along with thirty other cases,' she tells him, wearily. They meet with Elli and Bev. Karen is at college. They will have to see her another time.

Bev is tiny, bruised and monosyllabic at best.

Sometimes she cries while Elli is telling their story. Elli isn't all that much bigger, but a year older and gobby. Bent likes her. And the more he hears, the colder his anger becomes.

'So, yeah,' Elli says, 'yeah, I know about date-rape drugs; I just wasn't expecting we'd all get a dose with a fish-and-chips tea. I went upstairs with Amir. He needn't have given me that stuff. Well, not for him, anyway. But then there was somebody else.'

'Just one?'

'Whaddya mean, "just"?'

'Sorry.'

'I don't know how many. I know I ended up bruised and sore. Then, at some stage, this woman, this Mrs Atkins, hauls us off to the shower and gets us dressed. Then we go out clubbing.'

'All four of you?'

'Yeah, with Amir and some other friends of his. Or no, maybe just three of us. And maybe Amir wasn't there then. Anyway, we end up in this hotel. Nicer than the B&B. And I'm with Bev and this man. And he wants Bev to do something and Bev says no. So, he hits her. And Bev says, OK, OK, she will, but he doesn't seem to want it anymore and he just keeps hitting her. And Bev's shouting and screaming and her nose is bleeding. Then some more men come rushing in and pull this bloke, he was a fat, old bloke, off Bev.

'Then one of them tells us to get our clothes on. Bev's all curled up and crying, so I help her, like, and we go out into the corridor and Karen's there. They say they're going to take us home. And I say, like, "Home?" and they say back to the B&B, and where is it? So, I say I don't know, but the woman's name was Atkins. But they've never heard of her and they all start asking about Amir and where the fuck he is, 'cause he's supposed to be "handling" us.

'Then they say there's no use wasting time and if Amir isn't here, that's his fault. And they start pulling us off to different rooms again. Then Bev goes nuts, hysterical, like. And that freaks them out completely. So one of 'em gets on his phone and they get this taxi. Well, maybe not a proper taxi. Anyway, they want to know if we know the address of the hostel here and I tell 'em of course we do.

'So this "taxi" brings us back here and they drop us off outside about four o'clock in the morning and there's hell to pay with the warden. Me and Karen are all right, you know, kind of, but Bev isn't saying anything, is she? Fuck knows what happened to Sarah. She was with us to start with.'

'I am so sorry,' says Bent. 'That all sounds like an absolute nightmare. Sarah's back home with her foster-parents, by the way.'

'Oh, good for her! She would be!'

'Do you think you'd recognise these people again?'

'Maybe one or two. I was pretty out of it most of the time. I can tell you the ones I know, like that bastard, Amir, and his mates.'

'What about the one who was beating Bev?'

'I didn't get that much of a view of his face, He was fat and hairy, I know that.'

'OK,' says Bent, looking at his notes. 'Maybe I can get you some faces to look at. Will you be prepared to give evidence in court? Perhaps by video link?'

'Oh, I'll give evidence all right. Look at 'er! Look at Bev! It's not right, is it?'

'No, Elli,' says Bent, 'It's not. We will nail these bastards. We just need the victims to come forward and testify.'

'So, when are you going to start arresting them?'

'Like I say, we need people to come forward and we need to gather some more evidence.'

'You're not starting now, then?'

'Not right this minute, no, but it won't be long.'

Elli looks at Bev, looks at Bent, looks at Bev again. Back to Bent.

'This is going to be a complete fucking waste of time, isn't it?'

'No, Elli,' says Bent quietly. 'These people are going down for what they did to you and Bev and the other girls.'

'Oh yeah? And maybe as far as Bev is concerned, maybe you're just another big, black bloke with promises. I mean, really, why would you give a flying fuck about what happens to the likes of her? Or me? Unless it's, "Let's get 'em down the station and see what tricks they've learned." We know about you lot, as well. Word gets around, you know.'

'You may not believe me now, but remember, on the day the sky falls in on these people, that I told you, today, it would.'

'Well, I'm ready when you are, copper,' says Elli. 'But then, it's like I've got a dog in this fight, innit? And I'd probably be better off with a bloody dog than waiting for the law to be looking out for me.'

'Stay with me, Elli,' Bent says, looking her levelly in the eye. 'I hear what you are saying. Maybe better than you think.' He gives her a card. 'Anytime.'

'Whatever,' she replies.

* * *

The same case is being discussed simultaneously among a group of well-dressed, middle-aged men in the coffee lounge of a city-centre hotel.

'Who is this Amir?'

'He is nobody.'

'Excuse me. He was nobody, but now he is somebody. He is the somebody who is the cause of all this trouble.'

'I am not so sure of that. The poor young man has explained that he was beaten up by a gang of whites.'

'Yes, but what was he doing there? He was supposed to be looking after things in ... somewhere else.'

'Yes, there was a problem there, and then he tried to do the right thing to sort it out.'

'Gentlemen, there are three problems to consider.'

When Kutab Zahid speaks, the others fall silent and pay attention.

'First, this young man was being too ambitious. For his own good and for ours. It is not his place to decide for his betters what dish they would like. They can make their own orders according to taste. If he had not tried to make connections beyond his station, this one bird would not have flown. From this, our other problems flow. Perhaps he can become useful, for which of us would be where we are today without having shown some initiative? But first, he will need to be disciplined.'

The others nod.

'Second, while this young man was away from his duties, a person known to us damaged goods delivered to him. Not for the first time. There must be a financial penalty and reparation arranged. Also, this person will no longer receive deliveries.'

'He will not be happy about this, uncle.'

'That is correct. This is also the intention.'

'But ...'

'Third, as you know, we benefit not only from the deliveries that we receive but also from the patronage and protection of those to whom we make deliveries.'

'Absolutely.'

'Yes.'

'Of course.'

'Should those people ever think of themselves as being at risk because of their dealings with us, how do we think they would react?'

'They would flush us down the toilet.'

'A very unpleasant turn of phrase, Daoud,' but it captures the spirit of their likely response.'

'So, we need to step back, downsize for a while, tighten up.'

'My thoughts precisely, Adnan. And yet,' Kutab Zahid pauses, 'Without throwing all the babes out with the bathwater.'

The group chuckles at the witticism.

Acknowledging their appreciation, Kutab Zahid looks at his watch.

'I am sure we all have other things to attend to. We

need a more private meeting in order to plan practical action. May I suggest Saturday? The usual place?'

The others agree. Diarised. The meeting disperses.

* * *

Back home from hospital, Amir is in no mood to take a phone call on his parents' landline.

'He says his name's Husni and he has found your driving license,' his father tells him.

They arrange to meet at a local café. The caller is easily identifiable by the fact that Amir's phone and notebook pages are lying on the table in front of him. As Amir approaches, he puts them back into his shoulder bag.

'As-salaamu alaikum, mother-fucker,' Amir greets and sits down.

'Alaikum as-salaam wa rahmat Allah wa barakaatu,' Husni replies. 'Cup of tea?'

Amir shakes his head, looks around, changes his mind.

'Two teas, please, love!' Husni calls to the young woman behind the counter, who responds with a smile, pours two teas and brings them to the table.

'What do you want?' says Amir. 'And before you answer, you ought to know that I have some very nasty friends.'

'Well,' says Husni. 'That's direct! Let's keep it that way, shall we? From now on, you shut up and listen until I tell you otherwise. Or else, I might just pop you one on what's left of your nose.'

Amir deflates. Swallows, with difficulty.

'I can imagine that your very nasty friends would be extremely unhappy to discover that someone,' Husni emphasizes the *some*one, 'has got hold of your phone and notebook. You have, I have to tell you, been getting a lot of calls and messages and texts. They do sound less than happy with you and they are getting very impatient.'

Amir swallows again. Husni takes a sip of his tea.

'Now, I'm going to give them back to you.'

Amir's eyes narrow as he waits for the price.

'You are right about your friends. They are not nice. The good news is that you are all in deep shit and I, personally, am looking forward to watching you all go down in it. You, Prince Amir, are going be submerged in shit. You are going to breathe it in, swallow it and drown in it.' Husni takes another sip of tea. 'Just imagine.'

Amir waits.

'Yes,' Husni continues. 'Yes, to your question about if there is a way out for you. You do exactly what you are told, say exactly what you are told to say and report back on everything that you hear. Then, if you are lucky, we can perhaps keep you out of the worst of it when the rest of them go down. Understood?'

'Why are you working for them? Why are you working against your brothers?'

'If you ever, *ever*, suggest again that I am in any way related to you and scum like you, I will truly wipe the nose off your face.'

'Well, you're not a white man, are you? ONOROL?'

'How true. Nor will you hear from me or see me again.'

He takes Amir's phone, license and pages from his

bag and pushes them across the table.

'The pages are all there. There is a new name and number on your phone. The name is Wahid Aswad. You take orders from him. You report to him. The tea's on me.'

Amir watches him get up, go to the counter, pay for the teas and leave. He checks his things. Yes, they are all there. But where does that leave him?

'Better off than half an hour ago, anyway,' he thinks to himself. 'I can beat these fuckers.'

* * *

On his way back to the station from Greenlands, Bent rendezvous with undercover officer, Husni Barakat. They talk through their open car windows, side-by-side at the back of a supermarket car park.

'Thanks, Husni. I owe you one.'

'I don't think so, my man. You're still ahead on my count. You OK?'

'Yeah, sure' Bent replies. 'I've felt better, but hey. You're out on the street in the middle of all this madness.'

'Yeah, did you hear about the young lad last night? Just waiting for a bus home?'

'Yes, I did. Gang jumped him. Decided he was an immigrant, or an asylum seeker. Or maybe just black. Turns out he's a student here, comes from Birmingham.'

'Yeah, still, they were right about the black part, eh? Half a street of people but nobody sees anything for sure. Just a kid lying in a pool of blood and a bunch of yobs chanting over him.'

'Chanting?'

'Yeah, you know, this ONOROL stuff.'

'Husni, do you sometimes think about going to the mattresses?'

'Man, you have some strange expressions!'

'Yeah, but you know what I mean. Seriously giving some back.'

'I *think* about it. But it's not what we *do*, is it? If we could *do* anything, what I'd *want* to do is remind people what they're in danger of forgetting: It's that lot who're the real problem— the boot boys and the serious political thugs behind them. We have to believe people in general are basically good-and-lied-to, don't we? Otherwise, what's the point?'

Bent gives him a long look.

'Thanks again, Husni. Keep the faith.'

They bump fists and drive on.

Chapter 15

Bent stands at the end of an alleyway diagonally across from The King's Head. His mind is churning, straining his ability to codify and analyse options. So much at stake. But stakes are made to be won. Damn it.

There is something in what she said.

No, it's hare-brained.

And yet exhilarating. He experiences a feeling of himself as more than an individual. Or is it less than an individual? A sense of inheritance. His place in a story. A longer story. In a history. He does not have a plan and that disturbs him. All he has is a next move.

He wants information and he wants it quickly. Are these Great Whites really a part of something more sinister than just a gang of thugs? If they are connected with neo-Nazi groups in Europe, as Mason has implied, that would be less reason for anyone to think of them as local heroes. Not that that would justify Mason's misguided suggestion. Nothing could ...

It is just past one in the morning. The staff left before midnight, but a light stayed on for a while in the bar. Now the pub has been dark for half an hour. He focuses on the calculation of risk: the likelihood of his being caught, balanced against the consequences if he is. And he factors into that his grudging recognition that he is angry and excited and simply wants to do something.

He is angry with Mason and appalled at her idea of goading white racists into beating up members of an ethnic minority. And he is angry with himself, because he does not want that 'members of an ethnic minority' label to be used to protect in any way these vile exploiters of vulnerable children. And he is angry with those senior officers who always nod in his direction when they talk about the importance of taking account 'ethnic sensitivities.' And he is angry about Mason's accusation that he is bottling something. And he is absolutely frozen livid about letting himself get so angry.

Risk. Likelihood. Consequences. It is, anyway, a long shot. If he is caught, or even just seen and possibly identified, the consequences will be bad at best and catastrophic at worst. For him. So, he just has to back himself not to let that happen. And why not? He smiles to himself, seeing an old Mexican friend shrug out that same question that was always also a challenge:

'¿Como no?'

He leaves the alleyway and, keeping his head down, crosses to The King's Head. He is dressed all in black, from the jacket with its raised hood, down to his steel-capped, rubber-soled boots. He is also wearing very thin, black, simulated leather gloves. On discovering them in a gym in Florida, he bought several pairs. Sensitive enough to handle paperwork and strong enough to protect his hands in combat, he has since used them for both.

Passing the entrance, he stops at a window and tries to make out what he can see in the bar. The reflection of a streetlamp turns the glass into a mirror and he sees only darkness. Against which, only himself and the street behind him.

Putting his head down again, he walks around the block to the rear of the building. Before entering the back yard, he pulls his hood further forward. He has checked for CCTV all around the building and found none, but it does no harm to be careful. There is a burglar alarm flashing on the rear wall. To Bent's eye, it looks as though it is only a fake box, put up to give the impression of a functioning system. At worst, there might be a fixed-time alarm that no one will respond to.

Carefully, he climbs the rickety fire escape to the first floor. The window is old, single-glazed, with a simple catch inside. Bent takes out a tiny, battery-powered glass cutter and inscribes a deep semi-circle above the catch. Then he puts the cutter away and brings out a rubber sucker on a short, wooden handle. He presses the sucker against the patch of glass until it grips. Then he punches hard and the semi-circle cracks, leaving the patch of glass on the sucker. Bent reaches through the hole, releases the catch and opens the window. He slips quickly through and closes it again behind him. He puts the piece of glass on the floor and the sucker back in his pocket. Then he stands very still and listens.

Nothing.

Using the torch in his phone, Bent works his way methodically around the room. The trays on the desk are empty, but in the waste paper basket are a number of envelopes. The stamps and franks include Holland, Poland and Ukraine. There are names and initials of organisations that he does not recognise. Strangely old-fashioned, he thinks, as a mode of communication, but perhaps these people are. He lays the envelopes out on the desk, photographs them on both sides and throws them back into the basket.

Also on the desk, apart from the telephone, is a heavy glass ashtray with two cigar stubs in it, and a mug holding a few biros. There is a large cupboard and a filing cabinet. The cupboard is unlocked. Inside are small piles of a variety of leaflets and posters. They are also in

Dutch, German and what he takes to be Polish. Bent cannot understand the writing, but the images of tall, muscular men with blonde hair and square jaws, sometimes armed, sometimes staring bravely into the future, sometimes defending frightened women from threatening dark figures, allow him to make a safe guess at their message. He photographs samples of them and puts them back.

At the bottom of the cupboard is a large pile of new posters still partly wrapped. Bent takes one off the top of the pile. The slogan reads:

Great Whites Defending Our Nation

over a map of Britain, on which stand three outsize figures wearing the shark emblem and reaching out a hand to repel stereotypical images of Africans, Asians and East Asians.

'Or, "Blacks, Pakis and Chinks," as we like to say among our own,' Bent murmurs to himself.

As he moves around, he keeps a listening brief for non-ambient sounds. At one point, he thinks he hears snoring, but the moment passes. He spots a laptop and decides to take it. Even if there is nothing on it, its theft could provide a plausible motivation for the break-in.

After ten minutes, he has found nothing else of any interest. But he has discovered that the filing cabinet and one desk drawer are locked. He turns his attention to the filing cabinet.

It is a cheap, standard model from Staples. He pulls a bunch of keys from his pocket and starts trying them. The fourth one moves a little. He jiggles it and the key turns.

The files in the top drawer are all labelled, but

haphazardly — some labels typed, others written with various types of pen or marker, no obvious sequence or logic to any of it. He runs his torch over them: Bills, Demos, Cuttings, Committee, Bank, Travel, Police . . . and then, under that last one, a new plastic folder with a newspaper cutting and a few hand-written notes.

The cutting is recent, reporting rumours of under-age girls being groomed. The notes read:

Police came round.
Told us about 'Brothers'
Paki bastards fucking our girls.
Said we should check out Lotus and Paradise Garden
Payback? Could be popular.

Bent reads the notes several times with growing disbelief. He folds the paper and pockets it. Then he drops the folder back into the filing cabinet, closes the drawer and locks it. He turns off his torch, waits, questions ricocheting around his head. What was Mason thinking of? Has she really been leading on this already, pushing it along behind his back? Has she been playing him all along? No, it doesn't make sense to think that. But it has become possible. And that makes all the difference. Like seeing the spider at the bottom of your glass, he thinks. Where is that from? Never mind. Bracket all thoughts of conclusions and consequences. Complete the search.

He goes back to the desk drawer. Old-fashioned lock, but nothing out of the ordinary. His third key opens it. A brass knuckle-duster. And then a disturbingly familiar weight and shape, wrapped in oilcloth. He unwraps it.

'Now we are into some seriously dangerous shit,' he mutters to himself. Running briefly through a number of possible scenarios, he cannot come up with a good reason to leave the weapon in the hands of its current owners. He tucks it into his waistband and drops the oilcloth back into the drawer, which he relocks.

Time to leave and then think about what to do next. But that thought is getting in the way of immediate action. What is next? What to do next?

The answer is taken out of his hands. The door flies open and a large, hand-held spotlight finds him.

'Eeny-meeny-miny-mo,' the voice is excited, as though the speaker has something to look forward to.

'What have we got here? Somebody who's put his big, black toe somewhere he shouldn't have. That's what I think. Well, well, we don't often have one come looking for it, do we? Usually, we have to go out and hunt them down. I am really going to enjoy this one.'

There are steps on the stairs. The figure in the doorway calls back over his shoulder.

'Bazza, Matto, bring the bats. We've got a very violent burglar here who is definitely going to attack us. I think we will just have to fight him off. With maximum prejudice. '

Then to Bent again.

'Do you like that, Sambo? "With maximum prejudice"? I think that's funny, don't you? Maximum prejudice. Funny. Get it?'

Bent curses himself for having let his attention wander. He pulls together all the confused emotions that he has experienced on finding the notes on Mason's visit, along with his thoughts on finding the handgun. He takes a deep breath and blows them all out. Freed again into the situation, mind and body come back together. In concert. In focus. Extreme focus.

'Con perjuicio máximo? Oh sí, señor, muy divertido!'

Counting on his stage-Mexican Spanish to have some slight, disorienting effect, he puts one hand on the desk and vaults over it. Landing, he throws his arms out wide and leans to the left. His right hand reaches back, scoops up the glass ashtray and hurls it into the darkness above the flashlight. He is immediately rewarded with the sound of impact on flesh and bone. A half strangled scream of pain. The beam of light flies upwards and backwards as the torch clatters off down the stairs. The stumbling figure, retreating with head in hands, collides with one of the men turning onto the landing. Counting on the fact that only two more men are left in the building, Bent moves forward, taking a chair with him.

The two on the landing are still disentangling themselves as Bent's first swing of the chair lands on the shoulder of the latecomer. He staggers, pushing his bloodied comrade, still clutching his face, out of the way. As he pulls his baseball bat back to swing, Bent stabs the chair legs into his chest and stomach. His head jerks backwards, then forwards and Bent brings the chair down onto the back of his neck. He drops.

The third figure, stopped at the edge of the landing, turns and runs down the stairs. Leaning over the bannister, Bent throws the chair into his retreating legs. The man goes headfirst down the last steps into the hallway. His head hitting the tiles sounds like a dropped coconut. As he scrambles, dazed, to get up, Bent's grabs him from behind by his belt and collar.

'I give up, I give up!'

'Sí, señor,' says Bent, again in his best movie-Mexican accent, 'Y con perjuicio máximo.'

He half-swings and half-pushes his unresisting opponent face-first into the wall, following up with his whole body weight in a shoulder charge into the man's back that crushes him against the rough plasterwork. His cry of pain is cut short as the breath seems to burst from his body and he crumples to the tiled floor.

Bent thinks about the upstairs room. Risky to go back. But the laptop idea is still a good one. Up the stairs at speed. One unconscious body. But the first one — where is he? No sign. Into the office, snatch up the laptop. Back to the landing. Is that a sound from the end room? Good. Let him hide in there and see nothing. Could be phoning for reinforcements. Never mind. Bent moves quickly back downstairs to the front door. Just an internal Yale. He unlocks it and opens the door. He pulls his hood further down over his face. No one around. Eyes down to the pavement, he walks deliberately along the street, leaving the door wide open behind him.

He feels his state of extreme focus relax. Slowly, thoughts return. Mason has been in that room. Has she taken things further than he had thought? What does that mean? Where are things heading now?

'In more directions than one!' is the only response that occurs to him.

Emotions return, too. Was that pleasure that he had experienced? A sharp hit of satisfaction, fleeting, but pure? File that one.

His body is also telling him that he needs some sleep. Tomorrow is going to be complicated. At best.

Chapter 16

Kyle, Nick and Terry are sitting around the coffee table in the Great Whites' office.

'There's no point in getting into a blame game now,' Terry says. 'We all knew the security was rubbish. No CCTV, not even a proper lock on the window.'

'That's why I told Ryan to sleep in the bar!' Kyle shouts. 'To have some fucking security!'

'And a lot of use he was,' Nick adds, 'Even with two of his mates dossing down with him.'

'I've got people coming round to replace the window later today,' says Terry. 'We'll do the whole top floor. And the security people are coming to set up a proper alarm system, with phone-alert and call-out. We can replace the computer and the filing cabinet was locked.'

'But that's not the problem, is it?' says Kyle. 'The real issue is who was it and why?'

'Thank god they didn't manage to open the desk drawer where the — you know — was,' Nick says a couple of times. 'That would've been well fucked-up, eh?'

Kyle has told Nick to shut up about the gun, especially in front of Terry. Kyle isn't altogether sure about the relationship between Terry and Mr Collingwood.

'Give it a break!' he snaps and tries to think.

Who and *why*, they are the important questions and that's what London is going to want to know about. Will it be enough to say this was just a random break-in? Thieves saw stuff being moved into an old building and thought there might be something worth nicking? Was the laptop it? Just something to flog for a bit of drug money?

That made sense enough, but then who are these people? How do you explain two black ninjas that speak a foreign language? OK, forget the language. If you've got two black ninjas, why wouldn't they speak a foreign language? Ryan thought it was Spanish, but what sense did that make? Unless it was an immigrant thing. They'd turned some immigrants out at the opening Great Whites' meeting. Had they got some muscle together to get back at them? That also made some sort of sense at least.

Bastards. Nobody from around here would be stupid enough to risk thieving from The King's Head, especially after that meeting. Whether or not this was something more than just a robbery, there would have to be payback ...

Even though he is waiting for it, the phone call still spooks Kyle. It's Mr C, as expected. He asks all the questions they have been struggling with, plus one more. He asks if there have been any visitors. Visitors? Nah. Only the police.

He doesn't like that at all. So Kyle tells him about the visit and the warning. And about this Paki sex ring they've been told to keep away from.

'Collect some information,' Mr C. says. 'Get hold of one or two of these girls and see what they tell you. I'll send you some questions to ask.'

'Thanks a lot,' Kyle thinks to himself.

'The shark circles its prey and attacks when it's ready,' says Mr C.

That was another big help. And Collingwood couldn't

make any sense of these Spanish-speaking black ninjas, either. What did they mean, 'black', he wanted to know.

Well, Kyle's asked the others that, but they aren't sure. Ryan saw one of them best and he says, 'Afro,' but he didn't see the other one who hit him from behind. Matto says it was too dark to tell one black from another and anyway he had Ryan in his face. Bazza hadn't seen anything except the floor coming up to meet him. They've all been kept in hospital overnight.

Mr C says if the police come back, they should all say as little as possible. If the press come around, tell them the burglars were definitely black and foreign and leave out the ninja stuff. He might send up one or two people to help out if it's needed. Kyle says they can handle things by themselves, but they'll need some more money. That was when he tells him about the computer and he has to go all through that again. Bloody hell. Nick and Terry keep making 'calm-down' signs at him while he has to suck up all the bile coming down the phone line. By the time it's over, Kyle is fair ready to hit somebody. Hard.

* * *

DS James Bent is also in a mood that he recognises well enough, one he does not like at all. The violence of the previous night has something to do with it. He quite enjoyed putting those pieces of human junk into hospital. Yes, even though he knows they are victims in their own way. At some point, the rational explanations and the endless protocol and the careful strategies get tuned out and people get what is coming to them. No. That can't be right. He is a professional. He needs to get himself together. He breathes. He clears his mind. He is ready to talk to Mason.

What he is not ready for is the next phone call.

'Sergeant Bent? It's Alice Thompson.'

'Mrs Thompson?'

'You have to come round. You have to come round now.'

'What's the matter, Mrs Thompson?'

'It's my husband. It's John. He's in such a state. You have to come round. He says he's going to Tanner's house.'

'Tell him I'm on the way. Keep him there and tell him I'm on the way.'

'All right. But hurry up.'

On his way to the Thompsons', Bent thinks more about Elli than he expected to. He likes her. Things have happened to her a person of her age should never have to experience. She is not blameless. Nor is she apologetic. She doesn't always help herself. She doesn't know who her friends are, either. She'll probably end up being crushed, one way or another. Either by people who con her and exploit her, or by the everyday pressures of what society won't put up with. Or a combination of the two. Or through her own bloody-mindedness.

Bent shakes his head in exasperation. She is unpredictable, unreliable ... Or is he judging her in just the same ways that he would criticise others for judging her? Damn! Sometimes, you really do want to step outside the frame and simply make something happen. But how could that ever work?

And isn't that what Mason has been arguing? He sighs. Ironic that he finds himself now pulled in that direction because of someone who calls him just another big, black bloke with promises. There is something about the totality of how Elli and Bev have been abused that engages his sense of the long arc of historical violence — men against women, race against race. The thought, 'I feel your pain,' goes through his mind and he laughs out loud to think of how Elli would respond if he said so.

Or Mason. Yes, he has felt it with Mason, too, but she is a powerful adult, so it hasn't been so keen. And then it is as though he sees and feels the thirteen-year-old in Mason. Not separate. They speak as one. The defenceless girl and the battle-hardened veteran are one. The woman can't help the girl and her attempts to do so might mean that the girl would destroy the woman.

Bent feels that he is getting close to something that might help him understand his own demons. But the auto-pilot that allows a person to drive without remembering any of the decisions or actions that got them there has led him to the Thompson's. He turns into the next side-street and parks.

Mrs Thompson opens the door almost before the bell stops ringing and hurriedly waves him inside.

'I tried DI Mason, but she's not answering,' she says, once the door is closed. 'But it's good that you're here,' she adds, quickly.

'That's fine, Mrs Thompson. Is something the matter? Where's Mr Thompson?'

'He's at the allotment. He's better off there. He is in a state, though, and I'm ever so worried.'

'Tell me, please.'

'Yes, yes. Cup of tea? Milk no sugar?'

Bent pauses on the verge of saying, 'No, thanks.' He takes a deep breath and says,

'That's very kind, Mrs Thompson. Yes, please, I'd love one.'

'Have a seat, then.'

She relaxes a little, busies herself in the kitchen and comes back with two mugs.

'What's up, Mrs Thompson?'

'Well, it happened, like you said.'

'Like I said?'

'Yes. And it was in the paper. There was a picture of the smashed window. John didn't like it being called "vandalism," you know, but it made him laugh when the reporter said it was probably "gang-related violence" and said about how Billy Tanner was in trouble with the police and, "in breach of a control order" or something like that. And John says it was a waste of a good, old hammer, but it was worth it. Now Tanner knows what it's like and he could clean up his own mess.'

'I see. So somebody got in touch and this was your "satisfaction" event.?'

'Yes, it was.'

'But?'

'Did you see yesterday's paper?'

'No, I didn't.'

She returns to the kitchen and brings the previous evening's paper back with her, opened to a small article on an inside page.

The story concerns Molly Calderwood, aged 84, who has been hospitalised following an attack on her home.

Mrs Calderwood suffers from multiple sclerosis, which severely restricts her mobility. She now sleeps downstairs in the house, which meant that she was close to the impact when a large object was thrown through her kitchen window. She is also on long-term medication for her anxiety and panic attacks. This incident seems to have tipped her over the edge and she is currently in hospital under sedation.

'I thought John was going to die,' says Mrs Thompson. 'He went so pale, and then so red. And he grabbed his chest, and fell back in his chair — that chair,' she nods to it.

'How is he now?'

'Better this morning. But he kept saying he'd have to go round and see what he could do. I told him it didn't make any sense. She's in hospital and all he's going to find there is young Billy. Seems like he must live with his Gran.'

'That's very sensible, Mrs Thompson.' Bent sips at his tea. 'Nice cuppa.'

'Not too strong?'

'No, I like it strong.'

'I thought you might,' she smiles. 'So, what do you think?'

'Well, it's not what anybody would have wanted.'

'That's what I told him. But it's not all our fault, either. Billy Tanner brought this down on his own head. And on his Gran's.'

'In a way. '

'Perhaps we should have thought about it more before we said, "Yes."'

'I wish you'd got in contact then.'

Mrs Thompson seems close to tears. Before she can respond, the telephone rings. She answers it. The colour drains from her face and she sits down.

'Oh, John, what have you done now?'

She turns to Bent and covers the mouthpiece of the old landline.

'He's round at Tanner's.

Bent sits back and drinks his tea while she listens. Her face brightens. After a few minutes, she says, 'OK,' and hangs up. Bent looks questioningly at her.

'You wouldn't credit it. He's gone round to Tanner's and banged on the door. No answer. So he's just about to leave when young Billy shows up, back from the hospital. His Gran's better. They reckon she's got dementia as well, so she's not always, you know, quite with the rest of us. But she's calm and wants to go home.'

'He must have been surprised to see John.'

'Yes. He starts off with, "What do you want?" and John says he's read about what happened in the paper and first he thought, "Serves him right." But then when he read about his Gran, he thought, "I wonder if the little bastard (sorry) has learned anything from all this." And then Billy bursts into tears. So they go inside and put the kettle on. The kitchen window is all covered with a sheet of plastic. John has a look and he tells Billy that if he can get the glass, then John will put it in. He's good like that, our John. Practical, you know.'

Bent stays silent and drinks his tea.

'So then there's a knock at the door. A couple of the neighbours have come round to ask about Mrs

Satisfaction in Times of Anger

Calderwood and can they go and see her? And they've had a whip-round up and down the street to collect some money to replace the window. So John says he'll measure it up and asks Billy if he's got a tape measure and Billy says yes and gets one out of a drawer and gives it to him. And, of course, it's John's. Had it for years. So he looks at it. And he looks at Billy. And then Billy gets it and he starts crying again and says, "I am so sorry, Mr Thompson, I am so sorry."

'So John measures up the window and writes it on a bit of paper and tells Billy to go off to this place he knows of round there and order the glass. Tell them we want it as soon as. Ask if they'll deliver. Otherwise, John will pick it up. Meanwhile, he says, if that's all right, he'll stay on and knock out the broken glass. Asks Billy if he's got a hammer. There's a moment when John thinks Billy's going to give him his hammer back, too, but Billy says, "No, sorry, the police took it." And John doesn't know whether to laugh or what. So, anyway, they decide Billy will go and order the glass while John picks up what's left of his tools. And if they can get the glass right off, John will go back and fit it this evening. And one of the neighbours says her husband will be back home by then and he'll come round and give him a hand.'

Then Mrs Thompson starts to cry.

'I haven't heard our John sound like that for I don't know how long.'

Bent stands up and gives her the tea mug.

'I think I'll be off, Mrs Thompson. I imagine your husband will be back soon.'

'I'll tell him you've been.'

'Right you are. But this isn't over, Mrs Thompson.

You know that, don't you?'

'You mean they'll be back. Those people who did this for John. For us.'

'Yes.'

'Let him put the window in, please. Then I'll tell him. And we'll call you. I'll call you myself.'

Bent nods his agreement and gives her a card.

'Give my regards to DI Mason. She'll be pleased, won't she?'

'I will. And yes, she will be pleased, in a way.'

'You never know, do you, how things will turn out?'

Bent shakes his head and smiles. Once outside, he checks his watch. It's time to meet up with Mason. They have a lot to discuss.

Chapter 17

They meet this time at a franchise restaurant called *Joey's Diner*. The food is reliable, if not exciting. Once again they take a corner table. It has the disadvantage of being directly under a speaker, but they both implicitly share a desire not to be somehow exposed in the middle of a public space.

They search for a way to begin.

'Who would choose this music to eat by?' says Bent.

'Don't listen,'

'Easily said.' Bent lifts his hands, fingers outstretched, and puts on a rapper mime:

'Ee sayyit widda riddim

An ee sayyit widda snap

Bu' i' doon really matta

Cuss ee's only talkin' crap.'

Mason laughs,

'I'm not sure you're going to make it as a soul brother.'

'It's more that I am cursed with an inability to tune out muzak,' says Bent, ruefully. 'Whatever reason people have for playing music that most people don't hear, and those who do hear, would never choose to listen to, I think it's a sign of cultural decay.'

'Ah, you are a philosopher, DS Bent!'

They smile briefly. They are back in the case.

The waitress comes. Neither of them is a picky eater, so sirloin steak with fries, washed down with a glass of pilsner, is just fine.

While they wait, Bent tells her about the Thompsons and they agree to leave it as something to come back to.

The food arrives. They continue to talk as they eat. Bent tells her about Elli and her story.

'She got to you,' Mason says. 'She got to you in a way I didn't. Maybe I'm jealous.'

'You got to me,' Bent replies. 'Maybe Elli was channelling you. Without you, I would not have heard her so well. And OK, yes, maybe without her, I wouldn't have been able to hear all that I can hear now. The long haul of it.'

'The long haul?'

Bent is quiet for a while.

'Yeah,' he says. 'The long haul. My version. Do you have time for this?'

'Do I look as though I'm in a hurry?'

Bent takes a deep breath and begins.

'In the American war of independence, a lot of Native Americans fought on the side of the British. That is, they fought against the settlers who had already driven them off their land and infected their people with their genocidal diseases. They thought that their enemy's enemy was their friend.'

'A common mistake.'

'For them, it turned out that today's friend is tomorrow's enemy. The British had to leave, but the Native Americans had nowhere to go. The victorious New Americans rounded them up and, just to show that there was no ill will towards the British, they sold the Native Americans to the British West Indies as slaves.'

'Really? I never heard that.'

'Mmmm. Nor had I. It came up in my searches. From Georgia, a group of Cherokee were sold off to a plantation in Jamaica. You already know the plantation owner's name.'

She looks at him.

'You're going to tell me it was Bent?'

'Mmmm. Among the Cherokee was a young couple, their child and the man's mother. They begged to stay together, but the profit lay in the resale of the young adults, so that's what Master Bent went ahead with. Even the two adults were sold to different owners. But before the deal went through, the couple decided to run away with their child and jump off a cliff. It was their only way of staying together and saving their child from that life.'

'That's dreadful.'

'Yes. The cliff was a place where the Cherokee liked to gather at sunset. The legend was that some days, when the light was just right, and the sun sank into the sea, they could see their old tribal lands back across the great water. Perhaps they did.'

'To kill your own child ...'

'But there is more to the story,' he goes on. At the last minute, the woman changed her mind and gave the little boy to her mother-in-law. Then the two of them carried out their plan. They sprinted away from the guards down there, hand-in-hand, and jumped. One story is that Bent didn't even bother to collect the bodies for burial. But the guards were whipped.'

'And the boy?'

'Ah. When he grew up, he married into the local slave

population. Genetically, you can still see the Cherokee inheritance today if you know where to look. And the view from the cliffs is breathtaking.'

'You've been there.'

'Oh yes. You can see a lot, but you can't see Georgia.'

'And you stick with your slave name.'

'Yes. I also have an honorary Cherokee name. I could tell you what it is. But then I would have to kill you.'

Bent takes it as a sign of their closeness that she laughs on the instant. This something between them is indeed part of a long haul. It is not simply personal. And it is deeply personal.

'Have you had a DNA test?'

'No,' he pauses. 'I've thought about it, of course, but I don't need to. I am a part of that story and it's a part of me.'

'And that's what you mean by "the long haul?" Where oppression by race and oppression by gender come together?' Mason probes.

'Mmm. And not only,' he adds. 'I thought I heard different echoes of the long haul earlier today when I asked DCI Shriver about those telephone numbers, including City Hall, and she said, "That's all in hand." Just a bit too quickly. The struggle takes many forms.'

'I don't want to hear this,' says Mason.

'Moving along,' says Bent, indicating the canvas bag by his chair, 'I've brought you a present. Kind of a thank-you for Amir's phone and notebook.'

He shows her the laptop and the photos of the envelopes.

'I don't know what's on the laptop, but the photos

show that they are in touch with neo-nazi groups in Europe — I checked out their websites.'

As Mason's eyes grow wider, he explains that this was his reason for going to The King's Head.

'I needed more good reason to target the Great Whites. I don't want them to come out as the avengers of white girls wronged by black rapists. They have to come out as violent racists who are a danger to everyone.'

'I get that,' says Mason, 'But what about if you were seen, if you were recognised, if you were caught, if you have given them a warning that someone is onto them?'

'Yeah, my call,' says Bent. 'A bit like you taking out Amir.' Then he tells her the rest of the story about the confrontation at The King's Head. At the end of it, she has her head in her hands.

'Bloody hell, Bent. Where does that leave us?'

'It leaves us with more information and it leaves them, my guess is, angry and scared and ready to be provoked. Which you have already done, according to their files.'

He pushes the note across the table to her.

'It was …,' she pauses. 'It was one of those moments when … there was an opportunity … you do it or you don't. You make your mark, or you don't. I think I was a bit more subtle than that note suggests.'

As a silence develops, Bent goes on to bring Mason up to date regarding the situation with Amir.

'He's not a big wheel in the Brothers' ring, but now at least he's our wheel. Perhaps we can use him to bring about a meeting of the people above him.'

'Or, if not, he might keep us informed about where

and when any such meeting might take place,' Mason adds.

They become thoughtful for a while.

Over coffee, they sketch as much of their not-quite-a-plan as they can foresee. Bent will keep Amir on a tight leash and also keep in touch with Elli, liaising with the social worker, McMahon. Mason will pay another visit to the Great Whites under the cover of investigating the break-in there. True, there has been no complaint, but it will be easy enough to invent a neighbour who has heard something, or thought they saw something. And then there is still the question of finding the youth in the hoodie caught on CCTV.

Hanging in the air, not repeated but alluded to, is Mason's proposal: While pursuing their official investigations, they will look for an opportunity to bring the Brothers together in one place, induce a Great White attack on them, and use this to justify a taking-down of the Great Whites, with maximum prejudice.

They tremble on their own cliff edge of premeditated violence, unable to justify it and unwilling to retreat. At least, they feel, they still have a choice and they are ahead of the game. Until the *Evening News* comes out next day.

Chapter 18

CARE HOME CHILD IN SEX HELL is a headline crafted to push a number of buttons: institutional neglect, paedophilia and sexual abuse being just those explicitly at the top of the list, with the racial element thrown in later. In this, the article is successful.

The whole thing isn't Elli's idea, but when this reporter turns up, it doesn't seem like a bad one. Sniffing around for a story for *The News*, she is, this Deborah (Call me, "Deb") Warburton. She's heard something about the scene at the *Lotus* and *Paradise*, but she gets properly excited when she hears about the Blackpool trip. Can't get her money out fast enough. So Elli thinks, yeah, she'll take it. Not as much as she might've got, maybe, but more than she would have thought to ask for. They won't use any names, Deb tells her, and the photo is only from behind, so nobody'll know it's her. So, she tells the story. It doesn't need exaggerating. It is horrible enough. And telling it like that, well, it brings it all back much worse than she expected.

So, now it's out. Elli thinks about buying a copy of the paper, but it's just as easy to nick one off the pile in the supermarket while she buys some Coke and biscuits. It's funny with the picture. You really can't tell it's her. Probably. If you don't know her, anyway. But if you do, it looks pretty bloody obvious. Still, why would Deborah Warburton give a toss about that? She paid up and got what she wanted, didn't she?

'And what about you Elli?' she asks herself? 'Well, you stupid bitch, you just get what you deserve, don't you?'

Elli looks down at the scratch marks on her arm. Not

bleeding. Yet. Been a while since she's done that. Not since she got in with Amir's crowd and they conned her into thinking that she wasn't a useless piece of shit. For a while. She presses a little harder. Watches the red rise to just below bursting point.

Gets a flash of that policeman. How he looked at her when he said, 'Stay with me Elli, these people are going down for what they did to you.'

Not that she believes a word of it. That's not it. It's not so much what he said as how he looked at her. Like this wasn't all her fault. Like she deserved not just sympathy, but ... what? Hard to say. It was like he talked to her as though she was ... somebody. Not "a somebody," but still another person, in her own right. With respect. Is that it? What does that even mean?

Absentmindedly, she fetches some moisturising cream and rubs it onto her arm. It feels soothing. But inside, she is boiling. Anger bubbling through the confusion.

And it's not even just the abuse, either. This isn't something that got out of hand. This was set up. This wasn't giving poor, sad Mohsin a blow-job for Amir's sake. This was a bunch of strangers standing in line to take their turn. Had they paid? How much? Never mind how much. That isn't the point. What is the point, Elli?

She stares into the mirror and asks again,

'What is the point, Elli?'

For the first time since that night with Amir and Mohsin, she cries. Two tears. One from each eye. She wipes them away with a fingertip and tastes them. Bitter beyond salty. Something has changed. In her. Physically and emotionally and whatever that adds up to.

Elli feels nauseous as she sits bewildered. She has a sudden memory of a lump of soft clay turning on a wheel, with wet fingers pressing on it, moulding and shaping. Now, she is the clay and the hands are hers, too. With a sharp intake of breath, she realises what she wants. It is unfamiliar to her. And not necessarily welcome.

She wants people hurt. She wants cut, she wants scarred, she wants broken. She wants looked down on. She wants shamed. She wants arrested. She wants banged-up. But most of all, yeah, she wants *hurt*.

'Not me,' she says, rubbing her arm. 'Not me. Not me anymore. Them.'

Maybe she should talk to that policeman again, sooner rather than later. Or get back to Deb. Or maybe just sit tight and let them come to her. She is scared, but also excited. And very, very angry. Any way you tell it, she has been fucked over enough. Like she's been walking around with VICTIM written across her forehead. Not anymore. It is other people's turn. And she knows exactly which people she has in mind.

* * *

As Elli leaves Greenfields, she sees two youths sitting on the wall opposite the hostel. Cropped hair, boots, jeans, denim jackets. They must have been watching out for her, because they get up immediately and the shorter one waves to her.

'Hey, Elli!'

She reaches into her bag as though she has a spray or alarm in it, and kind-of wishes she had.

'It's me, Ryan. Ryan Price.'

He has bandages across his face, which makes it hard

to tell what he's saying, as well as making him look weird.

'Ryan who?'

'Ryan Price. You used to knock about with a mate of mine, Joey Farron, had a red Honda.'

'Oh, yeah.'

'Yeah. He had a bit of bad luck. He's inside now.'

'Yeah, right.'

'This is Matto.'

'Right.'

'Saw your picture in the paper.'

'Maybe just looked like me.'

'Yeah, well, look, no hassle, but we read about what's happened and it's not right.'

No argument from Elli about that.

'So, we've been talking about it, with some of our mates, and we're maybe thinking of doing something about it.'

'Sending a message,' says Matto, 'about what happens to people who think they can mess with our women.'

Elli isn't too happy about the 'our women' bit and she certainly doesn't fancy the look of either of her would-be avengers. But she surely is in the mood for some head-kicking and who else is likely to come along with an offer to do just that?

'It's not like just "some mates" either,' Ryan goes on. It's like a proper organisation we belong to. We want to take you to our headquarters to meet the people in charge.'

'Oh, you do, do you? Do I really look that stupid?'

'Nah, look, Elli, this is straight up. It's a proper invitation. It's only over in Winton. We can give you a lift there and back in plenty of time for your curfew.'

'It's like, we don't want people to think we might be encouraging you to step out of line,' Matto says.

'Makes a change,' Elli thinks. And even if she feels like she is going through changes, that doesn't mean that she's about to start backing down when chances come her way.

'Yeah, OK, I'm up for that. You'd just better not be pissing me about.'

'No worries Elli,' says Ryan.

Matto manages something between a smile and a sneer.

The old Vauxhall, with its scrapes and dents and one odd-coloured door, is a disappointment, but it goes. They drive to a part of town she isn't familiar with, though the crappy housing is no surprise. They pull up outside a pub called The King's Head. Matto and Ryan lead her upstairs to an office with an image of a shark on its door.

'That's a Great White, isn't it?' Elli says. 'We did them in geography.'

'Yeah, that's us,' says Ryan. They knock and a voice tells them to go in.

'I've heard of you lot,' says Elli. You have marches about immigrants and that, don't you? I mean, not round here, but I've heard of you.'

'That's good to know,' says the man behind the desk. 'Our idea is to make sure people get to know us round here, as well.'

'What's that got to do with me?' asks Elli.

'Good question. Have a seat. My name's Kyle. This is Nick. Want a drink?'

Elli hesitates. 'No thanks.'

'OK, speak up if you change your mind.'

They settle around the table and Kyle lays it out.

'I'm not going to beat about the bush with you, Elli. We've read the paper and we've heard some other stories about the *Paradise* and the *Lotus* and we've had it up to here.' He jabs his flat hand up under his jaw.

'We, the Great Whites, are going to make a statement. We are going to make examples of people who carry out the kind of race crimes that don't get called that. In this country, of course, only white people can be racists. Other people can come here and lock their own women up and do what they want with our women, even young girls, like yourself. Social services don't care, the police don't care, and the newspapers just want another story to sell more papers, but the Great Whites care and we intend to show just how much.'

Then there are a lot of questions about the *Lotus* and *Paradise*. How many of 'that lot' usually turn up, which nights and what times were most people there? They want as many names of people as she can remember. Have there been other trips like this last one? Kyle is getting some of these questions from a list. He makes notes. They offer her a drink again.

'Am I all right with you lot?' she asks.

'Yeah, you're not just safe here, Elli. You are protected,' says Kyle.

So she says she'll have a cider and Kyle sends Ryan down to the bar to get a round in.

Funny thing is, she *feels* pretty safe with them, too. The one called Nick keeps looking at her breasts, but he seems harmless. Kyle is just interested in his questions. The other two keep quiet. Ryan pulls at his bandages and the other one just fidgets.

After about an hour, they've finished. She has told them everything she knows, as well as a few things she thinks, and they seem satisfied.

'So, what's up, then?' she asks.

'How do you mean?'

'What are you going to do? "Make examples," you said.'

'Yeah,' says Kyle, 'At the minute, we're just collecting information. We need to be prepared before we move in.'

'Oh, bloody hell, where have I heard that before?' Elli snaps and wishes she hadn't. She goes on quickly, 'Come on! Are you just going to turn up mob-handed somewhere and do some straightforward Paki-bashing, or do you have a "cunning plan"?'

'Like Kyle said,' Nick comes in, 'We're just gathering information. The main thing is you don't breathe a word about any of this. No warnings, get it?'

'All right, all right. But will you let me know when? I don't want to miss out on it all.'

'Well, we wouldn't want to put you in any danger,' says Kyle. 'But we can make sure you get an eyewitness description, even if you don't get a grandstand seat.'

'And if you have anybody in mind you'd like to send a special message to, like this Amir, just let us know,' Nick adds.

'I'll think about that,' says Elli. "I think I just might."

'Good,' says Kyle, and it makes Elli smile how he tries to sound formal. 'Thank you so much again for coming along and helping us out. Please take this for your time and trouble.'

He gives her a twenty.

'And remember not to say anything about this meeting.'

'Which meeting?' Elli smiles.

'Matto and Ryan will drop you back at Greenfields.'

The drive home is quick. Elli isn't sure if anything important has happened. Seem like another bunch of talkers and losers. But the cider was good. She knows about another pub. Knows a few more people. And she's picked up a twenty. Not so bad. And maybe, just maybe, some payback is on the way. Yessss.

* * *

Mason's response to hearing about Elli's visit to The King's Head is even more positive, although she keeps her satisfaction to herself.

'So, what's all this about then?'

'Hard to say, boss,' says DC Carpenter. 'It was definitely her. She's not exactly moving up in the world, though, if she's getting away from the likes of those bastards grooming her and ending up with John Matthews.'

'Do we know him?'

'Matto? Yeah, he's a crack-head of the feral, carrion-eating variety.'

'Political?'

'No chance. What we're getting with these Great

Whites, if you ask me, is radicalisation by free T-shirt or drug of choice.'

'And somebody is funding both,' Mason points out. 'Are they looking to give the foot-soldiers something to keep them busy?'

'Sorry?'

'Mmmm. So far, we've got a two-hander: Asians as villains and these girls as victims. If somebody steps in to take the side of the victims, what role do you think they're after?'

'Avengers? Vigilante stuff? Could go down well with some of the punters.'

'And that's two things we don't want: One, vigilante action, and two, these racist thugs doing something that might look popular. You're sure of your contacts on the street up in Winton and Drearden and that end?'

'Yes, boss. They're looking out for Great Whites activity and keeping us up to date.'

'Good. Tell them to keep a special eye out for any of those young girls visiting The King's Head. Can't be the normal clientele. If there is anything boiling up, we might have to call around there again and warn them off.'

'Will do, boss.'

* * *

Mason's next call is to inform Superintendent Barrett of her suspicions regarding a possible revenge link between Great Whites activity and the paedophile ring.

'Let's hold fire on the "paedophile ring" angle, he says. 'Simply feeds media speculation. As for vigilante action, more bloody déja-vu! Get on to DCI Shriver. We need joined-up thinking across these two cases. Best thing is you liaise with Bent. Vigilante stuff is what you do, isn't it?'

* * *

'I'm starting to wonder if there might be a god, after all,' Mason mutters wryly to Bent when they meet up to liaise.

'And,' Bent says, playing his top card with a slight smile. 'There's a meeting tonight. At the *Lotus*.'

'Tonight? That's too early. We can't set things up that quickly.'

'No, but Amir has been told to attend and give his version of what happened in Blackpool and after. He hasn't been to any of these meetings before. That means he will be able to give us some names of some of the bigger players.'

'Barrett only wants to hear about a small gang of Asian yobs on the street,' Mason warns.

'Yes, just a little like Shriver and those telephone numbers. It could all boil down to, "Let's keep it on the street." D'you think they're worried about upsetting some people?'

'Some people?'

'Just a thought,' says Bent. 'I'm a simple DS following orders. The politics of these things are beyond me.'

'Mmmmm,' says Mason. 'Quite so.' And then, flatly, 'So, you're up for this?'

'Yes. Let's make a noise. Let's make a grab into those long histories.'

They hold eye contact for longer than usual before parting.

Chapter 19

'It's not my fault! It's not my fault! They told me we were going to meet at the Lotus and then nobody came. Just them two and they wouldn't let me leave. They said I'd done enough damage. What did they mean, "done enough damage"? It was like everything was my fault. What was I supposed to …'

'Oh, shut up!' Bent snaps, doing his best to copy Amir's own accent and weary of listening to his complaints and excuses. 'So what happened then?'

'It was humiliating.'

'What was?'

'So, like, I'm waiting for an hour or so, then these two fellas turn up. Very heavy dudes.'

'What did they look like?'

'Heavy! I'm telling you, innit? Expensive suits, shiny shoes, sharp hair.

'Big, small?'

'Big! You don't send little people round to threaten folks, do you!?'

'Black, white?'

Fucking hell, Wahid! If they'd been white, I would have said so, wouldn't I?'

'Are you looking to get another beating?'

'What is your problem? Not very young. Spoke English with a local accent, like I do. My guess is they were circumcised. Anything else?'

'Amir Qureshi, if you are no use to me, then you are no use to me. I might just as well start calling some of these numbers.'

Bent hangs up. Amir rings back.

His mood has become more subdued.

'So they say, "None of this ever happened." And I'm like, "If you say so, but it wasn't all bad, you know." And they're like, "Are you trying to be funny?" And I say, "No, I mean, I get it. If anything ever happened, which it didn't, I can't remember what it was." Then one of them slaps me. Across the face. I thought he'd broken my nose again. Then the other one gets out a piece of paper and a pen and he says, "Write it down." And I'm like, "What?" and he's like, "None of this ever happened." Write it.' So I write it on this piece of paper and he takes his pen back off me and then he says, "Eat it." So, I do.

'I have to chew it till I can swallow it. It takes ages. And the other one's pulled out his phone and taken a picture of me eating it, with bits of paper sticking out of my mouth. Bastard. And then the other one, he takes his pen and snaps it in two. And he gives the bits back to me and says, "Now eat that." And I'm like, "I can't eat that." And he says, "Eat it!" And then he pulls out a gun. A fucking gun! Who has guns, for fuck's sake? And he says, "Eat it," again, dead quiet, like. So I put one piece in my mouth and bite into it and the plastic cracks and I can feel the tube bit with the ink in it between my teeth and then the two of them start laughing. They take another picture and then they just turn round and walk out of the room. And I've got this mouth full of bits of plastic and my tongue has gone blue and I hear them walking off, laughing.'

'This is the last time I'm going to bother listening to your crap, Amir. Last chance. Have you got anything useful to tell me, or not?'

'I'm telling you, aren't I? The word is, it's stopped. It

hasn't just stopped. It never happened. No girls, no drugs, nobody ever wanted a bit of white meat on the side. Nobody ever decided which ones was the dogs for the regular paying customers and which ones was the specials to get passed up the line for the VIPs. No bank accounts, no cars, no nothing. Fuck knows what we're supposed to do now, the ones who did all the work. Same as ever, innit? I'm just a working bloke, so I get humiliated by one lot, threatened by you — and who the fuck are you anyway? — and the money people just have their fun and then walk away. Is that right? Is it, eh?'

'And this girl in the paper, she was one of the dogs, right?'

'Too fucking right. Give her a Korean knock-off watch and you can line the punters up.'

Bent feels the familiar coldness of his anger envelop him from inside out.

'OK, you got anything else for me?'

'No! That's it. That's it! Don't you get it?'

'Are you scared, Amir?'

'Scared? Should I be?'

'Oh yes,' Bent says. 'Yes, I think so. I'm pretty sure you should be scared, Amir. I'll be in touch.'

Bent hangs up again and turns his 'Amir phone' off.

Waves of frustration. Anger. Relief? Relief?? No, this doesn't end here. The wind's too high. There will be damage.

* * *

At the station, DCI Shriver briefs that investigations into the numbers and addresses taken from Amir's phone and notebook are still being collated and analysed. They are a mixture of untraceable mobiles, the occasional private landline, a range of small businesses, including taxi firms, and a number of small, commercial hotels mostly focused in the north-west of England.

'Good we have our own copy of it all,' Bent thinks, noting the lack of any mention of the council building.

Mason reports on developments in the Great Whites operation.

'Three main points. First, some of them have been hanging around outside two local clubs, *The Lotus* and *The Paradise Garden*, which are not at all their usual haunts. Two, both clubs have gone very quiet since the "race sex hell" story broke. Three, something took place at the *Paradise* last night. That's to say, a number of older, ethnic Asian visitors arrived, usually chauffeur-driven, shortly before 11 pm. By midnight, they were all gone again, leaving singly or in pairs and picked up by their drivers.'

'If this was a deliberate meeting of these people,' Barrett comments, 'and if it is connected to the appalling sexual abuse case that we are closing in on, do we have any idea what was said or what the outcomes might have been?'

'No, sir,' Mason replied. 'With this sudden rush of publicity, it might well be that they want to go to ground, so to speak. Break off activity until things cool down.'

'Mmmm. Or we might be on the brink of closing the whole thing down, putting a stop to it. Or perhaps,' Barrett nods thoughtfully, 'some community leaders are pursuing exactly that same end.'

There is a silence.

'OK,' says Barrett. 'You all know what you're doing. Let's get on with it.'

As the meeting breaks up, Barrett takes Mason and Bent aside.

'Are you two liaising well?'

'Yes, sir,' they reply in unison.

'Excellent,' says Barrett. 'I particularly want the two of you to have special roles. This is big-profile stuff. Potentially very important for us. Woman DI, ethnic minority DS, very good for the media, very good for the force. Just be careful how you go. No loose implications that might get misinterpreted,' he glances meaningfully at Mason. 'Check with me, or with DCI Shriver, of course, before you strike out in any new directions and especially before you go public with anything. Otherwise, keep at it. Very impressed by both of you.'

'I almost thought,' Mason murmurs when he has left, 'that he was going to say, "Credit to your race, DS Bent."'

'And your gender, DI Mason,' Bent replies. 'Makes you wonder whether to laugh or cry.'

'Best neither,' says Mason. 'We need a quick decision on where this leaves us and how to take things forward.'

Bent briefly brings her up to date on what he has learned from Amir.

'Have we missed the bus?' Mason asks. 'Perhaps we have,' she replies to her own question. 'But there's always another one if you don't mind waiting.'

'Depends how quickly our actual official investigation moves forward.'

'Yes, indeed. Anyway, I can't see a good reason for changing the plan to revisit The King's Head. We aren't where we wanted to be. We just are where we are.'

* * *

Next day at The King's Head, Kyle is very far from where he wants to be. He is now under pressure from London to produce a response to the grooming stories.

'Yeah, we know about these people, Mr C. We're on top of it!'

'You know them? What do you know?'

'Well, we've been observing them, we ...'

'Observing them? The point of the Great Whites is to strike fear into the hearts of inferior races and make our own people proud. What is the point of the Great Whites when young girls are being passed around for a quick fuck by people who are not fit to clean their shoes?'

'Yeah, I know, well, we've ...'

'These people are showing contempt for the whole White race. And they keep their own women under wraps just to point out to White men that we have no control over our own women. And you have been "observing" them?' I gave you that little present because I thought you were a man of action, a commander! Now you tell me you are an observer? I can send some men up if you need them.'

'No, we can handle it! I said "observing" so as to find out where they meet! That's what I meant. And now I've got twenty blokes, troops, proper hard men lined up and ready for it. Bats, hoodies, balaclavas, the works, all set to go.'

'Well, that sounds more like it! That's the sort of thing I want to be hearing about. Action, Kyle! A little blood in the water.'

'Don't you worry, Mr C,' says Kyle, 'We ...,' but Mr C has already hung up.

Any mention of the Glock sets Kyle to sweating. Nick is always going on about it and wanting to see it again. Like some bloody kid who wants to play with a new toy. It's all very well having a neat gun, but a gun isn't what you need to crack a few dozen heads with, is it? And anyway, the fucking gun is gone.

And so were the fucking Pakis! We check the clubs and where the fuck are they? Disappeared. A few old men show up for an hour and bugger off again. Who are they? We've got car numbers, but what am I supposed to do with them? I could ask Collingwood, but that would just show me up again and tell him the only plan we had is off.

To cap it all, Terry calls up to say that bloody police woman is here again.

'Yeah, send her up, Terry. And tell Nick to come up, as well.'

'I hear you had a bit of trouble,' is Mason's opening line.

Kyle and Nick exchange glances.

'No trouble here,' Kyle says.

'Nobody comes here looking for trouble,' Nick adds, 'Or they get more than they can handle.'

Mason grins.

'Oh, right,' she says, 'I heard different. Something about people falling downstairs, I think they said at the hospital. But you can't believe everything you hear, can you?'

'You'd know about that.'

'Nice new windows. Alarm system. I suppose you'll be getting that fire escape replaced? Health and Safety, you know.'

'On the way.'

'Good, good. Should keep you safe in here, then, as long as you keep your heads down. Good to see that you haven't done anything stupid about all these stories in the press.'

'You think? Who *is* going to protect our people then? Where's the police when our girls are getting raped?' Kyle's temper is wearing thin.

'And when they're breaking in and beating people up?' Nick adds. 'They need showing who's boss!'

'Shut up, Nick!' Kyle shouts.

'How are the T-shirt sales going?' asks Mason. 'Have you thought about key-rings? Or little plastic sharks for kids to play with in the bath? Could be a nice little earner.'

'Bitch!' Kyle shouts once she's gone. 'Fucking women! Fucking police! Fucking Pakis!'

'What shall I tell the guys?' Nick asks. 'They're all pumped up for one. We can always find some Pakis.'

'Not the point, though, is it? Not just something random. This is supposed to be hitting back because of these girls. That's what Mr C wants, a proper eye for an eye.'

'You mean like, girls for girls?'

Kyle and Nick stare at each other for a long silent minute.

'Tell the guys to stand down,' says Kyle. 'Be ready to tool up when I give the word. Tell 'em again: This is a movement. We have discipline. Then come back here.'

'What are you doing?'

'Thinking,' says Kyle. 'Thinking and planning. Like a commander.' He unscrews a bottle of Jamesons and settles down behind his desk.

After a while, he unlocks the top drawer, ignoring the oilcloth, and takes out the knuckle duster. He slips it on and slowly starts to punch his fist softly into the palm of his other hand.

* * *

Mason looks at Bent and shrugs.

'They're mouthing off about this grooming situation and they're mad about the break-in, of course. And I couldn't resist winding them up a bit, but what's the point? If there's nobody for them to attack, we can't bust them at it, can we?'

'We could leak a few names,' Bent agrees, 'But the longer this drags on, the more obvious it becomes that the odd Amir here and Mohsin there are just messenger boys. We had a glimpse of some of the people behind this, but we're not going to get a good look at them now. Not without some serious police work, anyway.'

'So let's get on with that and then see if we can set up a clear, serious target for what is a pretty blunt instrument. Or perhaps we just get back on track. We have those car registrations.'

'Yes, I've got a feeling they've disappeared into the "sensitive and all in hand" area of operation.' Bent pauses before turning away. 'Anyway, we come out of this knowing more than we did before.'

'More about ourselves, you mean?'

'Yes. More about that.'

'Well,' she says, 'I think I've come out with more questions than answers, but yeah, they are worthwhile questions.'

'We have different pieces and maybe they don't make a picture, but I would like to work on finding out if they do.'

'Yeah, me too. Maybe the real lesson is to realise that whatever comes out is going to be a self-portrait.'

'Too deep for me, boss.'

'Yeah, sure. Anyway, there are still violent racists and child abusers out there, DS Bent, so it's not like we don't have things to get on with.'

'Yes, ma'am. Let's get back to some routine.'

Chapter 20

Choudry Bakht looks at his watch and sighs. He leaves his job, sorting vegetables, washes his hands and picks up the keys for the Toyota People-Carrier from the office.

The school run is not something Choudry looks forward to particularly, but at least it gets him out of the warehouse. At 8 am on weekday mornings, he sets off with Mr Ahmed's two daughters on board. He collects the girls from two other family members and two important customers and delivers all seven of them to the girls' school across town. At half-past three, he picks them up again and retraces his steps, dropping them off safely at their various homes.

'How they gabble!' he shakes his head. Aged between 11 and 16, they talk non-stop. He cannot always understand everything they say, and sometimes he thinks he understands things he wishes he had not. They are from good families and he wonders if he ought to tell their fathers about those conversations. But it is probably just childish foolishness and he has no wish to be involved in anything unpleasant. Still, he thinks it is time with one or two of them that their families pay some attention to getting them married. At least he is doing his part by driving them to and from school without any risk of them being molested by whites, or any danger of gossip among their own community that could spoil their chances. He also understands from some of Fawziyya's chatter (Allah, that girl can talk!) that her parents are planning a trip home this year, so perhaps things will be arranged then.

At 3.15, he parks outside the school. He is a little early, but it's better for getting a spot close to the gates before the rest of the school-run traffic turns up. Soon enough he hears the bell, then the doors open and the first girls appear. Why are 'his' always so slow? Ha! Here they come. Here they come. Two little ones holding hands. So sweet! Ayeee, that Fawziyya, how she walks! Oooofff! One of them is missing. Now what? At least the sensible one is here. Even if she is so very sure of herself. Never get a husband like that.

'Sorry, Uncle Choudry,' says Ayesha. 'Asma has to see Mrs Hussein. She'll just be a few minutes late.'

'Mrs Hussein?'

'The geography teacher.'

'Acha, not to worry.'

He turns on the radio and the sound of qawwali at least partly blocks out the girls' nonsense while he waits.

The other cars and minibuses have gone by the time Asma, a chubby twelve-year-old, comes running across the street.

'Sorry, Uncle Choudry, I had to see Mrs Hussein.'

'I hope you're not in trouble, or I'll have to tell your dad!'

'No!' she blushes, 'I got a message to go to see Mrs Hussein. And then she was busy, so I had to wait.'

'Is it about your prize?' calls out one of the waiting girls.

'Ay! What are you getting a prize for?'

'Eating puddings!' shouts another.

Asma's blush deepens. 'I'm not supposed to talk about it.'

'Is it for geography?'

'Is it for finding out which countries make the best

puddings?'

'Please stop that now! That is very unkind.'

'Yeeees, Uncle Choudry. Soooorry , Uncle Choudry,' the girls chorus in a cheerful parody of class responses. Asma climbs into the bus and Ayesha pulls the sliding door closed behind her.

'Seat belts fastened?'

'Yeeees, Uncle Choudry,' the girls chorus again

'Ready for take-off!' cries one.

'Off to Islamabad to find a nice boy for Amira!' shouts another.

'Let me out now!' Amira screams in mock panic.

'She's already got one!'

'Or two!'

Choudry shakes his head slowly from side to side, not knowing whether to smile, disapprove, or pretend he hasn't heard. Suppressing a mixture of all three, he starts the engine and reaches for his own safety belt.

This move is interrupted by a loud rapping against the window of the empty front passenger seat. Looking across, Choudry sees a large red face under a baseball cap. Choudry looks again. The face is a mask, the red face of a devil.

The man raps again with the coin in his hand and signals for Choudry to lower the window. Choudry raises his chin and lifts a hand in a gesture of refusal. As he does so, his own door is ripped open and he is pulled from his seat. He has a brief glimpse of a grotesque animal face. He lands on his hands and knees on the tarmac. The first kick winds him. The second knocks him unconscious. He knows nothing about the others.

'Get the fuck in and drive!' Ayesha hears the Devil's angry instruction above her friends' screams. The Pig obeys immediately. The doors lock automatically as he pulls away.

'Shut up! Shut up now, or I'll give you something to scream about!'

Devil is looking back from the front passenger seat. He has pulled out a knife and, with a flick of the wrist, snapped the blade into place.

'You all keep quiet. You all sit still. Phones on the floor. Now! All of them!'

The girls look to Ayesha. She obeys. They follow. Ayesha feels herself soaking up the fear around her like a sponge thrown into a bath. A fleeting image of herself in her bathroom magnifies her sense of vulnerability.

'Right,' Devil is speaking again. 'Now, then. You keep quiet, you sit still and nothing is going to happen to you.'

'Well,' Pig looks back at them in the driving mirror. 'If you're lucky, that is. If you're very, very lucky.'

Ayesha looks around and sees the terrified faces that Pig sees.

'And anyway,' Devil adds. 'They might like it. What do you think?'

'Oh, the girls I know like it a lot. Can't get enough.'

The two men-creatures look at each other and laugh.

Devil turns back again and winks bizarrely through the eyehole in the mask.

'Lucky girls, eh?'

The silence is broken only by the sobbing of the two youngest girls, Basima and Laila. Ayesha is saturated by memories of running home in tears after one insult, one attack or another. Always her grandmother would comfort her and then, when the crying was over, she would say,

'And what is your name?'

And Ayesha would reply,

'My name is Ayesha Sajjadi.'

'Ah, you are a Sajjadi?'

'Yes, I am a Sajjadi.'

'Then what shall we do?'

'We will hold up our heads and we will go on our way.'

'Acha, you *are* a Sajjadi.'

Ayesha returns to the sound of weeping. She finds her back is bent and her head down. She straightens herself and takes a deep breath. And then another.

'You had ... you had better pull over and let us out,' she says, her voice steadying as she speaks.

'And what's your name?' Devil asks.

Ayesha almost laughs at the echo.

'My name is Ayesha Sajjadi. And what is yours?'

'Very funny. Now shut up, Ayesha.'

'You had better pull over and let us out.'

'Shut up!' Devil bellows.

The two younger girls start to cry louder.

'And you shut up, an' all!'

'Laila, don't cry. Be brave. Don't let these animals frighten you. God is with us,' Ayesha says softly but firmly in Urdu.

'None of that! None of that! You speak English!'

'It is the language of her mother. She is young and

frightened.'

'Well she can bloody well be frightened in English.'

'ONOROL! ONOROL!' Pig chants.

Laila begins to wail.

'Yes, she *is* frightened in English, that's the point. I was trying to help her be less frightened,' Ayesha spells out.

'Well, do it in English!'

'ONOROL! ONOROL!'

'Oh, for fuck's sake, Pricey, leave it out a minute and just drive, will you?'

'Saba, put your arm around her, give her a tissue,' Ayesha continues in Urdu.

'Look, I'll make this dead simple.' Devil lunges back and grabs the nearest girl by her hair through her hijab. Fatima cries out. He pulls her head towards him, puts down his knife, and slaps her hard across the face.

'Every word of gibberish I hear that isn't English, I'm going to hit her in the face. Not you, not anyone else, just her. Got it?'

Ayesha, who flinches as the blow lands, looks Devil in the eye.

'Saba, put your arm around Laila, give her a tissue,' Ayesha says quietly in English, without breaking eye contact.

'Ah, isn't that nice!' Pig says to the rear-view mirror. 'Now we're all getting to know each other — Ayesha and Laila and Saba!'

'Yes,' Ayesha replies, 'Yes, we are, aren't we, Pricey?'

Devil and Pig exchange angry glances.

'Stupid bastard!'

'Later.'

'The sooner you let us go, the less trouble you will be in,' Ayesha says.

'Well, perhaps we aren't afraid of a bit of trouble,' Devil tells her.

'At the moment, it is only assault, car-theft and attempted kidnap. The longer this goes on, the more likely it becomes that you will have to kill us.'

'You are a right fuckin' little drama-queen aren't you?'

'Watches too much telly,' says Pig.

'We have all seen you, heard your voices, and we know one of your names. We can identify you, and we can see where you are taking us. Once we get there, you will not be able to let us go. So it is better for you if you let us go now.'

'You don't know what we look like!' says Pig.

'Of course I do, Pricey,' says Ayesha. 'You look like a pig. You should have worn a mask.'

In that moment, Ayesha recognises her own tendency to take things one step too far. She has been told often enough about being too clever for her own good. Especially for a girl. She is astonished by the way a mask can seem to change its expression, as the previous anger in Devil's voice shifts to an even more intimidating malevolence.

'You know what, smart-arse? We'll deal with those little problems one at a time. And I'll deal with you. In more ways than you can imagine. Nice girl like you.'

Ayesha lowers her eyes.

'That's more like it,' Devil sneers. 'Supposed to do

what you're told, aren't you, eh?'

In the silence that follows, Ayesha bites off the responses that go through her head. She chews them. Tastes the bitterness. Swallows them. She raises her head just enough to look around the group. She imagines herself throwing a cloak over them. Where she can make eye-contact, she sends out the message.

'We are being tested, but we are strong. Trust in Allah. And trust me.'

After several minutes, the people-carrier turns into a side-street and then into a yard behind the derelict remains of a small clothing factory. Pig pulls up alongside the only other vehicle there, a well-worn and windowless Ford Transit van.

'Get the door,' says Devil.

Pig walks to the van and opens the rear doors. The compartment is completely empty, with a solid partition separating off the driver's cabin.

'You get out of here and into that. No fuss, no messing about. Leave your bags behind. And your phones! Just get up and go.'

Devil tugs on Fatima's hair again, pulling her closer. Her face is already swelling, red before the bruising shows.

'She stays here till you are all in.'

'No, I will stay,' says Ayesha.

'Oh, that could be cosy. And you are a nice big, little girl, aren't you?'

She feels his eyes move down her body. She is grateful for the modesty of her clothing. Devil lets go of

Fatima. Ayesha takes her place in the seat closest to him. She looks back to the others.

'As soon as you are all outside,' she says quietly in Urdu, 'run in different directions. Bang on doors. Find someone,' Then to Devil, 'Sorry, I was just telling them not to be afraid!'

'Lying bitch!' Devil takes hold of her arm and picks up his knife again. He lays it against her cheek.

'Any trouble from them and I will cut my fucking initials in your face.'

'Just do as I told you,' says Ayesha.

The girls stare at her, wide-eyed. They get out of the car and stand trembling in a huddle.

'Come on,' Pig shouts. 'Get a move on. Get in here!'

'Now,' says Ayesha firmly.

The girls look at each other, back to the car where Ayesha still sits, and climb quickly into the Transit.

Devil gets out and pulls Ayesha through the side door. She resists, but then allows herself to be dragged to the Transit and pushed in.

'You,' Devil points to Fatima. 'Here, now.'

'No!' cries Ayesha.

'Now! Kneel down.'

Fatima kneels inside the open door.

Devil slaps her heavily across the other side of her face and she falls backwards with a whimper.

'I told you once,' he snarls at Ayesha. 'I don't want to have to fuckin-well tell you again.'

He slams the door and locks it. Stands for a moment. Takes off the cap and mask, runs his hand over the stubble on his head.

'Piece of piss,' Matto mutters to himself as he walks to the front of the Transit and climbs into the passenger seat. Ryan drives off.

Chapter 21

'Don't worry. It's all under control.'

Kyle can see from Terry's expression that he is not so much worried as, well, just about dumbstruck.

'You've done what?'

'Like I said.'

'Who, exactly, has done this?' Terry wants to know.

'Ryan and Matto.'

Terry stares at him.

'You said yourself Ryan Price is a useless wanker and Matto is a nutter, even when he isn't frying his brain on something.'

'I know, I know, but Ryan's shaped up on the last couple of jobs I've given him. I mean, I wouldn't want him minding my back in a knife-fight, but he's tough enough for a few schoolgirls.'

'And Matto's clean these days,' Nick chips in. 'Ryan says he hasn't been using for months. And he's hard as nails. He was in Iraq, you know. In that business on the stairs here, he says he couldn't get at the first bloke 'cause Ryan was all over him, and then the other one hit him from behind.'

'Yeah,' says Kyle. 'Point Matto in the right direction and he'll walk through walls for you.'

'And he's got biker mates. He's got the lend of a bike so either him or Ryan can get around without using the van again, once that's under a tarp.'

'What were you thinking?' Terry has his head in his hands.

'I'll tell you what I was thinking!' Kyle's voice is rising

with his temper. 'I was thinking of taking some action that would put the Great Whites where they belong — out in front protecting their people. An eye for an eye! They mess with our girls, well, we can mess with theirs! We are sending out a message!'

'You're absolutely stark raving mad!' says Terry. 'Kidnap, rape — you'll go down forever, and the Great Whites with you.'

'We're not talking about real kidnapping. And nobody said anything about rape. Nobody's fucking anybody.'

'So, what's your message, then? "You fuck our girls and we'll take yours for a drive in a minibus?"'

All three men are standing by now. Kyle stares at Terry, then at Nick, and then sits down again. The other two follow suit.

'If you've got your head round the first half of the idea, I'll tell you the rest,' Kyle says. 'There's always demands, isn't there? When somebody gets taken, OK, like, kidnapped.'

'Ransom demands.'

'Yeah, well, we stash the girls somewhere safe and then we say what our demands are.' He waits.

'OK, all right, so what are "our" demands?'

'We demand that they give up all these bastards who've been fucking our girls. I mean, they know, don't they? Them in their so-called "community." They all know who they are. They have to give 'em up. To the police. That way,' Kyle bangs on the table, 'we are helping the police do what they can't manage by themselves. And we show that stupid bitch that was round here exactly who we are: Great Whites — Local Heroes.'

'But the filth'll be all over us, right off, won't they?'

'We don't say it's us right off. But after, when it's all sorted, we just let everybody know how it went down.'

'What if they won't give anybody up?'

'Why are you so fucking negative? Anyway, I've thought about that. If they won't give 'em up, it just shows what a load of callous bastards they are, dunnit? We can let the girls go and show that we're better than them, 'cause we didn't do anything to 'em. Get it?'

'Hey, Kyle,' Nick says.

'What?'

'Them two black bastards that broke in and did Ryan and the others over. We want them an' all. I want them, and not for the police.'

Kyle gets up and starts pacing the room.

'Nick, Nick, Nick,' he says slowly. 'I'll tell you what. I've just had another idea. They also have to give up all their fucking terrorist sympathisers. 'Cause they know who they are as well, don't they? Their Al Kayeeders and their Islamic Staters. Great Whites — National Heroes.'

'Fucking hell,' says Nick. 'Pull that off and they'll have to give you an AK47 next! Here, Let's have another look at that Glock!'

'Give that a break, will you? We have work to do.'

'Jesus Christ,' says Terry. 'Where are they?'

'Out at …,' says Nick.

'Hold on, Nick,' says Kyle. 'I don't know how much I want to tell you anymore, Terry. You're starting to worry me.'

'Oh, am I?' Terry replies. 'You've got a lot more to worry about before you need to worry about me. Where are they?'

'Well,' says Kyle, after a short pause, 'As you can see, it's a bit of a secret. Not a lot of people know about it. You tell him, Nick.'

'It's this old pub, was what they call a coaching inn, out on the road between Morbury and Sagwell.'

'Never heard of 'em.'

'Exactly. They was only ever little villages and there's hardly anybody lives out there these days. And the Britannia's been boarded up forever. People used to have the odd rave out there. Then Kyle had this idea, to take over, like, take control of what was going on. That was how most of us got together, before we called ourselves The Great Whites, you know.'

'Yeah,' Kyle comes in. 'From the road, it just looks like a ruin falling down. But round the back, we fixed up ways into the cellar: one through the old back entrance and one through the delivery trapdoor in the yard. It stinks a bit, but it's more or less dry. We knocked off a stack of old camp beds and blankets, paraffin heaters, hurricane lamps and that, so's we could doss there if we wanted to after we had a bash. Only ever used it in the summer. Nobody'd think about going there now.'

'Remember those immigrants we picked up last year?' Nick grins. 'How happy were they for a day's work?'

'Done a good job!' Kyle laughs at the memory. 'Even had a good go at cleaning up the so-called toilets. Jesus, that was horrible!'

'And then they were pleased enough just to be given a lift back to town instead of getting paid.'

'Once they'd thought about the other option!' Kyle laughs again.

'And that's where you're taking the girls?'

'Yeah. Ryan and Matto both know it. That was another reason it made sense for them to do the job. Me and Nick went out there yesterday and dropped off some paraffin for the heaters and lanterns. And we took a few dozen loaves of sliced bread and what looks like half a ton of cheddar a mate nicked out of the back of an Aldi.'

'These people might have funny eating habits, but anybody can get by on cheese sandwiches if they're hungry enough,' Nick adds. 'And they've got big bottles of drinking water and plastic cups. We even left toilet paper and some plastic buckets we lifted from outside a B&Q — they can fill them from the old rainwater cistern for flushing.'

'It's rough, but it'll do for a couple of days and that's all we need,' says Kyle. 'That's the beauty of it. It doesn't even matter if nobody gets given up. It's still the Great Whites leading the way, making the right demands, speaking up for our people. Anytime we want, we can call the television and say where they are. Just a bit scared. And if some of those people do get given up, Bullseye!'

'I'd like to see Mr Collingwood's face — Sorry, Mr C's face — when you tell him,' says Nick.

'And that's not all!' says Kyle. 'Those people he put us in touch with are totally up for it. We've just gone Europa League! The Poles've agreed to send emails via connections they've got so they can't be traced. They just bounce round the world and turn up where you want them to. Too fucking cool. They said, start the story local and let it build, so we're sending a message to local BBC radio.'

'No mention of the Great Whites?' Terry asks.

"Course not,' says Kyle. 'Not yet. We're not fucking stupid.'

'So, this is all on you, Kyle. You and Nick.'

'Yeah. You remember that, Terry. London wants action and, as far as this patch is concerned, I am the commander and we are in for some bloody action.'

* * *

It is already quite dark and a cold wind is blowing off the moors. The rain has stopped and the cloud cover broken up. A gibbous moon appears now and again between the racing clouds. As they pull around behind the ruined Britannia, Ryan breaks into a chorus of,

'Hey cowboy, better change your ways

Or with us you will ride,

Tryin' to catch this devil's herd ...'

'Shut the fuck up and get your mask back on,' is Matto's response.

When they open the back of the van, there is complete silence. No crying, no complaints.

'Out!' says Matto.

One by one, the girls crawl to the door and scramble down, the older ones helping the smaller. Fatima and Laila seem to be in a state of shock, staring ahead but apparently seeing nothing. The others all keep their eyes on the ground, as if by agreement.

'This way,' says Matto. 'Follow him.'

Price walks towards the back of the building. Some distance short of it, he bends down and unlocks a huge padlock that secures a large trapdoor in the ground. He opens it up on noisy hinges and climbs down an old but solid ladder into the darkness. After a few moments, a wavering light comes up from below.

'Down there,' says Matto.

The girls freeze. Then Ayesha points to Fawziyya. Trembling visibly, Fawziyya goes to the edge of the opening and looks down. She sees Ryan's mask staring up at her and lets out an involuntary cry.

'Go,' says Ayesha. 'Show no fear.'

'It's OK to be afraid,' says Matto. 'In fact, it's a very good idea. You can piss yourself as far as I'm concerned, just so long as you get down into that hole.'

'It is simply a cellar,' says Ayesha. 'This is where they would have rolled the beer casks down into the vaults.'

'What the fuck do you know about beer casks and vaults?'

'Very little. But I can read and I am interested in the social history of my country.'

'Your fucking country!? This is not your fucking country!'

'ONOROL! clap-clap-clap ONOROL! clap-clap-clap ONOROL!' comes up from Ryan at the bottom of the ladder.

'Shut up!' Matto screams down at him. He turns back to Ayesha, 'You have no fucking idea who you are dealing with here!'

'Of course, we do,' Ayesha replies. There is a brief silence before she continues. 'We are dealing with a devil and his pig. Go down now, Fawziyya.'

Fawziyya turns and, struggling a little with her ankle

length skirt, makes her way down the ladder. The others follow. Ayesha helps Laila make the start. When she offers the same to Fatima, Fatima shakes her head to signal she does not need assistance and indicates with a lift of her chin that she has recovered her sense of what is going on. Last of all, Ayesha descends. Matto closes the trapdoor and replaces the lock.

The girls watch the moonlight disappear and, in the flickering lamplight, they wait.

* * *

In a matter of hours, a photograph of the girls' faces, huddled together and strangely illuminated, goes viral. Along with its message:

We demand that those Muslim men responsible for the abuse of our girls give themselves up immediately.

The message is signed by a group calling itself, *Defenders of One Nation*. Kyle and Nick have decided that is as close as they want to go in claiming credit for the Great Whites at this point. This way, they can deny all knowledge for as long as necessary and take credit as soon as it becomes possible. The more they think about their strategy, the better they like it. They toast each other and the new computer screen.

When the call from London comes, however, it is far from congratulatory. Mr C himself is on the line.

'If you have anything, anything at all to do with this appalling act, then you will use all possible measures to get these girls released. And then you find a hole deep enough to hide in.'

Kyle's brain spins like the fruit on a slot machine, searching for a winning combination in a world where you hope chance is random, while really you know it is fixed.

'It's nothing to do with us!' Kyle assures him, while thinking, "At least Terry hasn't told him." 'But you can see why it's happened can't you? I mean, it's understandable. These people want to stand up for the same things we do: One Nation, One Race, One Language. Bloody hell, you wanted us to do something, didn't you?'

'We were talking about an act of resistance aimed at the defilers of our young women.' Collingwood's voice is icy. 'We were talking about direct punishment of the guilty. We were *not*,' the pitch of his voice begins to rise towards cracking point, 'We were *not* talking about creating sympathy for these aliens by kidnapping their children and frightening them out of their wits. What comes next? Beheadings? We are bringing ourselves down to their level!'

'Maybe that's what they understand!' Kyle shouts back, surprised by his own bravery. 'If some people give themselves up, it'll look different, won't it? And even if they don't, as long as the girls are all right, it'll just be a sign that we aren't like them, because nobody gets hurt.'

'You imbecile,' Collingwood's voice is calm again. 'It *is* you.'

'Tell him about the terrorists,' Nick suggests.

'What did he say?'

'He said about the terrorists,' Kyle is trying to speak despite a very dry throat. He motions to Nick to pass him something to drink. 'We were talking about what happened and we thought that maybe these people, these Defenders of One Nation, might also demand that the Muslims give up their terrorist sympathisers.'

'You thought that, did you?'

'Yeah. I mean, it would just be a reminder that they have these terrorists and they know who they are and they don't want to give them up. Even though the girls would have to be set free before that could happen, I mean, of course, it would just be a reminder ...'

'I am sending two men up there to take over. You will do exactly what they tell you. And you will give back to them the small item that I loaned you.'

'You said it was a gift. A gift in appreciation, that's what you said.'

'They will be with you by tomorrow night at the very latest. If those girls are still in danger, and if we find your fingerprints on this fiasco, prepare to say goodbye to your fingers.'

Mr C. hangs up.

Chapter 22

'I am trying not to feel too guilty about this,' says Mason, chewing furiously. 'And it's a losing battle.'

'Wasn't foreseeable,' says Bent. 'We did not cause this.'

'Not exactly, but I helped set it up. I made it more likely, rather than less. I stirred the pot. And I've heard you before on the subject of taking responsibility for unintended consequences.'

'Different thing,' Bent responds. 'You did what seemed right for good reason. Things have gone belly-up. Doesn't mean you're to blame.'

'OK, OK. Thanks. I appreciate it. Even though we both know that's bollocks. I've heard you on noble-cause corruption, too. We don't have time to talk about it now. We have to do something.'

'Yes, we still have to do what we think is right for good reason.'

'OK, OK,' Mason repeats, visibly controlling her temper. 'That vermin, Kyle Redwood, has been on local radio saying that the kidnap is a disgrace and the Great Whites want to stand up for the dignity of women. Whoever has done this is down at the level of those people "from another community who have been abusing young white girls," so he says.'

'And we still think they are up to their necks in it.'

'Correct. So, apart from beating the shit out of him till he says more, what options do we have?'

'There's Elli and there's Amir,' Bent says. 'They're both only on the periphery of this actual kidnapping, but we know that Elli was out at The King's Head with two of those goons ...'

'And whatever the response in the Muslim community, some people will be pointing the finger at Amir and his friends,' Mason completes the thought.

He waits for her to continue. They stand shoulder to shoulder on a quiet corridor, staring out at the clouds massing.

'There's something beyond irony that tastes too bitter to have a name,' she says.

He stays silent. There is the occasional sound of doors opening and closing somewhere else in the building. Some traffic noise outside.

'Those kids are picking up my tab. My unpayable tab. No, listen!' She raises her hand to ward off his interruption.

'I know about unintended consequences, I *know* that,' she taps her head with a forefinger,' but that doesn't change the feeling. These girls have been kidnapped, threatened and imprisoned, at the very least. I swear to you, if they have been sexually abused by the time this is over, I am going to get a gun. Just like my brother said. And I will hunt down every last one of these fuckers until somebody stops me. Even if they haven't been assaulted, who knows what kind of trauma they are going through and the effects it will have?'

'I've got a gun,' says Bent.

'What?'

'It's another story. Or a different part of this one. If we need a gun, don't concern yourself. We have a gun. And my visits to the land of my ancestors — well, some of them — have allowed me to learn how to use one. But you're right, it's not for now.'

'What's not for now? What do you mean, you've got ...'

'I mean this conversation about what we've done, how it tastes, and how we move forward.'

'What?'

'I know we are on a tightrope here and it's a very high wire. We're both here because we chose to be. A choice we made some time ago. When you were talking just now, I heard what you were saying. The tab. The guilt. The gun. I heard it. But I also have a feeling that it sounds like more of the same. Like *not* learning. Now maybe that's for the best. But maybe it's not. Maybe there is something else to learn, something different.'

'Like what?'

'Well, take irony for a start. Kidnapping schoolgirls? And I was worried these scumbags might come out of this looking good? So, that's turned to our advantage. But have I got what I wanted?'

'I'm not sure I know what you're talking about.'

'Satisfaction. It's got more complicated. Even more than it always was.'

'Ha!'

'But now, right now, things are relatively straightforward. We have to find these girls. It's police work.'

'Except that you and I already have our own involvements, don't we, that are not exactly police work? And what do you mean, "There's Elli?"'

'Yes,' Bent nods, 'we have our extra angles on this. Maybe they are problems and maybe possibilities. She might be one. And we'll use them all: official, undercover and downright illegal, as and when. That's how we take responsibility for what we're responsible for. All I'm saying is we don't come to any major conclusions at this point. We stay in the action and we roll with it.'

'Are you telling me to keep my nerve, DS Bent?'

'Wouldn't occur to me, DI Mason.'

'Good.' She refreshes her gum. 'I'm going to The King's Head.'

'I'll phone Amir. And Elli.'

'Dinner tonight?'

'Later on?'

'Yes.'

'Yes.'

* * *

Elli sits on her bed at the hostel, knees drawn up under her chin. She runs the prongs of the fork over the tender skin of her inner arm. They leave four light red trails. She presses a little harder. Back here again then.

She closes her eyes. Images form.

Life is an endless crowded procession around a mousetrap on a concrete floor. Mostly, things are hard and you are cold and there doesn't seem to be a lot of point. But sometimes, now and again, it's like your ticket has come up, or there's a special offer. You step up onto the platform and reach out for it. And that's when everything gives way under your feet. And the spring you hadn't seen jumps into action. And that metal bar you had no idea about comes winging down out of the sky and breaks your back, or your neck, or your skull. Unless you are very tough. Very, very tough. And then it just leaves another wound, another bruise, another scar, and you limp back into the crowd and drag your injuries on to next time.

She wonders where the memory of mousetraps comes from, but wondering is as far as she gets. So many half-memories that don't add up to much. Not to a life. Not even to a childhood.

Mmphhhh! Oh, that hurt. Yesss. Take it easy. Plenty of time.

Hurt. She knows she wanted Amir hurt. Amir and all his 'friends', or were they customers? And what's come of it? Half a dozen of those little girls in their headscarves and long skirts have been kidnapped. Was she a part of it? Not really, surely? Yeah, she never liked them, with their sticking together and stupid cover-up clothes. Yeah, she got it, all those Asian boys were frustrated as hell and that's why they threw their money around at girls like her. She wasn't stupid. But why wasn't that enough? If they wanted 'a girl like her,' why wasn't that enough? Did she even count as a girl? A person at all? Or just tits-and-cunt to be passed around? Yes, she got it. Finally, she got it.

And what has she done with it, now she's "got it"? She's lined up with these other men in order to get revenge. And what are they doing? They're harming some other girls who don't have half a clue, probably, of what any of it is all about. What's going to happen to them? At least she'd had some idea of what she was getting into. What about them?

Men. Fucking men. Yes, absolutely that.

Elli cries out. Her arm is bleeding. There doesn't seem

to be a lot worse can happen to her, she feels. And in the very next moment, she thinks,

'Nah. One thing you can be sure of is things can always get worse.'

Her phone buzzes. Those vultures from the press, probably. Then she looks. No, even worse. That policeman. Police + man. Does it get any worse than that? She ignores the call.

What to do? Nothing?

If anything, it has to start at The King's Head. Those creepy guys who picked her up and dropped her off. They had been OK in the sense they hadn't tried anything on, but still they'd been a bit weird. And those two at the pub, making out as though they were somebody. She knew their gang. Bunch of macho skinheads. She'd even been out to one of their parties once, miles out of town. Big bonfire, head-banging music and a big hole in the ground they'd gone down in for a bit and she was very glad to get out of. Not much fun and happy she'd had a lift home. Yeah, with Karen, that was it. Karen knew this bloke with a bike and they'd had three of them on it. Crazy. Amazing they hadn't got busted. Then they'd dropped her at the hostel and Karen had got off with him, turned around on the saddle in the car park, she said. Young love, eh?

So, it has to be The King's Head. And what? For perhaps the first time in her life, Elli realises that she is thinking more than one step ahead. It's strange. It's interesting. OK. Turn up. Say she wants in. They came to her first, didn't they? Said something about a grandstand seat. So now she can let on she's up for whatever's going on to pay those Paki bastards back.

And then see what she can do to protect those girls.

Her phone buzzes again. Him again. She thinks for a moment. Answers.

* * *

Coming down the stairs at The King's Head, Mason is furious and elated. Elated because it is very obvious that Kyle and Nick are up to their eyes in this sick affair. Furious because there is no obvious way to proceed against them that might not endanger the girls or get in the way of the official investigation. One thing for sure is that they are clearly scared as hell. Scared like children who have learned how to strike a match but have no idea how to put out a fire. What is that all about?

She has scared them some more. Pushed them on the business of the break-in, which Nick seems to have forgotten about, but which still sends shivers through Kyle. Pushed them, too, about the racial motivation of the kidnapping. They mouthed what sounded like learned responses about how this kind of thing was kind-of understandable but totally unacceptable. Mason has promised to return. She looks in the bar for Terry, but he is not to be seen.

As she walks out of the porch, a young girl across the street makes a swift hand-gesture to catch her attention. Mason looks, questioningly. The girl nods, gestures sideway with her head and walks away. Mason follows. In the next street, the girl steps into the doorway of a closed shop. Mason approaches. The girl beckons her in off the pavement.

'You're Mason.'

'Yes.'

'I just spoke to Bent. He says you're all right.'

'You believe him?'

'You're a copper.'

'So's Bent.'

They stare at each other for a moment.

'You're Elli.'

'Yes.'

'Bent says you're all right.'

'Do you believe him?'

'Yes,' Mason nodded.

'Why?'

'Because, in the end, if you can't believe anybody, you really are fucked.'

'As far as I know, it doesn't matter who you believe, you still end up getting fucked.'

Mason sighs, stares at the shabby contents of the shop window and turns back to the girl in front of her.

'Elli, that's pretty much my experience, too. And I can't argue with what you tell me about your experience. It's yours. I'll just tell you this. I don't think that you want this bus-load of girls to go through the same kind of hell that you have. They were just waiting to go home from school. Do you know why they got picked out?'

Elli shakes her head.

'Almost certainly because they were the last group to leave. No other reason. And they were the last group to leave because one of them had to stay behind to see a teacher, because she was going to get a prize for her geography. She *is* going to get a prize for her geography,' Mason corrects herself. 'She is twelve years old.'

'Are they letting on?' Elli asks, looking back towards the pub.

It is Mason's turn to shake her head.

'OK, says Elli, with a shrug, 'Well then, I've got an idea.'

'Tell me.'

'I go in there, I get all enthusiastic about the kidnap and offer to help out, seeing as how I want a slice of this on my own account. I already told them something like that. If they are behind it, I'll find out where the girls are.'

'No,' says Mason, 'You need to keep out of it. Let the police deal with it. It's what we're here for.'

'Not in my experience,' says Elli. 'And I'm not hearing a better idea from you.'

'What did Bent say?'

'He said I could trust you. He said I should do what you say. I shouldn't talk to the press. And I should keep out of harm's way.'

'And so?'

'*But* I've already pissed in this pool. I was out here before with these idiots. They were asking me about, you know, all that what happened, and I knew they wanted to go and break some heads. I was all for it, me, and I encouraged them. I never thought they'd do something like this. It's sick. And I think it is them or somebody they know. And if it is, it makes sense they'd believe me, see? With you, they're just going to deny everything anyway, aren't they?'

Mason hesitates, shakes her head, reaches for her nicotine gum, puts it away again.

'Trying to give up?'

'You should be a detective.'

'Yeah, fat chance of that. Anyway, I did something to make this happen, and now I'm going to do something to put it right.'

'Hell's bells, Elli. You're not the only person who's pissed in this pool. You've already suffered enough and I don't want to put you at risk of something worse.'

'Nobody's putting me anywhere. This one's all me.'

'Nobody puts baby in a corner,' Mason thinks, with regard to herself as much as to Elli. 'OK, look,' she says. 'Set up a text to me, so all you have to do is press Send. I'll be right in. Otherwise, I'll be watching the door. Try to come out by yourself. If you come out with them, I'll step in.'

'Only if you see me making a fuss,' says Elli. 'I can take care of myself.'

'You're a very brave young woman.'

'Of all the things I've been called,' says Elli, breathing in deeply, 'and that's a lot, I've never been called that before.'

'Brave?'

'Nah. A woman. You know what? It was my birthday yesterday. I just turned sixteen.'

'Not much of a birthday, I suppose.'

'Nobody baked me a cake, that's for sure.'

'I'll do you a deal, Elli Washington,' says Mason. 'We get this sorted and I'll bake you a cake. And I never said that to anybody before, either.'

Elli grins.

'Can we invite your friend?'

'DS Bent?'

'Yeah, doesn't he have a name?'

'Sure, he's called Bent. We can invite him. My name's Wendy.' She holds out a hand.

'You're kidding me, right?'

'No, that's it.'

'Bad luck!' says Elli and shakes the outstretched hand. 'OK. You're backup. Gimme your phone number and I'll go and see what's up.'

'Nice phone,' says Mason, and immediately wishes she hadn't as Elli's face tightens up.

'Yeah, I thought it was a present, idiot that I am. That's what I've learned, see? My trouble wasn't to do with brown men, or white men, or black men. It's just men. As far as I know, they can't even help it. It's just the way they are.'

'We're all learning, Miss Washington.'

'You're a riot, Wendy. Keep your phone on.' She pauses as she turns to leave, 'Please.'

Chapter 23

'I am a barrister,' says Tawfiq. 'I practise criminal law. It is a profession that brings me into contact with all sectors of society. If you are right that these trash calling themselves 'Great Whites' are the ones who have been threatening you, it may well be that they can be dissuaded. I have spoken to some people who know men specialising in this kind of work.'

'I didn't think you'd do that. I never thought you'd do that. Thanks, bro,' says Amir.

'What has happened to your tongue?' Tawfiq asks.

'Oh, nothing. It's ink.'

'Ink?'

'Forget it will you? It's not important.'

'No, indeed. What is important, of course, is what has happened to our young sisters.'

'Yeah, yeah, it's probably the same gang.'

'Well, that's not what I'm hearing. Unofficial spokespeople for this extremely unfortunate organisation are emphatically denying any involvement.'

'They would say, that, wouldn't they?'

'That is a very fair point, Amir. It's also a very famous line in the history of the British legal system. A high-ranking Conservative politician, a member of the Cabinet, I believe ...'

'Oh, don't start with your showing-off shit now!'

'My showing-off shit? What? Where would you be right now without what I do? And what do you do? Don't you see your direct involvement in all this? Your responsibility for it? Fawziyya! She is your cousin! Asma is the baby sister of boys you were in school with! Ayesha Sajjadi's grandparents are from the same village as ours! Have you no shame? Did I not say to you that these girls you abuse are somebody's sisters and daughters? Now we know! This is what it is like!'

'That's bollocks! If they'd had any brothers or parents who gave a toss about what happened to 'em, they wouldn't have been out giving blow-jobs for the price of a cheap pair of shoes, would they?'

Tawfiq is silent for a while. When he speaks, all passion has gone from his voice.

'For the sake of our parents, I have broken the law in order to have you protected. If I am called on by the law to account for that, so be it. If those poor white girls had no family to care for them and teach them right from wrong, so much greater the shame on you for taking advantage of them. If our sisters come to harm, may God, who is compassionate, have mercy on your soul, for I will never forgive you.'

Tawfiq looks up at the sky for a moment before continuing.

'Do not come to my house again. Do not speak to my wife or children. Do not speak to me outside our parents' house. When I visit them, I expect you to leave. If I am there and you come, I will leave.'

'Brother ...'

'No. No more. If the men who go tonight to see these Great Whites come one day for you, do not turn to me.'

Amir knows those men already. He thinks about them as he watches his brother walk away.

'You pompous, selfish twat!' he murmurs to himself.

* * *

Kyle and Nick have been drinking steadily as they work on future strategy.

'It's these soft southerners. They haven't got the balls for it. We can just tell 'em to fuck off,' says Kyle.

'Yeah, I suppose.'

'Best thing now is just sit tight another day and then drop the girls off somewhere safe. Put out a statement from the 'Defenders of One Nation' about how they'd just wanted to show they are looking out for their own people, and this was meant as a warning.'

'Yeah, that'll do it.

'*Or*, we go for broke, give the Pakis a deadline and see what they come up with.'

'Yeah, *or* pull the plug right now — just tell Matto to get out and tell the police where the girls are.'

'Yeah. Bit fucking feeble, that though, innit?'

'Yeah, I suppose.'

'On the other hand, we've already got a result, haven't we?'

'You reckon?'

'Yeah, lots of noise, lots of publicity. There's no such thing as bad publicity — that's what they say.'

'Main thing is not to let these characters coming up from London take over, no matter what Mr C says. This is our patch.'

'That's right. *Or*, maybe, better let them call the next shots and it's on them if things go tits up.'

'Yeah, but ... Bloody hell. This isn't easy.'

The phone rings. Terry.

'It's Ryan. He's on the way up. He's come in on the bike. Looks excited. Something about a picture.'

Ryan knocks before he comes in. Then he launches straight into his story.

'We go down there and they're all eating cheese sandwiches. Funniest thing you ever saw. Matto tells 'em to line up again for their next group photo. He's high as a kite, man, like steam coming out of his ears and his eyes popping. You know the way Matto gets.'

Kyle and Nick exchange looks. Yeah, they know the way Matto gets.

'You said he was clean.'

'He was. He was. But he had that money you gave him and he said he just needed something to keep him sharp. Didn't want any slip-ups. Anyway, that's not the point ...'

'Isn't it?'

'Nah, listen. So, then he tells them to take their headscarves off for this one. They say, "No," of course. Matto tells the one he always hits to step up and the bossy one, she says, "No," again and she steps forward. Matto just puts his hand on her chest and pushes her backwards, so she ends up on her arse. Then he grabs the other one, the one he always hits, and makes like he's going to punch her in the face. So then the bossy one says, "Stop. Don't hit her. We will do it."'

'Then all the others freak out and say they won't. One of them says they'll be shamed and the bossy one gets dead nose-in-the-air, the way she does — you really ought to hear her, she sounds like a dictionary talking sometimes — and she says you can't be shamed by something you are forced to do. You can only be shamed by what you choose to do. And then, get this, then she quotes something from the fucking Koran, she says, so Matto whacks the other one anyway, 'cause that wasn't English and that's his rule. Then the gobby one says, "The Holy Koran is written in Arabic."

'And it's like Matto is waiting for her to translate what she said, but she just stands there as though there isn't anything else to say. So Matto hauls off like he's going to whack this other one again. But before he can, the bossy one steps up and she takes her scarf, this johab, or whatever they call it, off and it all goes quiet, dead quiet.'

'Then she shakes her head and all this black hair comes down around her shoulders. I mean, it's dark down there anyway, right? But this hair is *so* black it sort of looks like blue where it shines in the lamplight, know what I mean?'

Ryan pauses as though recalling the memory.

'I'll tell you what, I mean, not my cup of tea and that, but if you liked black women, you'd have to say she is a right fucking looker.'

'Then what?'

'Well, so they all take these jabbies off and stand there looking miserable. So Matto tells them to smile for the camera. Then the gobby one says something dead snooty again, like, "It will not suit your purpose for our parents to see us smiling." And Matto says, "You could be right, sweetheart, you could be right," and he takes the picture. And they all put these hijbas back on again. Any chance of a drink?'

'Help yourself' says Kyle. 'And listen up. We have a

situation here.'

'Thanks,' says Ryan and pours himself a stiff scotch from the bottle on the table. 'Got any ice?'

'Downstairs,' says Nick, 'But you can do without for now. Put a bit of water in that. You'll have to get back out there again pronto. Things have changed.'

'All right, all right. Just let me finish the story. You haven't heard the best bit yet.'

'Fine. Get on with it.'

'Fucking hell, man, what's your problem? All right, this is it. Matto says it's time to crank the pressure up a bit, that's why he wants this photo. So he tells me to come back and check in with you two, but first, he says, send the photo off to the guys in Poland.'

'The what?' Nick and Kyle shout together.

'Yeah. We know how it goes. We were here, remember? Different Internet café every time. Send it off, the Polskis pick it up, bounce it off round the world and it comes out here.'

'You fucking idiots! Why didn't you check with me first?' Kyle screams.

'"Radio silence except in the case of emergencies," that's what you said. "Radio silence," very movie-star! And this wasn't an emergency.'

'Well, it fucking well is now!'

'I still haven't even told you the best bit.' Ryan sulks.

Kyle and Nick look at him, both already knowing that "the best bit" is not going to be good.

'You sent something else, didn't you? says Kyle.

'Yeah, you know, like a little message to go with the picture.'

'What was the little message, Pricey?'

'It was Matto's idea. He was dead pleased with it.'

'What did it say, the little message?'

'HAIR TODAY, TITS TOMORROW'

'And that's what you sent.'

'Yeah,' Ryan's grin fades. 'What's up? Don't you get it?'

The phone. Terry again.

'Listen, I'm shutting up shop. Bit too much going on. But that girl, Elli, is here again. Says she needs to see you. Wants to help out. Got an idea, so she says.'

Kyle has turned a sickly green-white. He takes a deep breath and shakes his head.

'Yeah, sure, send her up. Why not? I could just do with hearing somebody else's great idea.'

* * *

Elli is halfway up the stairs when the alert she's set up on her phone does its annoying bike-horn thing. She checks it and stops between steps. A new photograph of the girls in the cellar.

In the cellar.

In ... The ... Cellar.

Is it? Isn't it? The Britannia? She turns back, but there's Nick on the landing.

'You coming, or going, or what?'

'Nice to see you, too,' says Elli, frantically reviewing her options. Now she knows for sure the Great Whites are behind the kidnap. She knows where the girls are.

Stick or twist? Double or quit? That makes her smile. She doesn't even know what those phrases actually mean. Yeah, Miss Washington is making some changes, but becoming a quitter isn't one of them. She drops her phone back into her bag and takes a step down towards the bar.

'Be right with you. Just gotta pee.'

'There's one up here. Don't want you wandering around. Pub's closed.'

Elli shrugs and follows his direction to the room at the end of the landing.

From there, she texts Mason:

The Britannia, Morbury Road out of Sagwell. Cellar. Go. I'm fine.

She tries phoning Bent.

Nick bangs on the door.

'What're you doing in there?'

'What the fuck do you think I'm doing? Do you want to watch?'

'Well, hurry up!'

She flushes, whispers her message to Bent, deletes the text to Mason and comes out.

The atmosphere in the Great Whites' office is weird, she thinks. Nick sits back down with the other two. They leave her standing. Kyle and Nick look wasted and mean. Ryan looks angry and baffled. He's taken the bandages off and his face is a right mess. They look like men who don't know what to do and who would rather hit somebody than talk about it. Nothing new there, then.

'What do you want?' is Kyle's greeting.

'Like before — lend a hand.'

'What with?'

'Like I said, like before. You was all talking about getting back at the Pakis.'

'Yeah, we still are.'

'Getting a bit spicy, though, innit? With them girls in the cellar.'

Elli isn't sure if she really meant to say that.

Kyle's face contorts as he stands up. Then he sits back down and seems to deflate.

'Cellar?'

Elli decides to keep pushing, WTF.

'Yeah, well, in this new picture, have you seen it? Looks like they might be in a cellar, dunnit?'

She offers her phone. Kyle and Nick look at the picture. Nick puts his head in his hands and says,

'Yeah, you could say that looks like a cellar.'

'You could say,' says Kyle, his anger building again, 'whichever fuckwit took that picture and posted it wanted everybody to know where they are!'

'You recognise it?' Elli asks, taking the phone back and trying her very best to feign surprise. Nobody answers.

'You didn't answer my question,' says Kyle. 'What do you want?'

'Yes, I did. I told you I want to lend a hand. And I want to get a bit of pay-back out of these people.'

'Right!' says Ryan. 'Somebody remembered what this

is all about!'

'Shut up!' Kyle slaps his hand on the table. 'We are one bad move away from being totally fucked!'

'What's going on?' Elli asks.

No response.

There is a banging from downstairs.

'What's that?' asks Nick.

'Probably somebody wants a drink,' says Elli. 'Your man downstairs was locking up, said he had things to do.'

'Somebody's going to have to do something,' Kyle mutters.

'OK,' says Elli. 'What about this?' Three pairs of harsh eyes in contemptuous faces turn to her.

'Do you know where they are?'

No response.

'OK,' she continues, 'Let's pretend you do know where they are. And let's pretend you know who's keeping them there.' She looks directly at Ryan. 'Somebody you know.' Ryan looks at the floor.

'But now, somebody else might be able to guess where they are. And they'll be going there, and they'll be coming here. That could be the police. Or it could be a big Paki or five, though I don't suppose they'd chance their arm here, would they? Mind you, there is a story going about that a couple of 'em were round here and did some of your lot over. Is that right?'

'What is your fucking point?' From Kyle.

'Yeah, right,' Elli continues. 'What if somebody had this really cool idea of snatching some little Paki bitches, and now it's all gone down the pan?'

'What if they did?' Kyle roars, getting to his feet again.

'Rescue them,' says Elli, and sits down.

'What?' says Nick.

'Rescue them,' she repeats. 'This new picture comes through. Holy shit! You recognise the place! Without stopping to think about your own safety, you jump in a car and drive on out there. There is a bit of a fight with some people you don't recognise — blacks, asylum seekers, illegals probably — and they run off. You free the girls. You are heroes. You say it was nothing. That's just how white men behave. That's why we want One Nation, One Race, One Language, and then we wouldn't have any of this grief.'

'Pass them fags over,' says Ryan.

'What's the magic word?' says Elli, adrenalin pumping.

'Please,' says Ryan. She offers them around.

Kyle looks puzzled. Runs a hand through his hair. Glances at Nick. Looks back to Elli.

'That is just so . fucking . brilliant.' He pulls hard on the cigarette and his whole body seems to relax as he exhales.

'Oh yes,' says Nick. 'Oh yes, it is.'

'One problem,' says Elli.

'What's that?' Nick asks sharply.

'You really do have to know where they are,' says Elli, deadpan.

The other three start to chuckle, then laugh, then howl almost hysterically.

They hardly notice Terry come into the room, but

when they look round, it is very clear he has blood running down his face. And that one of the two, large, well-dressed men of South Asian heritage who follow him into the room has a gun in his hand. The gun also has blood on it.

Chapter 24

After telling Elli about Mason's planned visit to The King's Head, Bent attends Shriver's briefing and is allocated his latest duties in the investigation. The new photograph, along with its explicit threat, has led to even more urgent media demands for a police response. Bent is also assigned a seat on a panel for a press and tv conference. His objection that he has nothing particular to say and would prefer to be actively involved in the search for the missing girls is dismissed by Superintendent Barrett.

'You've got a lot to learn, James. This is intercultural work. You'll be doing your part just by appearing on tonight's news. Look serious, focused. Nod at the answers given and, if you do have to say anything, stay positive but non-specific. No hostages to fortune, but confident about our progress. And don't worry. You'll be very good at this, I have every confidence.'

Afterwards, as they stand and leave the raised platform on which they have been sitting, Barrett comments,

'Good work, James. Very sound. You can probably loosen up a little more another time. But safe, very good, gave nothing away. Nothing quotable. Good man.'

Barely able to unclench his fists, Bent's thoughts turn to the gym downstairs and the heavy punch-bag. But first, he turns his phone back on. Elli. The whispered message says only,

'Call Wendy.'

'Dammit!' He feels chemicals run through him like electricity through a neon sign in a dark place. And the sign reads, 'Missed The Boat.'

* * *

Holding the gun loosely, his finger resting lightly on the trigger guard, the first man speaks. His voice is deep, resonant, and in a strange way, calming, Elli finds, after the raucous exchanges of the previous conversation.

'Please excuse the interruption. My name is Mohamed. This is my associate, Mohamed. I should, first of all, assure you that your compatriot,' he nods towards Terry, 'made every reasonable attempt to warn you of our arrival.' He touches Terry on the shoulder. 'Please, take a seat.'

Terry moves slightly unsteadily to the table and sits on it.

'Good,' the speaker continues. 'We intend no serious harm on this occasion. So far as we know. We are simply here to clarify a situation regarding yourselves and our employers. Or perhaps two situations.'

'It's nothing to do with us!' says Nick.

'Shut up!' Kyle barks.

'No, no, this is actually not a time to be quiet,' says the first Mohamed. 'Too much silence might be harmful. What exactly is it that is nothing to do with you?'

'Those girls,' says Ryan. 'This kidnapping. It's shit. We were just sitting here saying what shit it is and wishing we could do something about it, weren't we?'

Kyle stares impassively at the newcomers. Nick and Elli murmur their agreement.

'What we heard as we came up the stairs sounded more like hilarity than concern,' says Mohamed.

'That was something different,' says Nick.

'You,' Mohamed turns to Elli. 'What are you doing here?'

'It's a free country.'

'Yes, so they say, although its freedoms have not always been to your own advantage, have they? What are you doing here?'

'I told you, it's a free country.'

'Very well, let us agree. This is a free country, this is a Colt .45, and I will ask you one more time.'

'You wouldn't dare.'

'Jesus, Elli!' says Nick.

Mohamed raises the weapon above his head and fires a single round. The noise is deafening. The bullet rips off up through the ceiling, sending down a shower of plaster, and thuds into a beam in the roof-space. The four around the table jump visibly. Elli lets out a small shriek.

Mohamed gives Elli a questioning look. She sits back in her chair and attempts a shrug.

'I came to see the guys to ask if they know anything about the kidnapping.'

'And do you believe their answer?'

'Yes.'

'Why?'

'Because in the end, you have to believe somebody or you really are fucked.'

'Given your background, I am not sure that your judgement on that issue is to be trusted.'

Elli flinches.

'What do you know about my background?'

'More than I would have wished to. Do you know a young man called Amir Qureshi?'

Elli's eyes narrow.

'More than I would've wished to.'

Mohamed smiles.

'Good answer. You are more intelligent than I would have guessed. This young man has recently been assaulted and threatened. Do you know anything about that?'

'No.'

'Do you believe that these people here had anything to do with it?'

'Not as far as I know.'

'Thank you. It is a rare pleasure to hear someone so obviously telling the truth. You,' Mohamed turns his attention to Kyle, 'Do you know anything about such an attack or threats?'

'Never heard of him,' says Kyle.

'Yes, or no?'

'No!'

Mohamed exchanges a brief glance with his companion, who nods.

'Good, we have clarified that. Just in case it is not obvious to you, we take a particular interest in this young man's welfare. If he should come to any further harm, we may need reassurance from you again. Or, we may simply decide to save ourselves the trouble and assume that you were involved. That brings us to the second issue, the one that you have raised,' he waves the gun casually in Ryan's direction. 'Unfortunately, and partly because of the noise for which I am responsible, it would be unwise to continue this interview here. You,' once more he indicates Ryan, 'will accompany us.'

'No fucking way.'

The second Mohamed steps forward, seizes Ryan's right ear and lifts him from his seat. As Ryan, arms flailing, mouth open, struggles to find his balance, Mohamed brings the flat of his hand up under his chin. Ryan's teeth crash together and, with a strange, whining sound, he falls to his knees, spitting blood. Mohamed grabs the same ear again and pulls him to his feet.

The three of them leave the room.

'Get the gun! Get the fucking Glock!' Nick whispers desperately.

'It's not here!' Kyle whispers back.

'Well, where is it, then? What's the fucking point of having it?'

'Call London, now,' says Terry. 'Collingwood has to know about this. All of it.'

Still no one moves.

Partly stunned, and also partly thrilled by the gunshot, Elli notices that she is listening and thinking rather than talking. Interesting. First, these wankers have a gun somewhere. Second, there is somebody called Collingwood in London who must be important to them. She waits for someone to speak.

'Fucking hell — Matto!' says Nick. 'What shall we tell him?'

Kyle goes to his desk and takes out a simple, red dumbphone.

'Do you think we can get out there and pull off this rescue idea before they find out?' he asks.

'Whatever else he does,' says Nick. 'Ryan won't rat Matto out.'

'You don't know that,' says Terry. 'Get him out, now. Just get away from all this as best you can.'

'But then they'll all come after us,' Kyle objects. 'Police, Pakis, they'll all be on our backs. If we can get in there as rescuers, we can still come out ahead of the game.'

'This is not a game. You are not going to come out ahead. You have never had a clue what you're doing.' Terry has wiped most of the blood from his face. 'Now give me the phone.'

'Piss off back downstairs and have one on the house!' is Kyle's retort.

Terry pauses, takes a deep breath, shakes his head and leaves the room.

Kyle punches Matto's number into the phone. When he answers, Matto's high-pitched voice crackles across the room so that Nick and Elli can also hear him clearly.

'Did you see it?'

'Yeah, I saw it. Listen.'

'Good, eh?'

'We're getting pressure here from all sides.'

'Too fucking bad! Great photo, though, eh?'

'You have to get out.'

'Out of what?'

'Matto, listen, will you? For fuck's sake! There's a big black man with a gun might be on his way to come and kill you. Geddit?'

'How would he know where I am?'

'Ryan might have told him.'

'No chance.'

'You remember that bit about the gun?'

'Where's Ryan now?'

'They took him.'

'Who did?'

'The fucking tooth fairy did! What do you mean, who? The Pakis.'

Kyle stares at the ceiling. Signals to Nick that Matto is off his head.

'What Pakis?' Matto shouts down the phone.

'Matto,' says Kyle. 'Listen, please. I'll explain everything later. Right now you need to do some stuff. Dead simple. Unlock the cellar. Get in the van and drive off. Just go somewhere else. Don't tell me where. Dump the van. Set fire to it if you can. Wait a couple of days and then get in touch. We'll look after Ryan, don't worry.'

'What was that you said about fairies?'

'Oh, Jesus!'

Elli held out her hand.

'Can I have a go?'

'What?'

'Let her,' says Nick. 'She can't do any worse.'

'Matto? It's me, Elli. You remember me?'

'No names!' says Kyle.

Elli rolls her eyes.

'Yeah. You're the little one was there.'

'Yeah. Listen, Matto. Very cool photo. "Hair today,"

huh?'

'Yeah! And tits tomorrow!'

'Good job! Hey, listen, we're worried about Ryan and he needs your help.'

'Why, what's he done?'

'He's in a bit of bother because of those girls.'

'They're all right. Bit sick of cheese sandwiches I should think and the bog stinks. Just wait till you see tomorrow's picture, though!'

'Do you want to help Ryan, Matto?'

'Sure.'

'OK, look, I haven't got much credit on this phone, so we'll have to be quick. OK?'

'OK.'

'Smart. I mean, you're the man. You're going to have to take control. And you have to do it right now, this minute. Ryan's depending on you. Let's get it right, yeah?'

'Absolutely.'

'Yeah, so, you're going to unlock the cellar, yeah?'

'Yeah. You mean, like, the inside door or the big trapdoor in the back yard outside?'

'Both. Unlock the cellar inside door and the trapdoor.'

'OK.'

'Cool. Then get in the van and drive off. That's your plan, yeah??

'Yeah, in the van and off.'

'Right. Keep driving till you come to a biggish town. Rashford, say, or somewhere like that. Dump the van and burn it.'

'Biggish town, burn the van.'

'Get yourself a B&B and have a good night's sleep. You've got some money, haven't you?'

'Yeah, off Kyle. Spent most of it, though. Some really good gear.'

'Well, when you run out, get back in touch with Kyle.'

'OK'

'Hey, Matto, it sounds like you've really got this down. Do you want to tell the guys here your plan? They can hear you if you tell them.'

'Unlock the cellar doors, drive to a biggish town, burn the van, get a good night's sleep, get back in touch with Kyle.'

'Elli, Elli, Elli,' says Nick, giving her a thumbs-up.

Kyle takes the phone back.

'You got that, then, Matto?'

'Piece of piss.'

'OK, talk to you in a couple of days.'

'Hey, Kyle.'

'Yeah, what?'

'Where's Ryan?'

'The Pakis took him. Don't worry, we'll get him back.'

'Fuck.'

'Yeah, I know.'

'Another thing.'

'What's that?'

'I've got some of my stuff round the place. I mean, it's not worth shit, but if anybody found it, they'd know it was mine. You know, fingerprints on it and that kind of crap. It'll take me a bit to get it together.'

'Have the girls seen you without your mask on?'

'Nah.'

'Then just leave everything and do what Elli says right now. As quick as you can. Don't say anything to the girls. Don't worry about your stuff. Once you're gone and the girls are out, we'll set fire to the place. That'll get rid of all the evidence and the Great Whites are the heroes of the hour.'

'Set fire to the place? Shit, I'd like to see that!'

'I'll take some pictures for you, Matto. But right now, you have to do those things: cellar doors, drive away, burn the van. Yeah, you get to see that go up, don't you?'

'Yeah, I suppose.'

'But you have to do those things right now and that'll get Ryan out of the shit. The sooner the better, eh?'

'You sure he'll be all right?'

'Yeah, trust me. The sooner the better for Ryan.'

'OK.'

'Right. Hear from you in a day or two.'

Kyle hangs up.

'What a fucking cretin!' he says.

'He's a crack-head,' says Nick. 'We knew that. The only time he's not fucked up is when he doesn't have any money. He's better when Ryan's around. He sort of looks after him.'

He turns to Elli.

'But you did a great job there, girl. Didn't she, Kyle?'

'Yeah, so shall we continue this celebration or get the fuck out there and hope we make it in time?'

'Good luck with that,' says Elli. 'I'm off back to the hostel. I'm in enough bother already and I don't need to be a hero.'

The other two watch as she picks up her bag and leaves. They stare at each other. Kyle shrugs.

'Fuck it. We can do this.'

He takes his Great Whites jacket from its hook on the back of the office door and puts it on. He walks to his desk, takes out the knuckle duster and drops it into a pocket.

'You got the car keys?'

Nick nods.

'So let's go be heroes.'

As they reach the hallway, they meet Elli coming back through the pub.

'Changed your mind?' Nick asks.

'No, not me,' Elli replies. 'But you might.'

'How's that?'

'You need to talk to Terry.'

'What about?'

'About Ryan. He's in the toilet out the back.'

'Thank god for that.'

'Looks like his neck's broke.'

Chapter 25

Matto's head feels like an overripe watermelon with serious roadworks going on inside it. Too much to think about. Mostly, Ryan. What's happened to him? What's the point of being here if Ryan needs help somewhere else? OK, but that is the point, he's supposed to be getting away from here. Yeah. OK.

First thing, unlock the cellar. Inside, yes. Outside, yes. He tosses the lock away. Next? Drive off in the van. Did Kyle say the Pakis have taken Ryan and the Great Whites are going to rescue the girls? What sense does that make? If they've taken Ryan, we ought to be keeping the girls. Do a swap if we have to. Bloody Kyle. Thinks he's so clever.

What was next? Drive off in the van. Can do. His mind flickers.

'What about taking one of them with me? For swapping. If need be. They can fucking well rescue the others. Which one? It'll have to be *her*, won't it? If I try to take one of the others, she'll kick up a fuss. But if I take *her*, it'll scare the shit out of the others and that'll keep 'em quiet.'

He goes back into the decaying building, along a corridor half-filled with rubble and refuse, puts on his mask and lets himself quietly into the cellar.

'Woah!' he shouts gleefully, 'You're all lined up for me! Don't move and I'll do the lot of you!'

The girls scramble to their feet.

'You obscene lout!' Ayesha snaps at him. 'We were at prayer. Go away. Let us complete them.'

Matto walks up to her. She straightens her shoulders

and raises her chin, which is where the punch catches her. She collapses like an empty collection of clothes. There are gasps and screams and tears. Matto bends down and sits her up, then heaves her over his shoulder. Without a word, he turns and leaves the cellar the way he came in. The wailing girls hug each other.

With some difficulty, he makes his way back along the partially blocked corridor, then out of the main building and across the yard to the tumble-down structure where the van is parked. As a still dazed Ayesha starts to struggle, he pulls the tarpaulin off the back end of the Transit and opens the rear doors. He tips her into the van and rolls her body forward. Then he closes and relocks the doors.

Right. Good. Jesus, his head hurts! What else was there? Oh fuck. What else was there? He hears Kyle's voice saying, 'Get rid of all the evidence and the Great Whites are the heroes of the hour.' How did that go? 'Once you're gone and the girl's out, set fire to the place.' Yeah, that was it. OK, the girl was out. Like he said, he wants to see that fire! Not a problem.

Matto sorts out a can of paraffin from the outbuilding and empties it onto and around what is left of the back of the Britannia, pouring a trail into the yard. Messy business. Then, congratulating himself on his carefulness, he reverses the Transit out of its hiding place and pulls it up to the road. He leaves the engine running and walks back to the rear of the building, where he lights the trail of paraffin. At first, there are just a few flames. Then, with a huge whoosh, the place goes up. Fucking brilliant.

Matto grins. He basks in the heat. Stands in wonder before the flames. Feels the smoke swirl around him.

Raises his arms and spreads his fingers.

'Beware the god of hellfire!' he shouts. Inspired, he drops into a half-crouch, just like that guy on YouTube, goes into the dance, throwing his head and shoulders forward.

'Start-a-fire! Start-a-fire!' he chants, mesmerised, into the sparking, fume-ridden, night sky. And he laughs, hearing the drumbeat urging him on.

Then, beyond excitement and strangely fulfilled, he turns, trots back to the Transit and drives away. Now he remembers the next thing: Burn the van, too!

* * *

As Kyle and Nick join Terry in staring at Ryan's lifeless body, Elli decides this would be a good time to get herself out of a rapidly deteriorating situation. She does not see how this is going to turn out well, or how her being there is going to make anything better — especially for her. She has a lingering worry there might be more information she should relay to Bent or Mason, but she's not sure what and her sense of self-preservation overrides those thoughts.

A block down the street, she looks back to see a large, dark saloon pull up outside The King's Head. Two men get out and go inside. What to do now? As a compromise, she decides to hang around for a while, step back into a doorway and observe from a distance.

It's not long before one of the men reappears and unlocks the boot of the car. He looks up and down the street and then waves to someone in the building. Kyle and Nick come out, struggling to carry what looks like a rolled-up carpet. They bundle it into the boot of the car and go back into the pub. The other man closes the boot, locks the car and follows them.

After another few minutes, all five men come back out. The two strangers are pushing Kyle and Nick, who don't seem to be making any effort to resist. They both get into the back of the car. The newcomers spend some time talking to Terry, who is nodding a lot. One of them goes back into The King's Head with Terry. The other one gets into the car and drives off. Elli presses herself back into the doorway as he drives past. Is he slowing down? Is he stopping? Has he seen her? She doesn't think so. She doesn't think so. She takes in the registration number. Breathes again as the car turns a corner.

She wonders, with a shiver, what it's like to sit in the back seat of that car, knowing that you are only inches away from your friend's corpse. What about the other stranger? Why is he staying here? Suddenly, everything feels a lot more than a bit too much. She walks a few streets away and calls a taxi. Good she still has some of the newspaper's money. Not for the first time over recent days, her bed at the hostel seems quite an attractive place.

Once there, she texts Bent,

`Back at Greenfields`

turns off her phone and tries to do the same with her thoughts.

* * *

'I've called it in,' says Mason. 'Armed response on the way. You keep out of it.'

'Not likely!'

'But the smart, helpful and necessary thing to do, DS Bent.'

'How close are you?'

'About ten minutes, as I remember it.'

'And the others?'

'Bit longer. I got a head start.'

'You delayed calling it in.'

'I just wanted to make sure I wasn't the last to arrive and find other people picking up loose ends and making unfortunate connections. But that doesn't mean I intend to go solo and unarmed into a hostage situation. And anyway, there's no chance of you being here in time to do anything. Stay away. It's less complicated.'

'OK, OK,' grudgingly from Bent. 'Just got a text from Elli. She's OK.'

'Good. Good. We're getting there. Later, then . . . Oh, sweet Jesus, now what?'

'What?'

'Looks like a fire up ahead. I'll call it in. Talk to you later.'

She breaks the connection and calls in the fire brigade. No rain tonight, just a fiery glow on the underside of the deep, rolling clouds. Not a garden fire, then. Not a campfire. Not a bonfire. Not a small fire at all.

* * *

When the two men who like to identify themselves, in the Anglo world at least, as Mohamed and Mohamed deliver their report, it is not well received.

'Your initial task was to make sure these "Great

Whites" have no involvement in the pressure being put on this unfortunately well-connected young man, or that they desist from any such activity in future. Frightening them was certainly in order and, in this, you have doubtless succeeded.'

Kutab Zahid sighs wearily.

'You apparently failed to grasp, however, that pursuing all avenues which might lead to the rescue of our kidnapped girls has, in the meantime, become much, much more important. And the actual killing of one of this gang, who might have had some information, seems inexplicably stupid. It might, even beyond the question of rescuing the girls, put a lot of quite important people in jeopardy.'

The two men stand for a while in obviously frustrated silence. Eventually, one of them speaks.

'It was an accident, sir.'

'An accident?'

'At first the usual abuse. Then more about our faith. Our prophet. He would not shut up. I lost my temper. It was unprofessional. And then he surprised me.'

'Surprised you?'

'Yes, as I raised the gun to strike him, he jumped at me and tried to take it from me. It was foolish, possibly even brave. I did not expect it of him. I was angry and he struggled. It seemed better not to remain longer.'

'I see.' Kutab Zahid stares across his desk at the two men. 'My friends, I am deeply disappointed at this outcome. I understand, however, that you are obliged to deal with creatures that seem human, but where we are faced with a challenge to understand God's purpose in allowing them to exist.'

The two men standing opposite him relax slightly.

'That leaves, however, our more immediate situation.'

They stiffen again, watchfully.

Kutab Zahid removes his spectacles and rubs his eyes.

'First of all, pray and then get some sleep. Then pray again.'

'Yes, sir,' they reply in unison.

'Then, this girl. This slut. This Elli. She was there. And she was with this imbecile, Amir. And she was talking to the newspaper. Why is she everywhere? Go now and sleep. And then find her. Find out what she knows. Without getting angry.'

* * *

To Mason, coming over the hill too fast to be safe and swooping down through a dip in the road to the bend, the Britannia looms like a giant, ramshackle pyre. Clearly, no one still in that building is going to be saved.

Through the fingertips of flame reaching out sideways across the entrance to the car park, she drives as far back from the blaze as she can. Out of the car, it is almost impossible to move forward and approach the building. The broken-down structures to her right are also starting to burn. There is no sign of life. Except for the demonic flames.

She sees a bucket lying on the ground. Running to it, she finds the cistern half full of rainwater. She fills the bucket and turns back to the building. Accepting the futility of her actions brings on a sense of nausea.

The scene is one of nightmare. She feels the rising

tide of panic. Nightmare — a once all-too familiar experience, recently returned. Before succumbing to the trauma before her eyes, her mind tries to escape. In desperation, her thoughts bolt through a mental wormhole that takes her back to her bedroom; the footsteps, the door opening, the light from the landing . . .

'No! No! Go away!' she screams. In a frenzy of fear and horror, she screams again, as she has never been able to before,

'Get away from me! GET . AWAY . FROM . MEEE !!!'

And the scene dominating her consciousness wavers like an image on a faulty screen, freezes, fractures, dissolves, disappears. She screams again, wordlessly this time, at the agony of what is ripped from her. Her next scream chokes into a sob that sets her whole body shaking as if in a fit.

And then there she is, back in the living furnace of the Britannia backyard. Her face is burning and her clothes are sandpaper against her skin. She upends the bucket over her head and stands there, a pillar of steam. She tips another bucket of water over herself and tries, pointlessly, to get closer to the building.

'Inferno' is the word that is going through her mind now. Inferno — the flames of hell. As a sense of helplessness threatens to overwhelm her, she realises she is hallucinating. She can actually hear the screams of the damned rising from below her feet. She drops to her knees, her head bowed. Still she hears them. The doomed, suffering in hell for their sins. Tears of rage, tears of grief — they all evaporate before they can leave her eyes. She raises her head towards the conflagration before her.

From this angle, however, there is a difference in what she sees. A square patch of ground marked out by smoke rising thinly along its sides. The gateway to hell. On hands and knees, she creeps forward. It is as if that very gate were moving, bobbing up and down as the damned souls below make their futile attempts to escape, screaming, into the earthly night.

Trapdoor.

Her rational mind insists on regaining control of her perceptions. And it tells her again, *A trapdoor*.

She crawls closer, sucking the blast-furnace heat into her lungs. No sinners suffering in hell, this new voice tells her, but innocents suffering the crimes of this world. And then, a realisation that comes with the force of an instruction, an instruction that comes like a release:

"Stop it. This time, you can stop it. *You* can *stop* it."

She sees there is no lock on the trapdoor, but the hasp is still in place over the loop, stopping the door being opened from below. Now regaining full control, her rational mind also throws up warning signs that flash by in less time than it takes her to act: Add a flow of air to a combustible situation and you are likely to increase the blaze —perhaps spectacularly. She computes, like Bent before her, the meaning of risk that they all learned in training: the likelihood of something happening in combination with the consequences if it does. Likelihood: high. Consequences: possibly fatal. Outcome: better odds than inaction is offering. She puts a hand flat on the trapdoor. It is hot, but not burning. She lifts the hasp free and heaves the trapdoor open.

Below her is the bruised and startled face of Fatima, wreathed in the smoke that is now spiralling up through the open space. Mason holds out her hand.

'Come!' she shouts.

'No, no,' Fatima calls and backs off down the ladder. 'You must take the young ones first.'

Frustrated, but seeing no alternative but to wait with her hand extended, Mason stares down into the smoky pit.

Soon, a much younger girl appears, barely able to climb through the hole, her face a rictus of fear. She is followed by another, and another. After them, two older girls crawl, coughing and almost blinded by the increasing smoke, into the night air. Then, the girl Mason saw first reappears, takes a single step away from the trapdoor and collapses onto the car park.

'One more! One more!' Mason shouts. 'There are seven of you! Where's the other one?'

The girls, sitting and lying together in an inchoate jumble of limbs, give no answer.

The air makes Mason retch. But it is the only air available. She takes a series of shallow breaths and forces herself forward, swinging her foot down onto the first rung of the ladder.

It is Asma who sees her.

'No, come back! Come back!' she shouts.

'Where is the other one?' Mason screams back at her. 'There are seven of you!'

'No, he took her!' Asma crawls forward to where the top half of Mason's body is still visible.

'Who took her?'

'Devil! The devil took her!'

Uncomprehendingly, Mason stares at the terrified girl in front of her. Then she shakes her head and takes another step down the ladder. One more. From somewhere below ground, there is the hollow, booming sound of a giant drum being struck, followed by a massive, raw belch.

Chapter 26

Matto wakes wondering if he is going throw up or shit himself. Or both. His head is lurching to no kind of rhythm and his eyes, even when he can get them to stay open, refuse to focus properly. Not morning yet. Not proper morning, anyway. He's parked up on some waste ground by a canal. There's what looks like a derelict little workshop. Yeah, that's right. They used to do repairs on the narrow-boats. Yeah, yeah, got it, he's just outside Rashford.

What is this stink? It's him. Paraffin. Smoke. Burn the van. Fuck. Yes, he was supposed to burn the van. What does paraffin have to do with it? He turns on the ignition and checks the petrol level. Fine, that'll do just fine. Just stuff a rag in it and set fire. Or should he syphon a bit off first? Doesn't want another fiasco like Ryan's "Molotov Cocktail".

Where the fuck is Ryan, anyway? He pauses and tries to concentrate on that question. But he doesn't know, and it seems more important now to get on with burning the van, even though he doesn't know why he is doing that, either. It's bound to attract attention, police attention, isn't it? And then he'll have no transport, 'cause Pricey has the bike. He checks his pockets. Yes, he still has his own keys to the bike. Could be useful in case Pricey's parked it up somewhere.

Anyway, back to the job in hand. Good enough spot for it. Best do it now. Does he have any tubing? Or rag come to that? Pricey always has bits of useful stuff like that lying about. He doesn't remember any in the back of the van, but it's worth checking.

Then find a toilet. Have a bit of a wash. Wake himself up and get rid of some of this smell. Then get back over to The King's Head and find out what the fuck is going on.

He has unlocked the doors and is twisting the handle to open them when they fly into his face. He tastes his own blood and staggers backwards. Ayesha jumps unsteadily to the ground and falls to her knees. She rights herself quickly and runs towards the streetlights on the road above the canal. She is stiff and her body obeys her urgent commands only reluctantly. Her coat and long skirt hamper her movements and she winces as the rough ground cuts into her stockinged feet. In desperate frustration, she unbuttons the lower half of her coat, pulls her skirt up above her knees, and runs again.

But by now, Matto has caught her. He pushes her from behind and she falls, face-first into rough grass, dirt and gravel. He also grabs her skirt, tears it along the seam and yanks it up around her waist. As she tries to turn, he drops his whole body weight onto her, forcing her face down into the ground.

He grabs her struggling hands and pins them above her head. He presses his hips against her buttocks and her movements stop. He pushes against her in a slow rhythm.

'Do you know what I've got here for you? Do you?'

Ayesha is silent, her body frozen, her mind on fire.

'Do you?!?' Matto barks into her ear. 'Answer me, or I'll arse-fuck you here and now.' He releases one hand and begins to tug at her underwear.

'You do not have anything for me,' Ayesha speaks into

the dirt.

Her words hit an unknown target. Among Matto's confused and violent response to what is happening, an erection plays no part. His anger escalates.

'We'll fucking well see about that!' he screams.

He gets up, reaches down and turns her over. He takes hold of her upper clothing and lifts her to her feet, tearing open her coat and the blouse under it. He readjusts his grip and, jerking his hands sideways, tears her clothes wider open. He pulls the coat and blouse over her shoulders and down to her elbows.

"Nice,' he nods. 'Just like I said, "Hair today and tits tomorrow." Except now it's tits today and hair next up. Or do you shave?'

Ayesha leans her head back and takes a deep breath. Just as Matto looks about to make a further comment on the effect this has, she brings her head forward and spits full into his face.

He punches her hard in the stomach. She doubles up and pitches sideways. Unable to use her hands to break the fall, she lands heavily on the stony ground and lies there, winded.

Matto looks down on her motionless body and tries again to make sense of the situation. He is not sure if some of the pictures in his head are memories or fantasies. There is a reason for this girl to be here, for him to have her, and it would not be in order to burn her in the van. He can't leave her here. He can't take her anywhere without the van.

He half-lifts her and drags her back to the Transit. Re-loads her and locks the door. Checks his cash. Just enough and he knows where he can score. He'll have to risk it again with the van.

He feels a wave of relief. At least he knows now what to do next. With a little boost, he can take it from there. That's always when he has his best ideas. He starts up the van and drives off.

* * *

Arriving at the hospital, Bent is met by DC Carpenter, back from the Britannia.

'It's OK, Bent, it's OK.'

'What's "OK" mean?'

'Well, burns up her legs and back at least. She was passed out. Doctors say the smoke inhalation is potentially more long-term dangerous, but they're not sure yet.'

'Doesn't sound exactly "OK",' Bent says grimly.

'Well it's a hell of a lot better than it looked when we arrived,' says Carpenter. 'She was full in our headlights as we hit the car park and it looked like some kind of bloody human cannonball experiment. She came blasting out of this hole in the ground on what must have been a jet of scalding hot air. Just as she hits the dirt and starts writhing around, this pillar of flame comes bursting out behind her, all red and blue and gold right up into the sky. It was more like a bloody volcano than a fire.' Carpenter pauses, her voice still in awe of the memory. 'The girls were pulling her clear and then the medics piled in.'

'Jesus,' is Bent's only comment.

'Plus we have one girl still missing and no sign of the kidnappers.'

'This is all a bit of a step-up from where we were, isn't it? Mass murder?'

'The girls say the last one there was acting like a crazy man. Maybe high on something?'

'Mmmm. And how are they?'

'All reasonably OK, too. Smoke inhalation again, but not too serious, it seems. God knows what the psychological effects will be. Parents are here and people are trying to set up counselling, but some don't want it, or they want Muslim counsellors, and then *we* have to talk to them, of course.

'One thing for sure,' Carpenter continues with a grin, 'Wendy Mason's an absolute nailed-on, bravery-medal, picture-in-the-paper heroine, of course, which she'll probably find very hard to take.'

'Any chance of talking to her?'

'You'll have to talk to the doctors about that. She's a tough nut. My guess is she is literally and metaphorically sore as hell.'

When Bent asks, it turns out Mason has been given a sedative after her initial debriefing and he is told to wait till morning before talking to her. He settles down in one of the waiting rooms.

* * *

Bent jerks awake to the sound of his phone. 7am. Elli. She brings him up to speed with events at The King's Head.

'Why have you waited till now?' he barks down the phone, failing to control his confusion of emotions. 'Why was your phone off?'

'Because I was knackered and I passed out, that's why!' she snaps back. 'I don't do murders for a living, you know.'

Bent smiles at the girl's spirit.

'You're right, Elli. And you shouldn't have to, either. I am sorry. And I am very happy you and I are on the same side. You are a good person to work with.'

'Hey,' she says, 'Take it easy. I don't have any experience of dealing with praise. Just keep shouting at me and we'll get on fine.'

Bent gives her an outline version of what has happened at the Britannia and thanks her again for her work. He tells her that Mason has been hurt, but tries to minimise the extent.

'Matto, that fucking reptile!' is Elli's response.

'And I'm a bit worried about you, too, Elli,' says Bent. 'Is there anywhere you could go, just to get out of the picture for while?'

'Why would you be worried about me?'

'You turn up in too many people's stories, Elli. And too many of those people are crazy or violent or both. And some of them have guns.'

'Well, you know what, copper? If I had somewhere to go, I wouldn't bloody well be here.'

Bent rubs his eyes, trying to see a way through.

'Look,' he says finally, 'Pack a few things, just for a couple of nights, and be outside the hostel at nine o'clock. I'll pick you up and drop you somewhere safe.'

'You're kidding, right?'

'Trust me on this, Elli.'

'Where are we going?'

'You can stay with a friend of mine. It won't be a problem.'

There is a long pause.

'Elli?'

'You want to pick me up and take me to a friend of yours for a couple of days because you are worried about me?'

'Yes. Nine o'clock. Sharp. Outside the hostel.'

There is another pause, shorter this time, before Elli speaks.

'Bent?'

'Yes?'

'Yes. OK. See you then.'

'Good.'

'Bent?'

'Yes?'

'Thanks.'

'You're welcome.'

They hang up.

'You have no idea,' Bent mutters, recognising his feelings of compound guilt and doing his best to pack them away.

He checks his watch and wonders when he will be allowed to talk to Mason. Apart from simply wanting to see her, they have to make sure any accounts they give are credible and coherent. Not identical, not contradictory, and not informed by details they have no obvious reason for knowing. It's not a problem as such; they know the ropes.

He decides to rest for a while longer. And suddenly it's 7.30 and his phone is ringing again. He rolls his eyes at the number.

'Hello, DS Bent here.'

'It's me, John Thompson.'

'Hi, Mr Thompson. Excuse me, but can I get back to you later? I've got a few things on at the moment.'

'Aye, right you are. Mostly, I just wanted to say thank you, but when you've got a minute, I'd like to tell you about it. There's nowt to worry about. It's all good news.'

'Mr Thompson, I could do with a bit of that. I'll call you soon.'

'Right you are, lad. Don't forget, I owe you one.'

'Changed his tune a bit!' Bent smiles ruefully to himself.

A text comes through. Barrett wants him at the station for the media. Three-ring circus. Three-line whip. Briefing at 8.30, panel at 9. Look smart. Keep quiet.

Bent is furious and frustrated. Not again! He can't ignore Barrett's instruction, nor can he explain why he wants to be excused in any terms that Barrett will accept. If there are reasons for Elli to be taken into protective custody, then she can be. The case needs first to be made and another officer can carry the procedure out. But Elli knows about things she is not supposed to, and about connections that, as far as Barrett is concerned, should not exist. Nor can Bent liaise with Mason in her current state, not even to agree an outline of an account. And still, Elli might be in danger and something has to be done.

Bent's mind dances around the situation while he rushes home. Use all angles, they said. Before showering he decides on what he sees as the best poor option. He phones the Thompsons.

'Oh hello,' says Alice. 'Er, did you hear about what happened? Mrs Calderwood coming home and everything?'

'That sounds good.'

'Oh yes,' says Alice, with relief in her voice. 'We see quite a lot of Billy now. It's funny how things work out, isn't it?'

'It is, Mrs Thompson, it is,' says Bent.

'There is something, isn't there?' she asks.

'Yes, there is,' says Bent. 'I wonder if I could have a word with your husband. Is he in?'

'Yes, yes he is. Just a minute. It's Sergeant Bent,' he hears her say. 'I think he wants something.'

'Hello?' says John Thompson.

'Hello, Mr Thompson. Look, I won't beat about the bush. I could use a favour.'

'Well, that didn't take you long! No, sorry, what is it?'

'Do you know where the Greenfields hostel is in Borsleigh?'

'On Goddesley Road?'

'Yes,' says Bent, feeling the relief in his own voice. 'Can you be there just before nine?'

'I can be there by half past.'

'OK, half past. Wait in your car in view of the entrance. It's a brown Micra, isn't it?'

'Gold, yeah.'

'Fine, a gold Nissan Micra. At half past nine, a girl with blonde hair will come out of the hostel with an overnight bag of some sort. I'll tell her to look for your car. Get out of the car so she can see you. Can you wear something bright?'

'I've got a yellow waterproof.'

'Please. She will come to you and get into the car. You don't need to talk to her. I want you to drive her to the big McDonalds in the centre of town. You know where I mean?'

'Aye, 'course I do.'

'Good. Drop her there and drive home.'

'That's it?'

'That's it.'

'Can I tell you something, Sergeant Bent?'

'Please.'

'You gave me very good advice and I didn't take it. And it's hard to believe how well things have turned out. It's changed our lives, Alice's and mine, and young Billy would tell you the same thing.'

Bent takes a long, deep breath.

'But the thing is, you were right. It were good advice. And I told those people I wouldn't have anything more to do with them.'

'How did that go down?'

'Not well. But I told 'em about old Mrs Calderwood and how I'd had to put things right. And I told 'em I won't rat them out, but I don't want anything else to do with them.'

'And they left it at that?'

'Aye, I believe they did. But I know you and DI Mason

could have been harder on me. And that would have been hard on Alice. So, I'm happy to do you a favour without asking any questions. Then we're even.'

'Yes, we're even. There is one more thing, Mr Thompson. Just a small thing, but an important one.'

'I think I know what that is.'

'You do?'

'Aye. The First Rule of Fight Club.'

'You've got it, Mr Thompson.'

'Aye, well, if you think on, we're not going to talk about it, are we? The last thing we want would be for Billy or his Gran to find out how all this started. Nor his neighbours, either. Did you know he's got a job?'

'No, I didn't. That is very good news. I'm going to leave you now, Mr Thompson. Please don't be late.'

'No chance.'

'Right. Goodbye, then.

'Goodbye, Sergeant Bent.'

Bent puffs up his cheeks and blows out slowly. He texts Elli:

```
Unavoidably delayed. Pick up still on, but
9.30. Gold-brown Nissan Micra. Old man, long
grey hair, yellow jacket. No need to talk. He
will drop you at McDonald's downtown. Stay
there. I'll join you as soon as I can. Please
confirm you get this.
```

Almost immediately, the response comes:

```
Unavoidably disappointed. Was just making
myself nice for you. Never a dull moment, eh?
I'll order you a big tasty.
```

Despite himself, Bent smiles and shakes his head. She has something, that girl.

"A Big Tasty!"

He is suddenly hungry. Checks his watch. Moving quickly around his tiny, well-organised kitchen, he chops an apple into a bowl, shakes some granola over it, adds some yoghurt, a little milk, eats it while the coffee brews. He focuses in on the fresh, crunchy, sour tastes and then enjoys their replacement by the dark, smooth spices of Colombia's best. A few minutes' release. He enjoys them fully.

Then his mood shifts as thoughts return of the girls that Mason has rescued from the Britannia. And of the missing one, Ayesha. And of Mason herself, still haunted by the nightmare experiences of her childhood. Will those girls all have to go through something like that? The young Mason probably put a brave face on her torment when it was happening, but the worm has been locked into her brain and laying its eggs across her subconscious ever since.

Was Elli's brave face also a mask over the traumas of her future? Bent feels an anger rising. An anger that he recognises, but has felt previously only in relation to the poisons of racism — a poison released in others by the face that you have no choice but to show and which no assumed mask could conceal, even if you wanted to. The face that is you and you are proud to be. He feels stupid as he contemplates the possibility that, sometimes, it might be just like that to be a woman.

***

'James! Good man!' says Barrett as he sweeps down the corridor towards the briefing room. 'Seems Wendy has made a heroine of herself. Good for her. The two of you are doing a power of good for our diversity stats. I say, are you all right, James?'

Bent nods and feigns a cough. He thinks again about masks and then deliberately clears his mind as best he can.

'Whatever you are doing, focus on it,' he tells himself. It is good advice, usually so ingrained that he does not have to repeat it to himself. And every time the gold-brown Micra drives into his thoughts, he nods in acknowledgement and wishes it on its way. And in this fashion, he makes every effort to engage with his senior colleagues' attempts to hold on to any information they have, while the representatives of the media try to fashion a catchy headline out of whatever has not been explicitly denied.

To Bent's surprise and intense relief, Barrett keeps the session relatively short, with only an almost tolerable amount of grandstanding. Once away from the room, Bent calls Elli. No response. He calls the Thompsons. Likewise.

Chapter 27

Elli swings her rucksack onto her back and strides out of the hostel door thinking,

'Bloody hell. This must be what they mean when they talk about "having a spring in your step."'

It really is as though her body is talking to her, if not in a new language, at least with a different accent. She feels she has found something inside herself that has either not been there before, or she has not dug deep enough to discover. All the abuse, the humiliation, the threats and the very real presence of violence over the last days has given her a sense of self. Her self. Core. And based on that, she feels a sense of growth that has come from her dealings with Mason and Bent. How they talk to her. The bloody police! All too much.

When she thinks of the stupid, shameful, irresponsible and sometimes mean things she has said and done, along with all the other shit that has happened to her, she does not try to deny any of it. Nor does she hang her head. She says to herself, as if she were saying to the world,

'Guilty as charged. But I have learnt some stuff. And I am still Elli Washington. And I am still moving along. Watch out, people, and make a little space. Not a lot, maybe. But a little, anyway, for sure.'

Even the fact that Bent has pulled out of their arrangement has not subdued her spirits. If Bent says 'unavoidable,' she believes it. It isn't an easy excuse. And the main thing is he hasn't just left her hanging. He has taken the trouble to make alternative arrangements and he's got in touch about it. How cool is that?

She scans the street for a Micra. She knows what they look like. Little round things. She doesn't see one. Not gold, not silver, not red nor yellow.

'Nice!' she says and hitches up her rucksack. 'Come on, Bent. Fucking hell!'

She sees a car door open about a hundred metres down the road. It's no Micra and it's blue, but the bloke getting out is wearing a bright yellow waterproof. He waves. Elli waves back and starts walking towards him. Yep, he's definitely old. And yeah, he has that kind of long, wispy, grey side-hair that men his age have. Ancient hippies and all that.

Then she stops. Another car door has opened a little further down the road. Looks very much like the old banger Ryan and Matto picked her up in that time. With the odd door. But this bloke is wearing a dark suit. Looks a bit out of place. He's striding very purposefully in her direction, with the guy in the yellow jacket unaware he's being approached from behind.

Elli turns and thinks about heading back to the hostel. But there she sees the two Mohameds coming from the other direction. They have already passed the hostel and are walking towards her. She turns again. The man in the dark suit has reached Yellow-Jacket. Dark-Suit pulls something from his inside pocket and swings his arm. Yellow-Jacket collapses to the pavement. Dark-Suit beckons Elli to join him. She is pretty sure that what he's holding in his other hand is a gun.

Once again she turns, the Mohameds have stopped. One of them signals to her to join them, while the other pulls out his own weapon. Elli hears a crack from behind her that she realises must be a gunshot. As she turns to look, the other door of the blue car opens and a young man of about her own age runs around the car to help Yellow-Jacket.

From behind, she hears the sound of a motorcycle accelerating towards her. She spins. The bike has mounted the pavement and it bursts between the two Mohameds. They fly apart like pins on a bowling alley, just as one of them looses a shot towards Dark-Suit. The bike skids to a halt by Elli.

'Get on!' the rider shouts. 'Get on, you stupid bitch! One of this lot's going to kill you!'

Not much to argue with there. Elli throws a leg over the pillion and wraps her arms around Matto's waist.

Matto drops the clutch, twists the throttle and they roar away. Elli holds on tight, fearing the sound of another shot and imagining what it must feel like actually to have a bullet hit you.

There are no more shots. As they accelerate away, she sees Dark-Suit (the man from The King's Head last night?) running back to his car, probably intending to chase after them. She sees Yellow-Jacket getting unsteadily to his feet. And she sees the young man who must have been driving Yellow-Jacket lying very still on the ground. He seems to be bleeding from the neck. And then Matto throws the bike down a side-street and they are gone.

* * *

Elli pulls her head away from Matto's back and tries to get some clean air into her lungs. She knows only too well what that stink of paraffin is about.

She has no idea where Matto is heading, or indeed

where he has come from. And who was the old man in the yellow jacket? Or the young man on the ground, perhaps shot? Perhaps dead?

At least no one seems to be following them and Matto has slowed down to a more sensible speed. She is not wearing a crash helmet. She wonders what Matto will do if the police try to wave them down. But then, she thinks, when do you ever see police on the street?

As Matto rides on, she realises to her surprise where her thoughts are leading. She is less concerned about her own safety than she is about the others involved. Yes, those two men who Bent sent to help her, but also, and especially, the missing Muslim girl, this Ayesha.

'She must be scared shitless,' Elli thinks. And then the thought follows, ' ... if she's still alive.' But either way, alive or dead, who's going to know? Matto, surely ...

She sees a sign for Breardon. Not a part of town she knows. A lot of clearance work going on. Streets of boarded-up old terraces. Squats, she thinks. That would suit Matto. The roads are more or less deserted.

He slows down, turns into an alley between two rows of dilapidated two-up and two-downs and kills the engine. They both get off the bike. He takes off his helmet and turns to her. She sees his eyes and thinks,

'Oh shit, he's completely out of it.'

And then she smiles at the next thought,

'And I am still Elli Washington!'

Matto leans forward.

'What the fuck are you laughing at?'

'Not laughing, Matto. Just impressed. That was quite a stunt you pulled back there. Saved my arse, didn't you?'

'Yes, I did save your arse. And why would I do that?'

Elli is searching for a move she's not sure is there. She has never kidded herself she has many cards to play in anybody's game, but Matto, dangerous as he might be, is also clearly a few short of a full deck. She is up for this one. She goes for it anyway.

'Dunno. Maybe you fancy it?'

'What I fancy, you stupid little bitch, is knowing what the fuck is going on. And if you don't tell me right now I will spread your arse all down this alley.'

'Christ, Matto, I'm on your side.'

'On my side? What's that supposed to mean?'

'Look, you want to know what's going on, and I want to know what's going on. I can tell you some things and you can tell me some, yeah?'

He stares at her. She wonders if he even understands what she is saying. The point is to find Ayesha. She presses on:

'And well, for another thing, you're not looking too happy. Maybe I can cheer you up a bit?'

'Cheer me up?'

'Yeah, I know a trick or two.'

'How old are you?'

'Never you mind. Like old ladies, do you?'

'I've got things to look after.'

'Got a place where you have to look after them?'

He stops and looks at her.

'Yeah, I got a place.'

'Well, let's go there then and you can look after me. I

need a bit of looking after. And you look like a bit of looking after wouldn't do you any harm, either.'

Matto looks her up and down. He locks the bike and sets off down the alley. Elli follows. They leave the alley, walk past some hoardings promising a variety of executive homes, premier office spaces and retail opportunities and turn left. The houses on Marlow Street are empty and, for the most part, boarded up. Outside one of them, Matto stops.

'This is none of your fucking business. You don't ever come here and you don't talk about it.'

'Got it. All right. Jesus, man.'

He unlocks the door and they step inside, directly into what its earlier inhabitants would have called the parlour. The place stinks of something that died long ago in the damp. Matto clicks up the catch on the Yale lock and closes a bolt.

'Wait here,' he says.

'What are you up to?'

'Mind your own.'

She watches him walk halfway along a short corridor and stop outside a door that Elli supposes must lead down to a cellar. She has very early memories of old houses like this. Not good ones. Neither houses nor memories. He waves his hand at her dismissively and she steps back into the parlour.

Elli listens to Matto unlock the door, open it and close it behind him. When she hears him lock it from the other side, she feels sure her suspicions are correct.

She picks her way across the debris-covered floor to the furthest corner of the room and takes a deep breath. Not a good idea. She reverts to the shallow breathing that does not help her calm down, but at least spares her the nauseating stench. Listening intently for any sound from below, she takes out her phone and calls Bent. He answers immediately.

'Listen,' she says, in a low voice that is a little shaky, but still clear. 'I can only say this once. Number 18, Marlow Street, in Breardon. Most of the street is boarded up. This one looks abandoned, but it's not. Blue door. It's Matto. He's got something in the cellar. I think it's her.'

'I'm on the way. Get out of there.'

'Don't know if I can. He likes locking doors. Anyway, that'd give the game away, wouldn't it?'

'Are you by yourself?'

'Obviously not, dickhead!'

'Apart from him. And maybe her?' Even in this situation, Elli 's response makes him smile.

'Yeah. He thinks we're going to get cosy. That's why he's brought me here.'

'Elli, get out of there. Find a way. Tell him you've got crabs. Tell him you're HIV positive.'

'For a policeman, you say the nicest things. I've got to go. How long do you think it'll take you to get here?'

'Twenty minutes, maybe less. I'll use the siren till I'm close.'

'Cool. I can keep him good for twenty minutes, I should think.'

'Elli, get out of there! If he's got Ayesha in the cellar, he can't just move her ...'

'I think you're just jealous,' says Elli. 'I like it.' She hangs up.

Bent curses and breaks into a run to his car. He drives quietly out of the station car park. Two blocks later, he turns on siren and lights and puts his foot down. He is still not sure why he doesn't call in back-up. But he knows that this is personal, whether because of guilt, or fear of the consequences if everything unravels, or something else, this is down to him. And he is not sorry.

Chapter 28

When Matto comes back through the cellar door, Elli is still standing in what was once a living room. There is a two-seater, fake leather sofa, one half of which is completely broken through. Two plastic garden chairs complete the furnishing, except for a low wooden table that has on it a full ashtray, a crack pipe, a battered square tin and a couple of plastic lighters. A little daylight creeps around the sides of the boards across the window.

'You do like to lock doors, don't you?' Elli comments.

'Yeah. You can't trust nobody these days,'

'I know. I know. But locking yourself in the cellar? That's going a bit far, innit? Worried I might follow you and attack you in the dark?'

'Take more than that to worry me.'

'Tough guy, eh?'

'Tough enough. Come over here.'

'No hurry,' says Elli, trying not to let her revulsion show.' Show me around the place. I want to have a look.'

'You can have a close look at what's in here,' says Matto, pointing to his crotch. 'Come round here and kneel down.'

'Oh, don't be in such a hurry! Let's have a smoke first. You'll get more off it.'

'Haven't scored yet today.'

'I've got a bit of skunk,' says Elli sitting on the solid end of the sofa by the table. Let's have that, anyway.'

She pulls out some papers and cigarettes from her rucksack and starts rolling up.

'You some kind of cock-teaser?'

'I've never had any complaints about that.'

She finishes rolling the joint and lights up. Takes a light toke and holds it out to Matto.

'Here you are.'

He takes it and smokes.

'Not bad. Where d'you get it?'

'Market.'

'Jonesy?'

'Yeah, Jonesy,' she laughs. 'D'you know him?'

'Everybody knows Jonesy. Sells oregano to students.'

'And they smoke it,' they say together.

They both laugh. Matto sits on one of the chairs.

'But he's given you some good stuff.'

She nods, takes a toke and hands it back.

'It's all been a bit mad since this thing kicked off with the blacks,' says Matto.

'Yeah, a bit,' Elli agrees, wanting to keep him talking, but not remind him of her role in it all. If he even knows. It's hard to tell where you are with Matto, or where he is in his head at any given time. They sit in silence, passing the joint.

Matto stirs. He seems to be struggling to remember something.

'Where the fuck is everybody?'

'Who d'you mean?'

'Everybody! Pricey, Kyle, Nick. Pricey! Where's Pricey?'

Elli is surprised by the genuine note of concern in his

voice.

'I went back to The King's Head,' he says, 'but there was no fucker there. The bike was in the back yard. Then I thought about you. You was with them. You told me what to do. So I've come and waited for you to come out of your place and then all that shit started. Burn the van, you said, didn't you? Well, I did that. The rest of it's all gone a bit mad, though. Where's Pricey? He had the bike, you know?'

'What's through there?' Elli asks, pointing her head towards the back of the house.

"Nother room.'

'Can I have a look?'

'If you like.'

As she expects, the room is a small eating-kitchen and beyond it is an extension for a bath and toilet. The key to the back door is in the lock. Faking a huge cough, she turns the key to unlock the door. Checks the bolt. It has been broken off at some point.

'Elli, Elli, Elli,' she says to herself. 'About time you had a bit of luck.'

'Just going to the loo!' she shouts through to Matto.

He grunts a response.

Inside the bathroom, which is as filthy as she expected, she takes out her phone and texts Bent:

Back door open x

She tries flushing the toilet, but there is no water.

'Perhaps as well I didn't need it then,' she mutters.

As she steps out of the bathroom, Matto is coming into the kitchen.

'Is there an upstairs?'

'Of course there's a fucking upstairs.'

'Can I see?'

'No.'

'Why not?'

"Cause there's no stairs to go up.'

'Oh yeah, you're right,' says Elli, looking at the strange, piled-up wreckage. 'I thought there was something missing!'

They both giggle. It was weird, Elli thought, to see Matto giggle.

'Anyway,' he says. 'I suppose I could do with a shag, but I don't know about you.'

'You mean, if I fancy shagging you?'

'No, I mean I don't know about you. I was just thinking. You been fucking all those blacks. You might have caught all kinds of shit.'

'I had a check-up, I'm fine,' Elli blurts out angrily, before she can stop herself.

'You sure? That's all right then. Come on.' He leads the way back to the front room and takes off his jacket. He throws it onto one of the plastic chairs. It slips off and falls to the floor, the keys in one pocket banging on the old wooden boards.

Elli screams.

'What the fuck!?' Matto is genuinely startled.

'I heard something!'

'What?'

'I heard something downstairs. It was like somebody moving around. Falling over something, cursing or something like that.'

'You bloody didn't!'

'I tell you I did. There's somebody moving around down there.'

'Can't be!'

'Why not?'

"Cause she's all taped up!'

They stare at each other. For what seems like a long time.

'Fuckin' hell,' says Elli. You've got *her*, haven't you?'

Matto continues to stare. Elli does not like the look forming on his face.

'You've got that spare Muslim bitch! The one they can't find. God, I want to see that! Come on, man! After what I've been through with those bastards, I want to see that!'

Matto's expression changes. A little. For the better, Elli thinks. Hopes.

'Come on then.' Matto leads the way to the cellar door and unlocks it. He turns back to Elli.

'Maybe I'll do you both at once,' he grins.

Elli swallows. Opens her eyes wide.

'Lead on, big guy,' she says. 'And I want some payback off her as well.'

Matto picks up a small torch from the top step and goes down into the darkness.

'Lock the door behind you,' he says over his shoulder. He directs the beam of light back up to the door. Elli takes the key from the outside of the door, closes it behind her and makes as much noise as she can while pretending to lock the door. She mimes trying the handle.

'Got it,' she says.

'Bring me the key.'

She does.

Matto points the light towards a hurricane lamp at the foot of the stairs.

'Hold that,' he says, handing the torch to Elli. 'Keep it on the lamp.'

He continues down the steps, picks up a lighter from the floor beside the lamp and lights it.

In what has been complete darkness, the pale glow of the lamp seems at first very bright. Elli moves towards it. The smell of damp and things animal and vegetal that have been rotting for years, if not decades, is appalling. There are scurrying noises along the walls and in the corners of the room. Some of the shapes Elli can make out are old tea-chests, some were once cardboard boxes, some are soft and amorphous, some mechanical and angular. One shape is unmistakably human. And female.

Elli moves towards her.

'What the fuck are you doing?' Matto shouts.

'I want to look at her.'

'You'll do what I tell you!'

'You didn't say anything,' Elli replies, quietly. 'Of course I'll do what you tell me. I'm just having a look at her. That's all right, isn't it?'

Matto says nothing. Elli takes a few steps closer to the figure. Yes, this must be her.

Her black hair is down over her shoulders. A strip of masking tape covers her mouth. Other loops bind her wrists to the arms of a rusty metal chair. Her blouse has been mostly ripped off and there are scratch marks across her chest. Her long, dark blue skirt is still in place, but it has been torn open along the seam. Kneesocks are down around her ankles. Above them, more tape attaches her legs, partly open, to the chair. No shoes. From the change in the stink as Elli gets closer, it is obvious the girl has soiled herself.

The face is bruised. There is dried blood on her chin and around her nostrils. But mostly, it is the eyes that demand Elli's attention. She searches for words to describe the expression, but fails to find any. Elli knows what defeat looks like and she knows what despair looks like. She knows what anger looks like and disgust. She has seen them all in her mirror.

None of those sensations is to be found in these eyes. There is almost an absence of emotion combined with a staggering statement of will. As though this person has laid aside all flavour of feeling in order to concentrate on survival. No, no, more than that ... *This is only now. Do not fight this. Practice patience. Do not presume to understand. Endure. Believe. You are not entitled to anything better than this, but, in the end, righteousness will prevail. And its justice will be terrible.*

All of this runs only semi-comprehensibly through Elli's mind like unidentifiable shapes through a forest. She has incoherent flash-backs to something called Sunday School and scary stories. She blinks and shakes her head. What the fuck? All of this is alien to her. This is not her way. And yet, there is an affinity. Elli knows she has no quarrel with those eyes or the person behind them. There might even be something to learn. Elli can't remember the last time she thought about wanting to learn something from someone.

She leans forward towards Ayesha and, with her face hidden from Matto behind her, she gives an exaggerated wink, hoping that the gesture will be understood by this strange girl.

'Right, you dirty little Paki bitch, shat ourselves, have we? What are we going to do with you, then, eh?'

The eyes do not blink, nor the expression change.

Elli reaches forward and pulls the tape away from Ayesha's mouth. There is an involuntary gasp of pain and her split lower lip begins to bleed again.

'What the fuck do you think you're doing?' Matto shouts and lunges forward. Elli sidesteps him and grins wildly.

'Come on, big boy! Think of all the things she can do with that lovely mouth! And we're not going to have much fun if she's sitting on the other end, either, are we?'

In frenzied fashion, Elli drops to her knees and starts scrabbling at the tape binding one of Ayesha's ankles.

'You're fucking mad, you,' says Matto. "Ere, use this.' He pulls a bone-handled knife from his pocket and flicks it open.

Elli pauses for a moment, then reaches out and takes it.

'Nice knife!'

'Yeah, get on with it and give it back.'

Elli saws through the tape on one leg, then the other. She stands up and looks down at Ayesha.

'Now then, darkie, you stay right where you are till I tell you different,' she snarls, and starts to cut through the tape holding Ayesha's left wrist.

'You mean till *I* tell her different! I'm in fucking charge here!' Matto shouts.

'Yeah, till *he* tells you different!' Elli shouts back, now almost hyperventilating as she dances hysterically around the chair to release the other arm.

Having done so, she backs away, holding the knife in front of her.

'Can you stand up?' she says to Ayesha, who pushes down on the arm rests of the chair and rises unsteadily to her feet.

'Right!' says Matto. There is a silence. 'What now?' Another silence. 'Give me the knife.'

No one speaks. No one moves.

'Give me the fucking knife.'

Elli looks at the weapon in her hand and breathes in another lungful of stink.

'I think I like it better when I have the knife.'

'You won't like it if I have to take it off you.'

Elli breathes slowly again. Part of her mind is trying to calculate how long it's been since she spoke to Bent. She even wonders what the traffic is like between there and here and if people are pulling over to let him through. Funny to be wishing for the police to arrive. Funny to think of Bent as 'the police.'

Another part of her mind is trying to think what to do next. Getting Ayesha untied must have been a good idea, mustn't it? And now she needs another plan to keep Matto occupied and quiet for a while. She has to be careful. Distract him, keep him calm. Delay any further action.

None of this thought process, however, is what

connects with her voice as she backs off into the darkness away from the steps.

'Take it off me? You cretinous piece of dogshit. Why don't you come over here and try and take it off me?'

Which is exactly what he does.

Chapter 29

Bent opens the cellar door quietly and starts cautiously down the steps. What he sees makes him regret the quietness and the caution.

The confrontation below him plays out in seconds. Ignoring the deep cut that he takes to his left forearm, Matto steps forward and sweeps aside the knife Elli is holding out in front of her. With his right fist, he lands a punch in her face that sends her staggering. She goes backwards over one of the mouldering boxes concealed behind her. Her feet fly up into the air and her head impacts the cement floor with the sound of a dull axe hitting a tree.

Ayesha's incomprehensible scream of invective takes both men's attention for an instant, but as Bent rages down the final steps, Matto has time to scoop up his knife and turn to face him.

'My, you're a big buck, aren't you?'

'You're happier hitting little girls.'

'Don't really mind. What somebody should have told her,' he nods in the direction of Elli's motionless body, lying obscured in the murk beyond the eerie glow of the lamp, 'is never, *never* to wave a weapon around unless you know *how* to use it ...'

'... and you are *prepared* to use it,' Bent completes the sentence.

'Yeah,' says Matto, grinning. 'So, I'm alright. Where does that leave you, Sambo? Fuck! You're him, aren't you? You're the one was at The King's Head. I am really going to enjoy this.'

'Drop the knife.'

'Yeah, as if.'

Bent shrugs. Reaches around behind his back and brings out Kyle's Glock.

Matto stares. Blinks.

Bent chambers a round.

Matto drops the knife.

'Kick it over here.'

Matto does so. His body, tense till now, seems to relax, but then starts to tremble a little.

Bent kicks the knife over towards the bottom of the stairs. Still without taking his eyes off Matto, he speaks to the girl who is still standing, half-supporting herself against the chair in which she has previously been imprisoned.

'Are you Ayesha?'

'Yes.'

'Can you walk?'

'I think so.'

Bent moves more directly between Ayesha and Matto.

'Go around behind me to the bottom of the stairs, please.'

She does so, moving slowly and a little unsteadily.

'You,' addressing Matto now, 'Go over there and sit on the chair.'

He does.

Bent looks at the bits of tape on the floor.

'Where's the tape?'

'Don't have any more.'

'You better, or you have a real problem.'

'You say.'

'Yes. It's like this. I have to get these two girls to a hospital as quickly as I can. That means I have to carry that one,' he nods in the direction of Elli, 'upstairs.'

'Sounds like *you*'ve got a problem, then.'

'Yes. What to do about you. I can't carry her and cover you at the same time. I could shoot you.'

'I don't think so. What are you anyway? Some kind of nigger-paki?'

Bent notices the coldness inside him intensify. At the same time, he feels carefully learned rules and responsibilities peel away as he makes contact with what feels like an innate core code.

'Yeah, that's exactly what I am. I am a warrior of the Cherokee Nigger-Paki Nation.'

Matto sneers a response.

'We have a knife. I could just hamstring you. That would keep you still.'

Matto falls silent, his expression confused, his twitching more obvious.

'Give me the gun.' Ayesha walks forward, more steady now on her feet.

'That doesn't sound like such a good idea,' Bent replies.

'Time is of the essence, is it not?' Ayesha's voice is stronger and her precisely correct English adds to the strangeness of the atmosphere created by Bent's change of mood, their dilemma and her suggestion.

'I can make sure he does not move while you carry her upstairs. You can then return and take the gun.'

'Do you know how to use one? He was right about

needing to know how to use a weapon. Otherwise, you just put yourself in danger.'

'I have seen the movies. You hold it very tight with both hands and you don't pull the trigger, you squeeze it. Is there a safety catch?'

'It's built into the grip. You just point and shoot.'

'An interesting kind of safety feature.'

'You heard what he said. You also have to be prepared to use it.'

'You aim at the widest part of the body in order to maximise the likelihood of hitting the target. Then, once the target is down, it is possible to approach the body and deliver a head-shot.'

Bent and Matto look carefully at Ayesha.

'Don't give her the gun.' Matto's eyes are popping, his trembling more severe. 'Don't give her the fucking gun. Jesus!'

'How are my friends?'

'All alive. No thanks to him. He left them trapped in the pub and torched it.'

'Are you fucking crazy? Don't believe him! I didn't! It was an accident!'

'Give me the gun. Take her upstairs. Does she deserve to lie there?'

'Get a grip, you stupid, fucking monkey!'

Bent decides.

'Get down on the floor. Cross-legged. Do it. Now. Put your hands behind your head. Look at the floor.'

Matto does.

Bent walks around behind him and picks up the

chair. He brings it back to a position three metres in front of Matto.

'Sit down,' he says to Ayesha. 'If he tries to get up, or move his hands, shoot him.'

'No, don't! You can't do that!'

'Look at the floor.'

Bent puts the Glock carefully into Ayesha's hands.

'Keep your finger here, alongside the trigger, but not on it. We don't want to shoot him by accident.'

'That will not occur,' Ayesha assures him. 'What is her name?'

'Her name's Elli.'

'She is very courageous.'

'Yes, she is.'

'Go to her. I can take care of this cretinous piece of dogshit.'

'That actually sounds rather like Elli,' says Bent, through his surprise.

'Yes,' says Ayesha. 'I am a fast learner.'

'No, no, no ...' Tears are rolling down Matto's face. 'I'm begging you.'

'Keep your head down and don't move.'

Bent crosses to Elli and checks her pulse. It is steady. No obviously broken bones.

'Come on, trouble.' He picks her up in his arms and raises his left elbow so that her head nestles on his shoulder. He walks to the bottom of the stairs and looks across to Ayesha. She has her elbows tucked into her waist and the Glock pointing unwaveringly at Matto. He is still staring at the floor.

'I'll be right back.'

Bent carries Elli up the steps, through the door and along the corridor into the parlour. He puts her down, half-sitting, on the solid part of the sofa and lays her head back gently. With a frown, her eyes flicker open.

'Mmmm, that was nice,' she murmurs.

'Elli! Are you OK?'

'If I'm not, do I get another carry?'

Bent rolls his eyes.

'You can have another carry either way, but I have to get back down there.'

'Oh shit,' says Elli, remembering the situation. 'Is he still down there with her?'

Bent's response is interrupted by the sound of a gunshot.

Chapter 30

When the ointments are fresh, the dressings new and the painkillers kicking in, Mason can move around the hospital for brief periods. Alerted by DC Carpenter, she joins the Thompsons just as news of Tanner is delivered by a Doctor Green.

'Thank God,' says Mrs Thompson.

'No permanent damage?' asks Mr Thompson.

'No, he's a strong lad. He'll make a full recovery. As long as there is no psychological trauma, he'll have a cracking story to tell,' says the young doctor.

'He saved my life,' says Thompson. 'He's a hero.'

'Well, I think you actually saved his. You did a fine job stemming the bleeding. And heroes usually mean the press. We're not going to have a big invasion of reporters and photographers, are we?'

'Oh no, please!' says Alice Thompson.

'I'm sure it would help if you were to say he can't have any visitors, except Mr and Mrs Thompson, of course,' says Mason, joining the conversation.

'And you are?'

'Mason, Detective Inspector. We believe this shooting was accidental. Unfortunate case of bystanders being in the wrong place at the wrong time and getting caught up in violence relating to a case I have been investigating. Still am, in fact. We are closing in on the culprits and we would appreciate as little publicity as possible.'

'Oh, well, that certainly suits us,' says Green. She turns to the Thompsons. 'You'll have to leave the hero celebration till he gets home.'

When she has gone, Mason takes over.

'We need a very simple story,' she says. 'Why were you and Billy parked in that street this morning?'

'Can't I say we were waiting to pick somebody up?'

'Who?'

'Well, this girl Sergeant Bent asked us ...'

'We'd rather keep her out of it, if at all possible. And him.'

'But that's why we were there! Billy only took me because my bloody car was acting up ...'

'Yes, it's awkward.'

'"Awkward," you call it?'

'Mr Thompson,' says Mason, painfully straightening her back, 'We can do this one of two ways. One way is absolutely on the level, starting with explaining to Tanner that you and Mrs Thompson were behind his gran's window getting smashed in.'

'Oh no, we wouldn't want that!' says Alice Thompson.

They look at each other in silence for what seems like a long time.

'What if,' Alice Thompson begins, 'What if Billy was trying to find somebody, a girl he'd met and he thought she lived at the hostel. He asked John to go with him because he thought they'd take John more seriously. Just a girl. Jennifer. Short red hair.'

Mason looks at them questioningly.

'Will Tanner go along with that? Why would he?'

'He will if we ask him,' says Alice. 'And, you know, there's been once or twice he's said to us, "Don't ask me about that anymore, please. Can we just let it go?" And he's not a lad who'll mind telling the police a bit of a story.'

Mason nods.

'So we'll just keep saying that to anybody who asks, and to Billy we'll just say, "Trust us on this one."'

'Aye, it's better if he doesn't know,' John Thompson adds. 'And he will trust us.'

'Sounds good,' says Mason.

'One more thing, though,' says John, as she turns to leave.

'Yes, Mr and Mrs Thompson,' says Mason. 'The answer is yes. Fix this with Billy and we are done here. Thank you, both.'

Mason heads off back to her own ward. She can feel the soreness creeping up her legs again. The good news is that the boy will be OK. As far as the story goes, there is nothing more to be done but hope for the best. Even as she thinks it, she corrects herself:

'And prepare for the worst.'

She does not realise that she has said it out loud until she sees the shocked expression of a passing patient who has, for a moment, felt himself addressed.

* * *

At the door to the cellar, Bent pauses. Silence.

'Ayesha? Ayesha!'

No answer.

Bent takes a deep breath and launches himself down the stairs.

Matto is lying on his back like a huge, red-breasted bird that has failed to take off: arms outstretched, one leg bent under his body, the savagery of that fatal failure etched into the final desperate grimace on its face.

Ayesha is standing over him. The gun is pointing downwards, but she is unable to hold it steady enough to keep it targeted on Matto's head.

'Ayesha,' softly now as he approaches, Bent holds out his hand. 'Ayesha, it's over.'

She looks up. When she speaks, her voice is shaky and strangely robotic.

'The head-shot.'

'No. Not now. No need.'

She looks at him questioningly.

'May I have the gun, please?'

She frowns. Shakes her head as if to clear it.

'Yes, of course.'

She raises her trembling hands in his direction, finger still on the trigger. Bent steps forward and, holding the automatic by the barrel, gently pushes it to one side.

'Let go now. Slowly.'

She does.

Bent takes what feels like his first breath since re-entering the cellar. He ejects the clip and the round from the breech. Drops them into his pocket. Sticks the gun back into his waistband.

'What happened? Are you all right?'

'Yes, thank you. Al hamdu lillah.'

'He tried to get up?'

She pauses before answering.

'Yes. I think so. I think *so*. Yes, I am sure. At one point, he did, yes. I saw his face. His face!'

Bent wonders about the advisability, or usefulness, of asking for any more details, but old habits die hard.

'When ...'

Ayesha interrupts him with the force of her gaze. Then, in response to an unasked question that seems most important and explanatory to her, she continues, her voice now much more her own again.

'You see, although God is merciful, my prophet, may peace be upon him, did not bring a message of non-violence under all circumstances. I will take my punishment as necessary, but I do not feel myself enjoined only to turn the other cheek.'

'Bloody hell, girl, you'll have to tell me more about your prophet.'

They both turn to see Elli sitting on the top step.

'Bent, I'm not feeling so great. I think I could do with that other carry.' She starts to stand up.

'Don't stand up there!'

Elli sits down again.

'Ayesha, can you manage the stairs?'

'What about ... all ... this?'

'Leave it. Just as it is. Walk away.'

As she makes her way to the foot of the stairs, Bent retrieves Matto's knife, using a tissue to pick it up by the point. He returns to the body and, taking care to avoid the blood, he stoops down and wraps Matto's fingers around the knife handle a few times. He steps back, hooks his foot under the seat of the chair and lofts it away into a corner. It lands on something soft, followed by a flurry of squeaks and small feet.

Bent supports Ayesha up the stairs. Once at the top,

he helps Elli stand and picks her up again. To Ayesha, he says,

'Take the key from the lock there and lock the door from the outside. Leave the key in the lock.'

He carries Elli back into the parlour and puts her down on the sofa again.

'Please just watch that she doesn't fall off,' he says to Ayesha. 'And if possible, keep her awake.'

Returning to the cellar door, he empties the clip of all its bullets but one and drops the others back into his pocket. He pulls the front of his shirt out of his trousers and wipes the clip thoroughly before clicking it back into the Glock. He pumps the single round into the chamber and then wipes the whole weapon. He lays it on the floor outside the door and goes back to the parlour.

'Ayesha, I need this to be kept very simple.'

'That seems unlikely.'

'You remember everything until he hit the girl. You screamed. You must have passed out. When you came to, I was there. You don't remember seeing Matthews again. I told you to go upstairs. You did. I followed, carrying Elli. You locked the cellar door and we left.'

'But I am prepared to take my punishment.'

'Ayesha, I need your help.'

'You have deserved it.'

'There is more riding on this, from my point of view, and from Elli's point of view, and from a lot of other points of view, than your readiness to take punishment. I know you can take punishment. And ...' he continues as she tries to speak, '... as far as Matthews' death is concerned, I need you to sort that out with your god as you both see fit at the appropriate time. Which is not now.'

Ayesha looks at him for a moment and then she speaks.

'He hit the girl and I screamed. I lost consciousness. When I awoke, I was lying on the floor and you were there. You told me to go upstairs. You followed me with Elli and told me to lock the door.'

Bent nods.

'Just that, no matter how often you are asked by how many people, just that.'

'Very well, but please tell me one more thing.'

'What's that?'

'Apart from being a mighty warrior of the Cherokee Nigger-Paki Nation, what is your role in all this?'

'That part *is* very simple,' says Bent. I am a Detective-Sergeant in Her Majesty's Police Force.

'Truly, God is great and unfathomable,' says Ayesha.

'And I will have to take my own chances with my employer and with my conscience for putting you in that situation.'

They leave through the front door. Bent's car is parked outside. The two girls sit in the back, Elli with her head leaning on Ayesha's shoulder.

'Keep her awake if you can,' says Bent. 'Talk to her, pinch her ...'

'Don't you bloody dare!' Elli mutters. 'And what's my story? Don't I get a story?'

'You don't remember anything after he hit you. Otherwise, you can tell it just the way it went down.'

'Bent,' says Elli, slurring a little, 'we don't need to tell anybody that bit about you wanting to pick me up and take me to your friend's, do we? I like that bit. I want to keep that private. I just walked out this morning and all hell broke loose. Whaddya think?'

'I think you're a lot smarter than you like to let on,' Bent replies to the rear-view mirror. 'And I thank you, Elli Washington.'

'She's gone,' says Ayesha. 'Elli, Elli!'

'Ayesha,' says Bent, putting his foot down and the siren on, 'we have choices to make and very little time to make them.'

'Then let us begin.'

'Right. First, in my estimation, from a purely medical point of view, Elli needs immediate attention more than you do.'

'Yes.'

'So I am driving to the hospital.'

'Good.'

'It may be that you also need attention at the hospital.'

'Yes ...'

'But maybe it's more important to take you home and get you into fresh clothes and have those ones destroyed.' He pauses. 'I'm sorry, there are better ways of doing this, but we have to choose between gathering evidence of sexual assault and destroying evidence of having fired a gun. I need to know if you ... '

'I was assaulted, but not sexually. They boasted and bragged and threatened, of course. They enjoyed our fear. Perhaps that was our biggest danger.'

'What?'

'Where is the other one?'

'Also dead.'

'Good.'

There is a short silence as they both try to gather their thoughts into a useable form.

'Detective-Sergeant Bent?'

'Yes.'

'If you succeed in hiding the fact that it was I who put an end to that abomination, is it also the case that you intend to implicate someone else?'

'Yes.'

'Will you tell me who?'

'Someone who is responsible for having seduced, drugged, raped and sold for sex a number of defenceless, under-age girls, Elli being one of them. In my book, *he* is an abomination.'

'If I recognise the story from the press, he is perhaps a member of my community.'

'Yes, and also indirectly responsible for everything that has happened to you and your friends over the past few days.'

'He has a name?'

'The only name I know is Amir.'

'It is not an unusual name. I know one Amir. His brother is a successful barrister. Our grandparents came from the same village in another country.' She looks down at Elli. 'But even if it is he, then let it be so.'

'Then we'll go first to the hospital ...'

'Allow me to help you, Detective-Sergeant Bent. I tell you, in a state of great emotional distress, that I do not wish to be taken to hospital. I insist on my right to be taken home to my mother, so that I may release her from her torment and make myself clean again before I have to face any more people from outside my family. I become almost hysterical. Will that suffice?'

'Oh yes,' says Bent. 'That will suffice. As soon as we have dropped Elli off, you can phone them and say we are on the way. Please excuse me now. I have to make a call myself. It is not possible to get the timing right, but I have to get it as close to right as I can. As you said, time is of the essence.'

He takes out his Amir phone and calls.

Chapter 31

Amir answers immediately.

'What the fuck's going on?'

'Aswad here,' says Bent in his best northern accent. 'I've got a way out for you.'

'Way out of what?'

'A way out of all your Brothers finding out it's you who dumped them in it. Including a few of your VIPs with their 'specials.'

'I don't know anything about that.'

'Maybe, maybe not, but they know about you, don't they? You remember the pen? And the gun? Maybe you get to eat the gun next time.'

Bent guesses that Amir wants to say something in response, but is too scared to speak. All Bent can hear is his snatched breathing at the other end of the connection. So he presses on.

'Have you got transport, right now?'

'Yeah. I can take the van.'

Bent gives Amir the address.

'What? It's all crap round there, man! I don't want to be going ... '

'How long to get there?'

'Fifteen minutes. Twenty?'

'Make it fifteen. And listen very carefully. When you get there, it's a blue front door. It's on the latch, you can walk in. Leave the door on the latch. Cross the front room. You'll see a door to the cellar on the right. In front of the door, you'll see a gun.'

'A gun? Are you fucking mad?'

'The question is, Amir, how fucking mad are you? If you don't do what I tell you, I will just give you up: phone numbers, notebook pages, the lot. And then you can expect the guys with the sense of humour just one more time.'

'And if I do?'

'Then all that disappears and the people who pay those guys will think of you as a very fine fellow indeed. You will be a made man. Even more than your brother.'

Bent bites his lip. Wasn't meaning to say that.

'What do you know about my brother?'

'The thing to keep in mind, Amir, is how much we know about you. So, you pick up the gun. Now listen carefully. The gun is loaded. There is no extra safety catch. When you hold the gun in a normal way and pull the trigger, it goes off. Got it?'

'Yeah, I got it. So what?'

'OK. The key's in the door. Give it a twist to make sure it's locked. Then, you shout, "Keep away from this door. I'm going to shoot in five!" Then you count, very loud, "One, two, three, four, five!" That gives plenty of time for anyone on the other side of the door to get away from it.'

'OK.'

'Then you get a good grip on the gun, two hands like you see in the movies ...'

'Yeah!'

'And you fire one round through the door.'

'You're shitting me, innit?'

'No, it's important. Set yourself, feet apart, like in the

films, two-handed grip on your weapon and fire one round through the door. The stairs go straight down, so there's no chance of you hitting anyone, but that'll show him inside that you mean business. In fact, it'll scare the shit out of him.'

'So, who is inside?'

'You've heard of a group called the Great Whites?'

'Course I have. Bunch of skinhead trash. Scum. They're the ones that beat me up and kidnapped those girls. Pigs. Want wiping out.'

'That's what's inside.'

'Fuck! How many?'

'Just one.'

'Right.'

'But an important one. He knows where the last girl is.'

'Fuck!'

'He isn't armed, not with a gun, anyway, but he might have a knife and he's definitely dangerous. There's back-up from the Brothers on the way, but you can get there quicker and you can make sure that he doesn't escape.'

'What if he already has?'

'No chance. Anyway, it's easy. Once you're in the house, look along the corridor and you'll see the gun. If it's not there, turn and run like hell. If it is, like I say, pick it up and make sure the door's locked. I am 100% sure that he can't get out of that cellar without help and the only people who know he's there are you, me and the Brothers.'

'Why not call the police?'

'Allahu akbar,' says Bent. What is the matter with

you? Who do you think are going to be better and quicker at getting information out of him — the police or the Brothers?'

'I'm in the van now. So, you're on our side?'

'I'm helping you be a hero to your people, Amir. Do you know what you're doing?'

'Yes, I got it.'

'What do you do with the door?'

'Make sure it's locked.'

'How many shots?'

'Just one.'

'That's right. One will keep him in his place and show our Brothers that you took charge. But no more. We don't want a wild-west circus to attract attention. Just a show of strength.'

'I got it, bro. How long before they arrive?'

'About ten minutes after you. Just hold the fort. I'll tell them you're taking care of things.'

'No problem, brother. And thanks. Shukriyya.'

'My pleasure,' says Bent and rings off.

'You take a large number of extreme risks,' says Ayesha, 'based on a very far-fetched plan, the stupidity of one man and a belief that I will not betray you.'

'Needs must when the devil drives.'

'I do not draw much comfort from that expression.'

'Me neither.'

And then they are at the hospital.

Bent lifts Elli out of the back seat and carries her through the doors of A&E. He is quickly surrounded by a team of professionals who wheel her away. Bent identifies himself and gives what few details he has of the injuries she has received. In a few minutes, he is back in the car.

'Do you know how to get home from here?'

'No.'

Bent puts her address into his GPS and they set off.

'Fifteen minutes,' he says and gives her his phone. 'Call them on this. Tell them not to tell anyone until you are there. We do not want a crowd.'

Some streets short of the house, he pulls over.

'What are you doing?' she asks.

'Sorry, it's time to make another call,' says Bent. This time he gets out, walks away from the car and dials 999 on his Amir phone. Assuming a stage-Scottish accent, he reports he was just in Breardon and he is sure he heard screams and gunshots from 18 Marlow Street. No, he will not give his name. He has been in Iraq and he knows what a gunshot sounds like. And there might have been somebody shouting 'Allahu Akbar!' He knows what that sounds like, too. Bent doesn't want Ayesha to hear that part.

He returns to the car. As they pull up outside the house, he turns to Ayesha, now sitting in the front passenger seat,

'Remember, ... '

'Bathe and have all the clothes destroyed.'

'Yes. Good.'

'When asked why, I shall embarrass my questioners

by referring to my shame and the honour of my family. I shall hint at some highly sensitive Islamic requirements and challenge the questioner's intercultural sensitivity. That will probably do the trick.'

'Ayesha, I would surely rather have you on my side than against me.'

'Thank you, Detective-Sergeant Bent. The feeling is mutual.'

Once again, Bent identifies himself and leaves as soon as possible, explaining that other police officers will soon be in touch to liaise with the family and continue the investigation. His request that no one contact the press, but allow the police to make an announcement, is immediately agreed to. In the same spirit of cooperation, he acknowledges their need to contact all family members with the good news.

* * *

Once away from the house, Bent pulls over in the vicinity of Victoria Park and phones in to the station to give the briefest of updates regarding Matto, locked in the cellar, possibly armed with a knife, Elli, in hospital, and Ayesha, at home. Next, he texts Mason:

Girls safe. All good.

Then he tips the seat back and stretches. He closes his eyes and begins to focus his attention on his breathing. Once he has established his preferred rhythm: in to a count of four, hold to a count of four, out to a count of four and hold to a count of four, he focuses his attention on his toes, noticing how they feel. Slowly, he shifts focus up his body, pausing at the shoulders to start again at his fingertips. After moving up through his neck and head to his scalp, he lets his awareness escape into the car and then out into the street around. Then up and above the street. Sounds of the city move into his consciousness. He acknowledges them and lets them go. After a while, slowly, he brings himself back down into the street, the car and his body. He returns the seat to its upright position and gets out of the car.

Bent looks at his watch. He strolls along the street towards Victoria Park. The light is already starting to fade. On the lake, last spring's cygnets, large now but still a murky mix of grey-brown feathers with a few spots of white here and there, are still staying relatively close to their mother. An old man and small girl are ripping up rounds of sliced bread and throwing them in to the birds. The girl is keen to make sure that each of the five cygnets gets its fair share and she squeals with delight when her grandfather — Bent supposes — manages to throw a piece directly to one that has been missing out. Bent walks along to a quieter spot and looks around. No one. Scooping the bullets from his pocket, he throws them out into the lake, along with his Amir phone. A few wildfowl come to investigate. They paddle away disappointed.

Back in the car, Bent drives towards the station. Some things are going to happen now that he can't control. The point is to be ready to respond. His head feels clear.

Chapter 32

'No, I haven't exactly been suspended,' says Bent. 'Just told to take a few days off, check in with Counselling Services for some therapy, and keep myself available for further interview.'

Mason pulls a face.

'That last part sounds threatening.'

She moves in a tentative manner, with a stiff, upright posture. She sits and stands very slowly and sleeps only on her front. What remains of her hair has had her thinking about going the whole hog with a shaved-head look, but a few checks in the mirror have persuaded her otherwise.

'I don't think I'm vain,' she says to Bent. 'But if I can't stand the way I look, why would I force everybody else to put up with it?'

'And the redhead wig?' Bent counters.

Mason grins.

'A girl deserves a little fun now and then.'

'Good job I didn't say that.'

'Very true,' Mason acknowledges. 'And speaking of girls, how are they?'

'Hard to tell for sure, of course, but no obvious signs of damage or trauma. Yet, anyway. They are with their families. They've been checked out medically. None of them wants to see a counsellor. Oh, Asma, the little round one, was very upset with herself for telling you that the devil had taken Ayesha. Blames herself that you wanted to go back down into the cellar.'

'Yes, I know,' says Mason, 'She came to see me with

her mother. She said she felt so stupid, but they had all got used to talking about them as The Devil and The Pig among themselves and it just came out that way.'

'What did you say?'

'Told her it wasn't her fault. The only people to blame were the ones who put us all in danger. We were all in there trying to do the best we could and the best we could worked out pretty well.'

'Nice.'

'Yeah, though I have to say that things went downhill from there.'

'How come?'

'Well, then she said, 'Yes, thanks to God.' So, of course, I foolishly said it was a pity that God's will had got us all into that mess in the first place. She blushed a bit and looked at her mum and then her mum said they had to go.'

Bent smiles. 'Well, as crises of faith go, I'm pretty sure that any half-decent Imam will be able to help her with that one.'

'And what about Ayesha?'

'Oh, she has been going around to see the others at home and telling their parents how brave they were.'

'She's quite something, isn't she?'

'Mmmm. And that's not the best bit. Who do you think has been going with her?'

Mason looked quizzically.

'Elli. Except she prefers to be called Eleanor now.'

'Eleanor? How come that?'

'Says she doesn't want to be that old Elli anymore. She's moved on and she finds the name-change useful to remind her.'

'Don't tell me. She's been talking to you about names. Or you talking to her?'

'Maybe a bit,' Bent acknowledges. 'She said it was a stupid name, so I asked her if she knew where it came from. She didn't.'

'Makes me smile, Bent. So, my guess is you told her stories of Eleanor of Aquitaine?'

'Mmmm. And Roosevelt. Strong women.'

'So, how is our Eleanor going down in Ayesha's community?'

'Very well, apparently. Ayesha's rather simplified version of the story was that Eleanor found out where she was being held, called the police, but also went there herself and helped rescue her.'

'All completely true.'

'Yeah, Eleanor says she has never been made so welcome by so many people anywhere. And they are such warm people. And all the women want to give her cakes and sweets.'

'Very nice.'

'It gets better. Ayesha has concocted a plan for Elli ... Eleanor ... and herself to go around schools and hostels and wherever, talking about what just happened to them and what their lives are like.'

'That sounds so good.'

'Well, get this. The current plan is that, on each occasion, a different one of them will turn up wearing a hijab and the other one won't. Half way through the session, they will change over. Then at the end, they will ask people if what they say sounds different with or without the hijab.'

'They should be on tv.'

'It wouldn't surprise me if that's where they end up. What's really surprising is that Eleanor seems to be up for it. They have more or less nothing in common, those two, except twenty minutes in a cellar, and now they are as thick as the proverbial thieves.'

'They are both young women in angry times, Bent. They have more or less everything in common.'

Bent raises his eyebrows, shakes his head, looks ruefully at the floor.

'How is Ayesha going to feel about appearing in public without her hijab?' says Mason, trying to move on from the put-down.

'She says she's discussing it with her imam. I don't give much for his chances.'

They are quiet for a while.

'Yeah, that's the good news.' Bent's expression changes.

Mason sighs. 'And, on the other hand?'

'We have a meeting the day after tomorrow with Barrett and Peters, and maybe the Chief Constable himself. Just us. No federation reps, nothing official, Barrett said. "Just to clarify a few things."'

'Like what kind of medals to give us?'

'Possibly. Possibly not.'

'Do you think if we agreed to forego the medals, we could skip the meeting?'

'I think definitely not.'

'I think you're right.'

'It will be in our interests to be well prepared.'

'Right again, DS Bent. There are a few people we need to talk to.'

* * *

The meeting is to take place in the office of Assistant Chief Constable Conrad Peters. On arrival, Mason and Bent are held for a while under the stern eye of his secretary and then called in. For the most part, the room is standard issue, but it is impossible not to notice that Peters is standing next to large, framed photograph of a Royal College of Defence Studies Senior Course graduation ceremony.

'This is shot through with procedural irregularities and inconsistencies,' is Peters' opening line. 'And I don't want to hear any more of your fake apologies for, "misjudgements made under pressure".'

He drops the dossier onto a small side table, where it inevitably draws attention to a riot helmet with ACC badge of rank and a firearms officer utility belt.

Barrett waves Mason and Bent to two straight-backed chairs and resumes his seat by the side of Peters' desk. Peters takes his own chair.

'There is something going on here. If I decide to find out what it is, I can. If you two think you can keep secrets from your superiors and collude with witnesses to obstruct investigations into the apparent execution of one victim and the fitting up of a suspect, no matter what kind of unsavoury little shits they both might be, you must have forgotten what it is that the rest of us do for a living — we investigate, we find out. Yes, what is it, Mason?'

'Permission to stand, sir?'

'What? Yes, of course, go ahead. And you may sit down again at any time, without asking permission.'

'Thank you, sir.'

'You're very welcome. As I was saying, I don't know what it is that is so fishy here, but something stinks. At the same time, as Bill has pointed out, you are heroes in the press and very good for us, for our demographic bloody statistics. So let me put it to you like this. You can have your five minutes of fame, because it suits us for you to have them. What follows will, inevitably, be a variation on something else we do very well. That is, we shall craft a rather more skilful account of recent events that enables us to be seen to be doing our duty in the eyes of the public that we serve. Exactly what form that account takes will depend on what you two have to say when we meet again, tomorrow.

'In general terms, DI Mason, DS Bent, you have two options. One, you can come clean. In that case, we will put our heads together and see what we can work out. Two, you can carry on as you have been doing thus far. In that case, you will each find your request for transfer waiting here for you to sign. Those requests will be granted. If you are lucky, one of you will find yourself in an underground office collating traffic statistics in central Wales, while the other one will start compiling an index to complaints made against the police in Ulster between 1970 and 1995. Or, you might not be so lucky. Dismissed.'

Peters, Barrett and Bent stand up. Mason sits down.

'If I may, sir?'

'What?'

'With regard to your suggestion of a cover-up, we are already looking at one. The key figure is Collingwood.'

'What are you talking about, Mason?'

Peters sits down again. Barrett sits down again. Bent sits down again.

'Kyle Redwood and his friend, Nick, mentioned a Mr Collingwood on a couple of occasions, once in my presence, once in the evidence given by Miss Washington. They are, or perhaps I should say were, never the sharpest tools in the box, Kyle and Nick. There is no *Mister* Collingwood, of course, is there?'

In the absence of a response, Mason continues.

'There is a Sir Peter Collingwood. Made his fortune in the arms trade, knighted for services to industry, outspoken in support of law and order, generous in his contributions to any number of police charities, prominent —although that is probably not the right word — in the Freemasons, thought to have connections to far-right groups across Europe and believed to take a particular interest in, including providing financial support for, the activities of such groups as The Great Whites.'

Mason takes a breath.

'He is known to like to mix with the grass roots now and again and we believe that he might well have been at the launch event of the local Great Whites chapter at The King's Head.'

'DI Mason,' Barrett steps in. 'This is neither the time nor ...'

'With the greatest respect, sir,' Mason takes up her theme again, 'This seems very much like the place and the Assistant Chief Constable's ultimatum seems to allow us very little time. Sir Peter's visit may well have been set up to celebrate not only the launch of the local chapter, but also the attempted fire-bombing of the corner shop that first brought this group to our attention. That proved to be a bit of a damp squib, of course, but, since that visit, things really kicked off, including the appearance in the story of a sophisticated handgun. And since things have gone so very wrong, two local Great White leaders have disappeared, following the appearance of two armed criminals sent, we believe, from London. Excuse me.'

Mason winces and Bent takes over as speaker.

'On the other side of this story, we know the network of men abusing local young girls goes way beyond lowlifes like Amir Qureshi. We know there are contacts in the Town Hall. We know prominent members of the business community are involved. We know some kind of network called Al-Ikhwan, or The Brothers, exists and that it employs armed enforcers, who appear also to be murderers. We know some girls were singled out for "special" clients and that not all those clients were Asians. One key character here appears to be Tawfiq Qureshi, Amir's brother. He is a high-flying barrister, devout Muslim, disgusted by his brother, but under pressure from his family to be supportive, and possibly compromised by the shadier practices of some of his clients.'

'And how do you know these things?' asks Peters.

'It is what we do for a living, sir. And I am in touch with an undercover informant. Sir.'

'Are you, indeed?'

'What we need is a dedicated unit and more resources,' says Mason, 'if we are to start to uncover just what it is that is being covered up. Once again, Collingwood might be where all this leads. Or he might be where we start — that would be because of the underage girl that was provided for him during his brief visit here. Just a quickie in a hotel room. Simply groomed and served up for the paedophile predilections of a proto-nazi white supremacist.'

'Have you completely lost your mind, DI Mason? You are this close to immediate suspension!' Peters holds up his hand, thumb and forefinger almost touching.

'Honestly, sir,' Mason shifts gingerly in her seat again, 'I believe that my state of mental well-being is as good, if not better, than I can ever remember. As you will be aware, as will Superintendent Barrett, few, if any, of the above lines of inquiry are currently being pursued with any great vigour. I am sure that there are excellent reasons for this, in the light of cuts to the force. However, DS Bent and I would like to accept your invitation to meet again tomorrow. We would like to discuss further the setting up of a small unit dedicated to the investigation of the people and the forces behind this iceberg of semi-institutionalised child abuse and inter-racial violence that we have encountered in this case so far.'

She maintains eye contact with Barrett as she turns her request into a covert ultimatum of her own.

'We feel sure that this option will be seen by all right-minded people as preferable. Preferable either to the guilty going unpunished, or to more mayhem in the media should any or all of the above leak into the public domain. To the extent that we can proceed strategically along these lines, possibly covertly at first, we will, of course, be happy to go along with any kind of tactical accounting you feel is appropriate. May I be excused now, please, sir. I think that these dressings need to be changed.'

'You are both excused, as you put it, until tomorrow morning at ten,' says Peters, icily. 'Bill, stay on for a moment, would you?'

* * *

'Did I overcook it?' asks Mason as they leave the building.

'Just enough, I would say,' Bent replies. 'Just enough. All you can do is look ready to play the cards people believe you're holding.'

'I meant what I said about never having felt better — mentally. It all sounds a bit too psycho-babbly if I try to talk about it, but something happened back there behind that burning building.'

'Coffee?'

'Sure.'

The sun throws long shadows through mostly bare trees. They walk slowly through the park, coffees in hand.

'I had the dream,' she says quietly. 'The one I told you about. I had the dream, awake.'

'The light from the landing?'

'Yes.'

After a brief silence, Bent prompts her to go on. 'And what happened?'

'I told him to leave me alone.'

'And he did?'

'That's it. There wasn't a 'he' anymore. It was ...'

She pauses again.

'Previously,' — she says it as though introducing the latest episode in a tv cop-show, but immediately afterwards her tone becomes serious.

'It was always as if there was the me in the bed and the other me, outside, watching. It wasn't either/or, they were both me. I was both. But this time, it was as though there was a third me, one step further back, another me, watching me watching me. But then, and that's the point, not being the child in the bed. That's where it all changed, you see. Not being the child in the bed anymore. As if I was now able to escape that part.'

'Escape it?'

'Yes, and not in a sense of denying it. Maybe trying to deny it is what I have been doing all these years. But this time, I was able to accept it. I mean, acknowledge it happened, and now I am big enough and old enough, yes, and ugly enough if you like,' she smiles at Bent, 'to say all that stuff really happened to that child who I was, and I couldn't handle it then, but now I can, and I will not carry it around with me anymore, and I will not be hurt by it anymore, and I am free of it. I am not in that bed anymore and that child is not in me.

'And, Jesus, it really was something like an exorcism as I felt all that happen. Felt it, physically. The whole scene in the bedroom just cracked apart and shattered and there was nothing left to look at. That was one me gone. So, the first 'looker-on' had no purpose and suddenly she was gone, too, and all that was left was this me. This me. And god knows I was in a bad enough place right there and then, but that was something I could act on and change.'

'Acting and changing sounds about as good as it gets.'

'I think, if I've got this right, the shrinks would say I got back into that repressed childhood trauma, but in a kind of adult-state that made it possible for me to deal with it in ways I couldn't then. And I did, in some way, and that freed me. It's gone. It's gone, Bent. And that changes everything. I saved myself in that moment when I saved those girls. I got some satisfaction, Bent. It's nothing to do with payback. There should be a word for it, but I don't think there is. Mostly, it feels like a liberation. And nobody can threaten me with anything that will make me want to stop using the freedom I now have.'

Mason reaches for a tissue to wipe the tears from her face. She sees that Bent's eyes are also shining.

'It's all good,' she says. 'Don't cry.'

'Yeah, it's good,' he replies. 'The crying is good, too. Some of it's for you, because I feel so ... happy for you. And happy that what you just described is possible, it's real.'

'And the other part of crying is for you?'

'You are a deeply intuitive detective inspector.'

They both smile and blow their noses.

'Yes, the other part is for me, because I am not there, where you just described, and I don't think I ever will be. The pictures in my head, they aren't me. They are my people. And what I am isn't hidden, it's there for all to see, and I have no idea what it is they see when they see me. And, at my best, I feel sorry for them, too.'

He holds up his hand.

'Please, let's leave it there for now. I am not where you are and I want to concentrate on enjoying you being where you are, right now.'

'OK,' says Mason, nodding acceptance. 'And isn't it good to think of where Eleanor and Ayesha are in terms of people learning to want to be with people who are different to them?'

'Yes,' says Bent quietly, 'it is. Just so long as I don't let myself start thinking of how Amir liked to treat people who were different from him, or how Matto liked to treat people who were different from him, or how Ayesha ...'

'Ayesha? — Oh. Anyway, I'm so pleased I had the chance to meet her finally. Even if it was only in the context of that press event. We had a few minutes to talk and I hope there will be more. She certainly is impressive.'

'Oh yes, she is. They asked if we could meet.'

'Is that a good idea?'

'I think so. I mean, aside from making absolutely sure our stories tally, I actually think it would be good for them. They're trying to reorient themselves in their very shaken-up worlds and, for better or worse, they see us as important in that process. Maybe especially you.'

'I don't see why you'd say that last part, unless you mean it's a woman thing. It is, of course, but there's more to it than that. But anyway, yes, I get it. They are trying to hold on to new perspectives flashing by and they probably want to double-check what they think they're seeing.'

'Yes. What *they* are seeing. And we have to take responsibility for the truth we tell them, and the truth we don't.'

They sit quietly for a while. Then Mason nods.

'And be around if they need help with the after-effects of what we got them into ... OK, more tomorrow. I don't think I'm up to a debate right now about when truth is right and when it's just not useful, or even what all that means. And yes, something huge has shifted for me, and I'm not sure exactly what that means, either. Mostly, right now, I'm tired, and I need to fix these dressings.'

'I'm sure you do. You are a very striking mixture of red and white.'

'That's the only skin I have, DS Bent. And colour-prejudice is a terrible thing. A terrible thing.'

Chapter 33

Two of them. He rings the bell. She looks down at the crumpled tarmac pavement. They wait together as another November evening drizzles in. At the rattle of the safety chain, they exchange glances and smile.

'Oh, come in, come in out of the rain!' says Alice Thompson. 'How are you, Billy? John could have picked you up, you know?'

'I'm fine, really, Alice,' says Tanner. 'It's still sore and I have to be careful, and I am being. And if you and John aren't reminding me, then Elli is. I mean, Eleanor is.'

'Good for you, Eleanor!' says Alice.

John Thompson appears and takes their coats. They go into the living room and sit down.

'Tea?'

'Yes, please.'

When they are all sitting with their mugs, Eleanor begins.

'About what you said. About me moving in for a bit and seeing how it works out.'

'Yes?'

A pause. A deep breath.

'Yes, please, I'd like to try that. But ...' she continues as Alice's face lights up,

'But if you find out I'm too difficult, or annoying, or too much trouble, or too loud, or messy, or anything at all, please just tell me and I'll do my best to change. And if I can't, I'll just move out again and that'll be fine. But please don't wait until you're so angry with me that we have to fight, because even if I can't live here, I don't see why we can't be friends and if we have to fight, we can't be friends and I don't know how I can change if you don't tell me what I'm doing wrong ...'

Eleanor bursts into tears. Billy wants to put his arm around her, but has second thoughts. Alice squeezes between the two of them on the sofa and puts her arm around her.

'Don't cry, little one,' she says, as she strokes Eleanor's hair. 'I don't expect you'll be doing so very much wrong. Not more than us, anyway. And when we find we do things the other one isn't so keen on, we'll talk about it. Just talk about it. I learned a bit about that trying to be a mum before, you know. I wasn't that good at it then, but I think I can make a better job of it now. Let's have a go at making this your home. And like any young woman, you'll want to leave it again one day, soon enough.'

'I don't much want to think about that now,' says John Thompson. 'I'm sure we'll have our moments, but as long as we're all doing our best, I fancy we'll be all right. How about if I put a bit of Led Zeppelin on? 'Stairway to Heaven?"

But before anyone can respond, he adds,

'Only kidding, lass. I'll give anything a go, just so long as it isn't rap!'

'And you can play what you want in your own room!' adds Alice.

Once they have eaten, Eleanor and Billy do the washing up.

'Oh, I could get used to this!' says John.

'Right,' says Alice, when they are all sitting together

again. 'How are things with Ayesha?'

'She's fine. She gets in really dark moods sometimes, but then she comes out of them. She's always planning things.'

'She wants to be a lawyer, you say?'

'Oh, yes. Says she always has.'

'And she's going to help you with GCSEs.'

'She's going to try!'

'You can do it!' says Billy. 'Anybody can tell you're clever.'

Eleanor looks off into the middle-distance.

'Yeah, sure. Mason said I should be a detective. Maybe I will.'

'Do you see anything of those two?' John asks. 'Right funny pair if you ask me.'

'How do you know them, anyway?' Billy asks John.

'Yeah,' Eleanor replies. 'She was joking at the time, but, you know, the idea's not so daft. She's changed, it seems to me. Her and Bent are worried, I think, that all this stuff that's happened is going to mess me up. Me and Ayesha.'

'Well,' says Alice, 'You have been through a lot.'

'Yeah,' Eleanor takes up her thoughts again. 'I think that's what I learn from listening to them. ... So far, anyway. ... And from talking with Ayesha. ... What's been done to me has been done. I don't intend to forget, because forgetting gets in the way of learning. I don't intend to forgive, because forgiving still ties me to those people, to the Amirs and the Mattos and what they did. And what they did was pretty horrible. There's no need to forgive it. But the big thing is, I don't intend to carry any of that shit around with me. Sorry, Alice, I can't think of another word for it. It's theirs. It's not mine. If I hold onto it, it hurts me, so I refuse it. And as for them, all of them, I've dismissed them. They have been dismissed. They're gone.'

There was a silence, before Billy says,

'You mean, like, deleted?'

'Yeah, smart!' Eleanor grins. 'Like "deleted". I'll try that out on Ayesha, It fits with her computer stuff.'

'Eleanor's doing classes,' Billy nods.

'It's not important to me,' Eleanor goes on, 'whether Amir goes down for killing Matto or not. It's not unimportant, either. It's just not anything. I have taken what I want, they have been deleted, and only I remain.'

'Sounds like you've learned a lot, young Eleanor,' says John.

'You don't want to get too hard, love,' Alice adds.

'I know,' she replies. 'And I know I still have a lot to learn. Wendy and Bent haven't got things sorted out, either, but they are working at it and that's great to see. You know, it's like you never get yourself sorted once and for all. Not because you're stupid or bad, but because there's always more to learn. How cool is that? And I think being in the police puts them in a place where working at sorting yourself out is, like, part of the job. Maybe that's wrong, I don't know. I know they've had a lot of grief with their bosses. It looked for a while like they were going to quit, or get kicked out, or something.'

'Really?'

'Yeah. In the end, they've worked out some kind of deal. They say they're back working mostly on a project they were on before. Something to do with Restorative

Justice. Sounds really interesting.'

She looks around the room, sensing a difference in the quality of the silence.

'I like that idea, Restorative Justice. Ayesha and me talk with them about what it means, or what it ought to mean. It's like they want to help us get our chance to get some stuff right.'

'Not easy,' says John. 'We've all got us skeletons in the cupboard. Best bet for you young 'uns is try and keep your cupboards bare — of skeletons, anyway!'

'No secrets, then, John?' Billy smiles.

'As long as we're all doing our best,' John replies. 'And with a bit of trust.'

'That's the hard bit, isn't it?' Eleanor says. 'Trust is so powerful that secrets can live in it and do no harm. But if those secrets get out, trust hasn't got a chance. You don't want to act like a mug, and you don't want to get cynical.'

'I am so much looking forward to having you living here with us,' says Alice.

* * *

Eleanor and Ayesha meet next day at *Fresh Ground*, an independent coffee shop in a leafy suburb with a bohemian clientele. Ayesha is introducing Eleanor to a side of the city that is unfamiliar to her, and Eleanor has a survivor's ability to learn quickly. She is not up to speed with Ayesha's conversational topics of Fair Trade, global warming, or cooperative business models, but Ayesha has a way of explaining things that opens her eyes and, most importantly, does not make her feel patronised. She is hungry to learn. She is attracted, too, by how Ayesha seems to live according to a strict code that she finds, instead of restrictive, somehow liberating in the guidance that tradition offers her.

In return, Ayesha's steely intelligence is intrigued by Eleanor's fiery propensity for engagement, how she seems able to run before the wind, or tack into the teeth of a gale, all without any rule-based ballast to steady her, all spirit, all physicality, all now.

As Mason once observed to Bent, they are both young women of an age in their own time; they have almost everything in common. They just have to find it all. And they are consciously working on that.

Ayesha looks at the dregs in her cup and speaks as if out of its emptiness.

'It feels like they're passing something on to us, you know, like a baton in a relay. It's all connected to what you choose to carry and what you need to walk away from.'

'I know what you mean. Hey, it's funny, that. I'd forgotten all about relay races. That used to be my favourite at school.'

Ayesha leans forward.

'I wish you would take up my parents' offer of the gym membership. We can work out how you get there.'

'I think I'd stick out like a sore thumb at your gym.'

'They're not all Muslim. In addition to which, ...'

Eleanor laughs out loud.

'Sorry, Aye. I never met anybody who says, "In addition to which," but when you say it, it sounds fine.'

Ayesha blushes, then smiles.

'Well, I have never met anyone who would call

someone, "a cretinous piece of dogshit," but, on the other hand, it sounded very persuasive at the time.'

Her smile fades. The mood darkens. Eleanor reaches across the table and takes Ayesha's hand.

'Are you OK?'

'Yes, thank you. I sometimes think about how bad I should feel. But I don't ever get so far as truly feeling that bad. I know I did something I had no right to do. In the same situation, with God's help, I hope I would act differently. I think about it and I pray. I do not think it would be accurate to describe me as traumatised.' She smiles. 'I haven't the time for it. There is too much to do.'

'Good. And you'll talk to me, whatever?'

'Oh yes.'

'Good. Now, what were you going to say?'

'Mmmm? Ah, sticking out like a sore thumb is an experience that many of us live with on a daily basis and it concentrates the mind wonderfully. *Plus* which,' she squeezes Eleanor's hand before releasing it with a smile, 'I want you to learn about the company of women, as we understand it.'

'I might have a thing or two to teach you, too, you know,' says Eleanor, opening her eyes wide, 'about the company of men.' Then, more seriously, 'Sometimes, it all still feels like overload. I mean, a couple of weeks ago, life was shit, but that was nothing new. I knew how that worked. Then it was Bev getting struck dumb and dead bodies in toilets and people getting shot on the street and kids trapped in burning buildings and knife fights in cellars ...

'In addition to which, they haven't gone away, the Brothers and the Great Whites, the rapists and the

racists and everything else that Wendy — who still owes me a cake, by the way — and Bent were fighting against, probably still are.'

'I know, I know,' Ayesha replies. But we have time, Eleanor, let us use it well. If not now, then when? If not us, then who?'

Eleanor pulls off her bright yellow baseball cap and runs her fingers through her short brown hair. She drops the cap onto the table. It bears the classic image of Ché over the inscription, *Hasta La Victoria Siempre.*

'Bent gave me this.'

'I know. You told me. I'm jealous.'

'Tough!' Eleanor shoots back. 'Anyway, you'd never get it on over your hijab.'

'That's all you know, white girl!'

They laugh. They look at each other. Their eyes swim together. They blink. They sniff. And then they order another coffee.

Acknowledgements

First and foremost, love and gratitude to Ingrid, who believed, encouraged, contributed and insisted. Without her, not.

My sincere thanks to the following for all kinds of support, great and small, whether critique or praise, reservations or enthusiasm, information or opinions: Abdulghani, Bill, Christina, David, Fiona, Helen, Henry, Isabelle, Jason, Juup, Louis, Margaret, Mark, Michelle, Mariam, Mohammad, Richard, Ronnie, Steve, Sylvia, Tim, Violet, Zeynep, everyone at Manchester Writers, especially Grace and David, all those involved with Orton, especially Beth, and the whole team at Michael Terence Publishing.

Responsibility for any faults found is mine alone.

Finally, my thanks to you, the reader. You have created this communication between us and made the writing worthwhile. If you enjoyed the book, I'd appreciate it if you'd post a review on Amazon. That can make all the difference between a novel being noticed by other potential readers, or getting lost in the crowd ...

Photo: Janie Cook

Julian Edge is from Stoke-on-Trent. He has worked internationally in English language education and as a counsellor in Manchester.

Available worldwide from

Amazon

———————

www.mtp.agency

———————

www.julianedge.com

Printed in Great Britain
by Amazon